THERE WAS LESS THAN A YARD'S SPACE BETWEEN THEM.

Besson had the shotgun tilted upward. Jack Sullivan seized it and slammed the barrel upward, crushing the Frenchman's nose. Bone splinters penetrated the brain and Besson slid to the floor, stone cold dead. Now Sullivan would hunt for the guards. He saw them standing together, their backs to him. It might be difficult to kill them both quietly but there was always a way. Sullivan's right hand whipped out a commando knife and his left hand, a half-second behind, whistled down overhand with the barrel of the Beretta. The heavy black pistol caught the shorter man on the head, poleaxing him; his eyes crossed and he crumpled. At the same moment, his friend was gurgling through the welter of blood gushing from his slashed windpipe.

Sullivan looked around at the flower bushes. Not a bad place to die . . .

D0556732

Thrilling Fiction from SIGNET

(0451)

- ☐ **ICEBOUND: THE VIKING CIPHER #1 by Rick Spencer.** (125460—$2.50)*
- ☐ **ALL THAT GLITTERS: THE VIKING CIPHER #2 by Rick Spencer.** (125479—$2.50)*
- ☐ **TRACE by Warren Murphy.** (125029—$2.95)*
- ☐ **THE CHINESE SPUR by Berent Sandberg.** (122305—$2.95)*
- ☐ **THE HONEYCOMB BID by Berent Sandberg.** (110692—$2.95)*
- ☐ **THE PROMETHEUS OPERATION by Mark Elder.** (113438—$2.95)
- ☐ **FALLBACK by Peter Niesewand.** (120531—$3.95)*
- ☐ **RED SUNSET by John Stockwell.** (119126—$3.50)*
- ☐ **DEATH BY GASLIGHT by Michael Kurland.** (119150—$3.50)*
- ☐ **THE PANTHER THRONE by Tom Murphy.** (118618—$3.95)*
- ☐ **YEAR OF THE DRAGON by Robert Daley.** (118170—$3.95)*
- ☐ **THE MAN WHO WOULD NOT DIE by Thomas Page.** (117638—$3.50)*
- ☐ **ROOFTOPS by Tom Lewis.** (117352—$2.95)*

*Prices slightly higher in Canada

Buy them at your local bookstore or use this convenient coupon for ordering.

THE NEW AMERICAN LIBRARY, INC.,
P.O. Box 999, Bergenfield, New Jersey 07621

Please send me the books I have checked above. I am enclosing $__________ (please add $1.00 to this order to cover postage and handling). Send check or money order—no cash or C.O.D.'s. Prices and numbers are subject to change without notice.

Name______________________________

Address______________________________

City ____________ State ____________ Zip Code ____________

Allow 4-6 weeks for delivery.
This offer is subject to withdrawal without notice.

THE SPECIALIST #1

A TALENT FOR REVENGE

John Cutter

A SIGNET BOOK
NEW AMERICAN LIBRARY
PUBLISHED BY
THE NEW AMERICAN LIBRARY
OF CANADA LIMITED

For Corby Simpson
. . . in gratitude for his invaluable research assistance

PUBLISHER'S NOTE

This novel is a work of fiction. Names, characters, places, and incidents either are the product of the author's imagination or are used fictitiously, and any resemblance to actual persons, living or dead, events, or locales is entirely coincidental.

NAL BOOKS ARE AVAILABLE AT QUANTITY DISCOUNTS
WHEN USED TO PROMOTE PRODUCTS OR SERVICES.
FOR INFORMATION PLEASE WRITE TO PREMIUM MARKETING DIVISION,
NEW AMERICAN LIBRARY, 1633 BROADWAY,
NEW YORK, NEW YORK 10019.

Copyright © 1984 by John Cutter

All rights reserved

First Printing, March, 1984

2 3 4 5 6 7 8 9

SIGNET TRADEMARK REG. U.S. PAT. OFF. AND FOREIGN COUNTRIES
REGISTERED TRADEMARK — MARCA REGISTRADA
HECHO EN WINNIPEG, CANADA

SIGNET, SIGNET CLASSIC, MENTOR, PLUME, MERIDIAN and NAL BOOKS are published in Canada by The New American Library of Canada, Limited, Scarborough, Ontario.

PRINTED IN CANADA

COVER PRINTED IN U.S.A.

1

Strangers and Fists, Guns and Old Friends

"Yes," said Malta, "I know the sort of man you mean, Madam Penn. Or rather, I know the sort of *profession* you are referring to. But you must understand that these men are not necessarily of a single type. They come from many countries, these mercenaries, and many cultures. Some things they have in common, such as the ability to kill. But some kill more than is necessary, and enjoy it; others kill only when they must, and regret it. And there is one—only one—who kills only those who truly *deserve* killing. And it is my advice, that this man is the one you should seek."

"I am indifferent to the man's attitude toward killing," said Julia Penn, lighting a cigarette. "I'm only concerned that he does it, and soon, and that he does it to the man I have in mind." She leaned back in her deck chair, adjusted her dark glasses with a pearly-nailed middle finger, and gazed into the azure Mediterranean midday sky. Her yacht, the *Justine*, rocked soothingly on the waves, at anchor a few hundred yards off the eastern tip of St. Tropez. They could see naked sunbathers on the ivory beach, enhancing their already golden "uniform St. Tropez" tans.

"But, madam," Malta continued patiently, "for every job, the proper tool, yes? And to kill Magg Ottoowa, the proper tool must be a man who is nearly *mad* with determination. Only Sullivan—"

"When I was a girl," Julia Penn interrupted, "I had a pet

cricket. I kept it in a little wicker cage, the way the Chinese do. One day a spider crept in and killed it, and sucked it dry. An ugly spider. I hate the creatures. I saw the spider still sucking on my little cricket and I told my father, 'Kill it! It's horrible! Kill it!' And he protested that he didn't have anything handy, no flyswatter perhaps, with which to kill it. And I said, 'I don't care what you use—your shoe, anything! *Just kill it!*' And that is how I feel about Ottoowa."

Malta nodded. "I understand. Still, if you want to be *certain* the job is done, best to choose the proper tool. Now, there is Sullivan . . . an extraordinary man . . . who has a very unusual condition for his being hired for mercenary work: he must be convinced that the man or men to be killed are entirely deserving of death. There must be no doubt in his mind. This is a very unusual attitude in a hired . . . ah, specialist. He is no Mafia hit man. He is a professional soldier, a veteran of two wars, but best known for his guerrilla work against the Russians in Afghanistan."

She looked at Malta with her eyebrows raised, mildly surprised. "*That* man? I thought that was all just a rumor, the story about an American among the guerrillas."

"No, madam. It's true. He was hired by an American millionaire, a strong anticommunist, to help train the Afghanistani guerrillas. He succeeded—very, very well. He led them in many successful campaigns. But they were betrayed into ambush, and he was captured. He was taken into the Soviet Union for interrogation. He escaped—he killed eight men, four with his bare hands, in making that escape, Madam Penn. Then he made his way across many hundreds of miles of hostile territory to the Black Sea, where he stole a boat and piloted it to safety. He was going to go back to Afghanistan, but he became enmeshed in a love affair with a young lady who persuaded him against it. She has subsequently died, killed by men attempting to assassinate Monsieur Sullivan. He also has another name—he is called The Specialist. He specializes in vengeance."

"How do you know so much about him?"

"When I worked for the CIA, they showed me the dossier on our Mr. Sullivan and asked me to recruit him. He refused. He was so arrogant that, when I saw him again later, I played a little joke on him. It was in Athens. There were four Greek cutthroats who cared for nothing but money—and their younger sister. This sister became pregnant and would not tell them who had done it. I lied: I told them it was our Mr. Sullivan. They took four more of their relatives and went to an inn he was staying at in Athens. Four of them went upstairs, the others remained below, hefting their weapons. They were there, of course, to force Monsieur Sullivan to marry their sister. There was a great noise upstairs, and two of the brothers came down the stairs headfirst. The other two went out the windows, also headfirst, and without opening them. Four more men went upstairs, and four more after that. It went no better for them."

He paused to sip his drink. He smiled and continued, "I was impressed. I had already begun recruiting men for mercenary work—I arranged a meeting in a safe public place with Mr. Sullivan and spoke to him with a very gentle tongue. He is an expert on weaponry, a leader, and a great marksman. He is—"

"Enough!" Julia Penn was impatient, and annoyed with Malta's talkativeness. She shrugged her glistening shoulders. She was too pale for St. Tropez. She was as milky-white as Malta was coal black. Her blond hair had been cut short; it was streaked with white, the product of an emotional shock: a gift from Magg Ottoowa. Moodily she spread more cocoa butter over her long, pale legs—Malta tried not to stare. She put the bottle aside, tugged the straps of her bikini top away from her shoulders, leaned back, closed her eyes . . . and said, "Hire him."

"Here come the amateurs again," Sullivan muttered, seeing the two young men approaching. They were tall, lean, darkly tanned men with white shirts open to show muscular chests, and khaki slacks. One man was taller and blond, wearing sunglasses; the other—like so many men on the French Mediterranean—had long curly black hair and a thick mustache. They were the same men who'd tailed him from his hotel the day before, sizing him up; the same men who, with a complete lack of subtlety, had looked at him, then at a picture taken from a manila envelope, then back at him, making painfully certain of his identity. Cops? No. Too obviously, they were local men; local police had no undercover. CIA? Maybe. Or . . . hired thugs? Probably.

Sullivan stood, fixing the man in sunglasses with a look that said: *No*.

The man stopped, unnerved, so that his associate bumped into him and swore.

Sullivan tossed a hundred-franc note onto the café table to pay for his lunch, and turned his back on the Whoever They Were. He stepped into the crowded shop-lined street fronting Bandol, facing the sea. He looked around distastefully, wondering how he'd ended spending the night in what was so blatantly a tourist trap. He blinked in the sunlight, turned toward the rented Renault in the row of parked cars across the street.

He felt them behind him. He supposed they were trying to shake him up now by tailing him so closely. He pointedly ignored them.

It occurred to him, as he unlocked the car and slid behind the wheel, that the two men following him might be representatives of some would-be employer. And it was true he could use the money just now. But he didn't want a job. He wanted to blow every cent he had doing nothing at all—very easy, in France—until it became necessary to sleep on the beach and pry mussels from rocks for his dinner.

He wanted to be left alone.

And when he was in such a mood, it was unwise to detain Jack Sullivan. Not only because Sullivan was a big man, a man of inhumanly refined reflexes; not only because he could shift from a languid slump to a cat-swift lunge in a split second; and not simply because he was never far from a lethal weapon—but because, glimmering behind his dusty-blue eyes, vibrating behind the perpetually mild expression on his scarred, tanned face, was an always waiting anger. Sheer, unadulterated volatility. And this brand of volatility was not to be mistaken for short temper; Sullivan hadn't so much as raised his voice to the café's snail-paced waiter. This was a volatility reserved for a particular kind of irritation from a particular kind of man.

It was precisely this kind of irritation that Sullivan felt when the man in the sunglasses opened the driver's-side door of Sullivan's rented car. The man bent down to speak.

"It is not now for you to be gone, Mr. Sullivan," said the man in the sunglasses, smirking and blond. "There is someone in Bandol who would like to see you. He said to tell you—"

The man was unable to finish the sentence, because it's difficult to talk with a mouthful of broken teeth.

Sullivan had slammed the corner of the car door into the side of the man's mouth. The thug fell on his ass, clutching his mouth, blood running between his fingers, his sunglasses askew.

Sullivan was out of the car in a single quick motion, turning to face the other . . .

But the two men had magically become six. They'd signaled four of their nearly identical friends (long hair, mustaches, bronzed skin, open shirts, white teeth, fists balled) while Sullivan had had his back turned.

Sullivan shrugged.

The five other men were just thirty feet from him. They rushed him, and it took them only about three seconds to come within reach.

In those three seconds, Jack Sullivan took note of several aspects of the situation: first, the men were not reaching for weapons, and anyway were too thinly clad to conceal guns, though there might be knives in thigh sheaths; second, there was the space of about a yard and a half between the cars, through which the men could come—only two could get at him at once, unless they came around behind; third, there was a man across the street running toward a pay phone in a way that was the same all over the world, his manner all official and self-important because he was calling the cops; fourth, there was an aluminum oar affixed by an elastic rope to the roof of the VW to his right, beside a rubber boat; and fifth, he would have just enough time to get hold of the oar and use it.

So there was no need to go for the guns under the front seat of his own car.

He'd unsnapped the elastic rope, leaped back, slid the oar off the roof, braced—in a second and a half, a blur to the men approaching him.

And just as he angled the oar at the man in the lead, he told himself: Don't kill them. The gendarmes will be on the way.

He jabbed twice with the blade of the oar, charitably opting for the bellies in place of the throats; two men doubled up; but one behind them managed to get hold of the oar.

Sullivan waited till the man had a firm grip, then yanked the oar so that the thug fell facedown. Sullivan twisted the oar away and cracked those three on the sides of their heads with it, wielding it like a long-shafted hammer, *crack crack crack* in quick succession. They slumped, stunned. The remaining two hesitated, crouching, wary of Sullivan now. Sullivan heard the warble of approaching sirens . . . and he noticed a girl of about twenty sitting in an open MG double-parked across the street. She was watching the fight with an air of rueful amusement. When she saw him looking at her, she smiled and inclined her head. She was tanned, with a spray of freckles, and her deep brown eyes and long auburn hair went nicely with her skin. There was something pleasantly innocent about her—with her freckles and dimples and white bikini—despite her obvious pleasure in watching the fight. It took Sullivan less than two seconds to take in all this. Deciding he wanted to continue amusing her, he began to replace the oar on the roof of the car it had come from; he hummed like a tourist preparing for a trip to the beach, deliberately turning his back to the two men crouching a few yards behind and to the left, about to spring on him—but never really ignoring them. Sullivan was too professional to be overconfident.

He strapped the oar in place under the elastic rope. Whistling, he wished he had a cigarette, mostly because it would make him seem even more absurdly relaxed if he were to light a cigarette as the crouching punks jumped him.

They jumped—and he was ready: he'd watched them from the corners of his eyes. He caught the first with his elbow, pile-driving it, crunching the man squarely between the eyes; an unpleasant shiver went through the bones of his elbows, but nothing broke—except the bridge of the thug's nose.

The man fell back across the three Sullivan had stunned earlier, who were just getting to their knees, flattening them once more; he was out cold. The last thug swung for Sullivan's kidneys; Sullivan had swiveled when he hit the other with his elbow, so the blow meant for his kidneys fell on his tensed leathery abdominal muscles—he hardly felt it. He caught the kidney puncher on the point of his jaw with a basic roundhouse right—the punk staggered backward. Sullivan was surprised: the guy should have fallen. Sullivan waited. The man reeled, scowled beneath his thick black mustache, blinked twice—and fell. He toppled backward, atop the others, who were once again trying to stand—carrying them back down. The man whose teeth Sullivan had smashed had bolted.

Nerves singing with adrenaline, Sullivan looked around for the cops. He saw the small French patrol car, its toy-like gum ball flashing down the street. There were four cops in it, looking for him. They hadn't seen him deal with his assailants—too many cars blocked their view. Just when they drew near, when Sullivan thought sure they'd see the stunned men groaning between the cars, the girl in the white MG stood up and dropped her bikini top. She let it fall away from two gloriously sun-ripened breasts. Shoulders thrown back, breasts jouncing with her every movement, she waved at the police. She had their full attention, so when they pulled up, they didn't see Sullivan or his victims. The eyes of the four gendarmes were fixed on her bobbling wine-nippled breasts. "That way!" the girl shouted in French. "Down the road, there . . . at the end of the avenue . . . in the casino parking lot! A man hitting another man with an oar! It was awful! Quick! Get him!" She pointed them away from Sullivan.

"*Merci, mademoiselle!*" they shouted in unison. Tearing their eyes from her, they drove on, siren yammering.

Sullivan sighed in relief. Cops were a complication. He preferred to work around them. He went to the white MG and said, "That was decent of you, getting rid of the cops. You saved me a lot of hassle."

"It was my pleasure, monsieur." Her English was clear, only mildly accented. "You were outnumbered, and you defended yourself with grace and . . . ah, it was impressive. You made them look like fools. And I know those tough boys. They think they are great fighters."

He shrugged. "They challenged me at my own sport. They're probably good at sail-surfing, and the one time I tried that I fell off the board and nearly drowned." He smiled.

She laughed. A sweet, honest laugh. "Everyone is equal in the end, that is true. You know, someone may have noticed your license plate. I can give you a lift and you can send for the car when it's safer for you."

"I'll change cars in the next town. It's rented. But thanks."

She seemed to hesitate. Then, as she replaced her bikini top—taking her time, Sullivan noted, though he tried not to stare—she said, "If you're in trouble and you need a secluded place to stay, there's a motel just outside Le Beausset called La Cigalle. I recommend it."

And she drove off.

He returned to the rented car, stepping over the thugs. They were just beginning to rise, rubbing their bruises. He got into the car, locked the door, turned the key in the ignition, and got the hell out of there.

Wishing again for a cigarette, Sullivan drove between the sea and the jade-dusty hills. He took long, slow breaths to calm himself, but it didn't help much because he was thinking about the girl. The girl with the dimples and the deep brown eyes. And the big brown breasts. A little too much like Lily, perhaps. And the memory brought a stab in his gut.

He seemed to see Lily again, on the little cabin cruiser, waving to him as he surfaced in his scuba equipment. He'd been in a hurry to get back, to tell her about the beautiful schools of fish he'd seen darting on the coral reef—she was afraid of diving, but loved to hear him talk about it. "It's like flying," he wanted to tell her, hoping she'd get up the nerve to go with him. "When you skim along under water, you see the sea bottom move past under you with all those colors. Makes you feel like a bird when it's flying over the ground." That's what he'd have said to her. If she hadn't been swallowed by the fireball from the explosion when the bomb went off—the bomb some cold-blooded animal had planted on the boat.

And the hell of it was, he'd never found out for sure who had done it. It might have been the family of Boss Angione, some nephew who'd sworn vengeance on him for executing the notorious Mafia hit man. . . . It might have been the KGB. They had probably identified him as the American who'd helped train the Afghanistanis in military strategy. . . . It might have been a lot of people. He'd probably never know.

He looked in his rearview mirror, expecting to see a police car. None yet.

The punks who'd jumped him might call the cops down on him just to get even.

He wondered if there was a connection between Lily's death and the encounter with the hirelings. Probably not—it had been nearly three years since Lily had died.

But then who?

He shrugged. He didn't want to know, really. He didn't want to get mixed up in anything new for a while.

But it was tempting to go to the motel La Cigalle just to see if, as he suspected, the young lady in the sports car lived there. Maybe her parents owned it. Odd that the cops hadn't reproached her for her bared breasts—but then, this was France, where the women commonly went topless on the beaches, and they'd supposed she'd been returning from a swim. . . .

He drove lazily on, musing, following the curving coast road north, watching the sea to his right go from aquamarine to indigo as the night came on.

To his left was a hillside seeming to swell as the growing breeze from the sea stirred the pines and brought him scents of brine mingled with pitch and earth.

He realized that something was worrying him.

Something just coming to the forefront of his mind.

It was the way the car behaved. It swung out a bit too much on the curves. Just fractionally too much. It might be the tires, of course, or the alignment. But he hadn't noticed it before.

It was as if there were too much weight in the car. Just as if . . .

As if there were someone heavy crouched behind the front seat.

He was just about to hit the brakes hard, which he hoped would disorient whoever it was, throw the person off balance long enough for him to get his Smith & Wesson out, when someone pressed the cold muzzle of a gun against the back of his neck.

"Stop here," said a deep, humorous, vaguely familiar voice.

He pulled over at the next road shoulder, atop a sea cliff.

He looked in the rearview mirror . . . but the man was positioned so that, looking in the mirror, all Sullivan could see was a big white-toothy grin. Like a goddamned Cheshire cat.

2

Close to the Edge

"Get out of the car, Jack. Very slowly and cautiously."

Sullivan complied—he could almost feel the man's finger twitching on the trigger.

He got out of the car, wondering if, after thirty-five years, this was how it would end: executed on the edge of a cliff and thrown into the Mediterranean. Well, it was a pretty spot, really; little yellow wildflowers around the edge of the cliff; the shadows of the headlands reaching across the foam-topped, tossing, wine-colored waves; the first few stars showing above the deepening orange of the sunset. . . .

Not a bad place to die.

But all the time he was trying to see the man in the reflection on the windshield, hoping he would see him look away just for a second, long enough to duck the gun muzzle, whirl, and kick.

He stood beside the car, glanced at the windshield, recognized the man reflected there, and blurted, "Malta!"

He heard Malta laugh, and the gun clattered on the hood of the car, thrown casually aside.

Exhaling windily, Sullivan turned and gazed at the tall bald Algerian. He shook his head ruefully. "Man, Malta, you've got a bizarre fucking sense of humor!"

Malta chuckled and leaned back against the car, crossing his thick arms, his muscles rippling under the blue silk short-sleeved shirt. "It was not humor, *mon ami*, not entirely—I was afraid you would break my face first and then look to identify this face later, you see? I had to get you out of the car and out of arm's reach before I felt safe. I know you to be a hair-trigger man, Jack Sullivan."

"But what the hell's the idea of hiding in the car?"

Malta laughed and took two cigarettes from his shirt pocket. He offered one to Sullivan, who accepted gratefully. Sullivan lit both cigarettes with his solid-gold lighter (which he was afraid he'd have to hock soon). Malta blew gray smoke at the sea. "Ah, Sullivan, my friend, it was partly a little humor, yes—you know I love my little jokes. But you know, I sent those beach bums to *look* for you, to ask you to come and see me. That's the only reason there were so many of them—so they could split up and find you quickly, you see? But when one found you, he called the others over, and . . . he *misunderstood* me, poor boy. He was supposed to ask you *politely* to come."

"Bullshit. You must have been nearby. You knew where I was—you were *hoping* that little 'misunderstanding' would happen!"

Malta showed his big white teeth in a grin; the last rays of the setting sun caught his hoop earring and glimmered on it. "Ah, well, perhaps it's true. Those boys have *so* annoyed me, strutting about Bandol, and it was *so* amusing to watch."

"And you sneaked into the backseat while they had me occupied. Okay." Sullivan snorted. "You haven't changed. How long has it been—four years?"

"Yes. I was sorry to hear about . . . your young lady. Who did this thing?"

"The bomb? I never found out. Someday I will."

"I have faith that you will. Aren't you going to ask me why I wanted to get in touch with you?"

"No. I'm not. I don't want to be hired just now."

"Ah, but your last job was three and a half years ago. I have reason to believe you are quite out of money now, Jack. The Specialist must work at his Specialty."

"That's my business, Malta, and my problem. I don't want to hear about it."

"Let me just tell you about a certain lady who has something in common with you. Two things in common, in fact."

"Don't say a fucking *word* about her. You know how I am, and it's not fair to get me involved like that, man; don't say a goddamned word—"

"This young lady has streaks of white in her hair—like you."

Jack's hair was a slightly overgrown tousle of black, streaked on the sides with white.

"And like you," Malta went on, "she got this mark because something bad happened to her. And here is the bad thing, which is what else she has in common with you: she lost a loved one to assassination. No, to *butchery*—at the hands of evil men."

"Damn you, Malta . . ."

"You once told me, Jack—you'd had a little too much to drink and you were unusually talkative that night—you told me that there are a lot of 'bad' men who are really only victims of circumstance, and can be changed, and they are not really so bad . . . but there are others who are 'bad seeds' from the start, who are deeply evil, perhaps possessed, and who will *always* be evil. I know of one such man—one famous for being that way. He took the sister, the twin sister, of this lady with the streaks of white hair—"

"I'm not going to listen to this and be badgered into anything!" Sullivan burst out, turning toward the car. He threw down his half-smoked Camel, got in the driver's seat, slammed the door, and started the motor.

Malta leaned over, resting his arms on the roof of the little car, and went on as if there had been no interruption, "This man took the girl's twin from her, when he had them both in prison, and tortured her simply for his own amusement, and made the twin of the tortured girl watch. And then he starved them, didn't feed them for two weeks . . . and he brought the lady—the lady who would now like to hire you—he brought her a big tray covered with beautiful things to eat. And the girl began to eat, and then the man lifted the cover from the centerpiece of the tray and there was the twin's head, the twin of the starving girl trying to eat—there was her head, severed and roasted."

"I said forget it, Malta!" Sullivan bellowed, scowling, throwing the car into reverse. He backed away, his tires spitting gravel. Malta watched him, looking like a Cheshire cat after it's just eaten: his eyes half-closed, his mouth shut but upturned contentedly at the corners.

He watched Jack Sullivan back the car away, shift gears, swing into the road, screech off down the highway . . .

. . . and come to a jerky stop just at the bend in the road.

The car did a U turn, drove back to the cliff's edge, and stopped. Sullivan sat, a meter away, hunched behind the wheel, glowering up at Malta. "Get in, God damn you. Get in and tell me the rest."

"First of all," Malta said as they cruised inland toward Le Beausset, between vineyards and olive orchards, "you must understand that the target is Magg Ottoowa."

Sullivan raised his eyebrows. "*That* son of a bitch? Now, there, categorically, I've got to admit, is a man who deserves death, and quickly."

Sullivan reviewed what he knew of Ottoowa. He'd been absolute dictator over the little country Maggia—named after Ottoowa's grandfather—in equatorial Africa. He had ruled for thirteen years, a reign of terror if ever there was one. More than twelve thousand "suspected assassins" had "disappeared." Sometimes he called them suspected assassins, sometimes "guerrilla provocateurs," sometimes "traitors." It might be someone who'd complained about the high taxes or the fact that M'lord Edge, as he insisted his servants call him, was wasting millions of dollars building a "copy" of Buckingham Palace; or it might be someone who'd sneered once at the military police; it might be someone who'd done nothing at all.

Ottoowa was an Anglophile, and believed in absolute-power monarchy and family succession. He insisted his servants and staff speak only English to him, and everyone had to address him as M'lord or Your Majesty or M'lord Edge, and no one was quite sure why he'd chosen "Edge"; an ambassador had once asked him why, and Ottoowa had broken into a half-hour fit of shrieking laughter. His chief recreation was torture—especially by impalement—and thinking up imaginative and grisly humiliations for his hundreds of prisoners or for one of his many wives when he fantasized an insult from her. The atrocities committed by M'lord Edge were countless.

"But Ottoowa was ousted," Sullivan said abruptly. "Right? They finally kicked his ass out, to everyone's immense relief—he was just gearing up for another pointless war. He ran to Libya or something, didn't he?"

"Only temporarily. A great many people with grudges sought him out and continually tried to kill him, so he fled

Libya. The trouble is," Malta added, glancing at Sullivan to see how he'd take it, "he got away with a lot of gold bullion and he uses the money to keep himself well protected. He's got the best bodyguards in the world, they say. And he himself is a formidable fighter. Always armed, always suspicious. After Libya, he came here."

"Here?" Sullivan was astonished. "France?"

"Yes. Illegally. Of course, your prospective employer *could* blow the whistle on him—the French authorities would arrest him. But she doesn't want him jailed or deported to where she can't get at him. She wants to know without a doubt that he is killed."

Sullivan sighed. " 'The best bodyguards in the world.' I suppose he's hired Marlow and Hayden?"

"He has."

"What a thing for you to drop in my lap." But he was secretly pleased. Suddenly the boredom, for months eating at him like rust eating the hull of a ship, had vanished. Maybe it wouldn't be so bad to have a little something to do, after all. A *little* something?

"I'll probably get my ass blown away," Sullivan reflected.

"I'll help you—from a safe distance," said Malta.

"You were always prudent that way."

"Too many cooks, you know . . . And anyway, I'm not getting the money you are getting, Jack. Two hundred thousand American dollars. The lady is a plastics heiress from New England."

"I'll take not a penny less than three hundred thousand," said Sullivan.

"I doubt you would take no less. I think you'd do it for free. But I will pretend that you are firm at three hundred thousand, and I will convey your terms to her. And I'll see that you get your usual seventy-five thousand dollars for operating expenses in advance. I trust you'll need special equipment?"

"We'll talk about that over drinks. I have to think about it. Depends on where Ottoowa's holed up, for one thing."

"M'lord Edge is on a rather sizeable yacht anchored a few hundred meters offshore, not far from here. The yacht is called *Essex Returns*—a reference to Ottoowa's desire to take up residence in Britain."

"And where are *you* staying?"

"On the yacht owned by the lady who is your employer."

"If it's docked, you can call her, after we make some plans, and ask her to send a car to pick you up."

"Pick me up where?"

"I'm going to get a room at a motel called La Cigalle. It comes highly recommended. We'll talk there—if I can find it . . . if the signs on this road haven't been switched by a guy with a sense of humor like yours, Malta."

The next morning, as Sullivan made arrangements at the front desk of La Cigalle to take a room for two weeks, he saw the girl. The girl with the deep brown eyes and the quick wits and the perfect sun-ripened breasts. Today she wore a sheer gold bikini and a white scarf holding her hair back. Her long brown hair flowed between her shoulder blades and fell glossy and thick to her waist. The eye naturally followed that flow of hair to her ass, which was fully as glorious as the orbs trying to burst her bikini top. She strolled past him without a glance. He thought: Good. Don't get distracted from the job. He signed over a traveler's check, then turned away from the front desk and headed for the door. He was mildly surprised to find her at the door waiting for him.

Don't get distracted. He smiled at her and said, "Good morning."

And putting on his sunglasses, he stepped past her out the door.

He paused to look around for Malta. Damn him, he was late. . . . The motel was a sprawling imitation-Spanish structure; concrete painted to look like stucco, roofed by red tiles; it was set atop a low ridge and surrounded by pine trees and wild roses. To the left was a small goldfish pond, the water deep green with algae, lilies opened white on its surface.

"Lilies are sexy, don't you think?" the girl asked him casually, coming up from behind. "Not as sexy as orchids, though. You know?"

"Yes. Where'd you learn to speak English so well?"

"My mother. She's American. She owns the place. My dad's French. He's not here much lately. What beach are we going to?"

"What?" Sullivan was startled.

"You're wearing a bathing suit and a T-shirt—you look

nice in them—and I'm wearing a bathing suit, so why don't we swim?"

"Ah, I'd like to. I can't. Got to see a gentleman about a boat."

He started to walk away into the constantly churning background sound of Provence: the maraca song of the *cigalle*, the French cicada, calling perpetually for its mate.

"Sullivan!" the girl called after him.

Sullivan came to an abrupt halt and swung to face her.

The fear showed in her face—when she saw what was in his.

"Who are you?" he demanded, his fingers closing on the butt of the Smith & Wesson .38 hidden in his rolled beach towel. "How did you know my name?" He'd signed the register John Vance.

The beach towel was tucked under Sullivan's left arm; he'd slipped his right hand into its folds.

She's so young, no more than twenty-one, he thought. How could she be working for them? But almost anyone could be.

"I know your name," she said haltingly, staring at his beach towel, "because . . ." She lowered her voice. Glanced around. They stood on the sun-washed terrace between the lobby doors and the parking lot. No one around. "Because my dad has bugged some of the rooms. He's a little perverted, my dad, I'm afraid. He likes to listen when people are making love. There's one in your room, and I listened when you went in there to talk to that black man. I wanted to find out what you're doing around here. I heard him call you Sullivan. And I know he's going to bring you some guns today, and some spying equipment, and you're doing something secret. And it's not safe. And you're being paid a *lot*."

Sullivan relaxed a little and took his hand away from the gun. He believed her. He'd have to clean the microphones from his room. What to do about the girl? Most men in his position would have killed her. But Sullivan wasn't like most "professionals." Still, last night in Sullivan's room Malta had mentioned the location of the temporary anchorage of the *Essex Returns*. So she'd know the objective, in a general way. If he ditched her, she'd probably follow him there, if he was any judge of character.

There was no choice—he had to enlist her.

Or was it, he wondered, just an excuse to get to know her more intimately?

"What's your name?"

"My name's Edvige, but everyone calls me Edie."

She moved closer to him and stood so near he could smell her perfume and her hair; he thought he might fall into her deep brown eyes. "Sullivan . . . let me help you."

"You don't even know what I'm doing. You might not like it."

"Then tell me and let me decide."

He shook his head. "Not now. Maybe later, Edie. If you promise not to get in my way today, I'll tell you tomorrow."

"Get in your way! You're a sexist, Monsieur Sullivan! I would be a big help to you!"

"Anyone, *any* gender, would get in my way. Even Malta won't be in close when . . . Look, forget it. But I'll talk to you tonight, okay?"

Malta was just driving up, watching the scene with open amusement from the air-conditioned interior of the Bentley.

"See you later, Edie."

Sullivan got into the Bentley. "You bring everything, Malta?"

"All I could get. Some will take a few days."

"I may not need it. I may get lucky and finish today. Head for the anchorage. Let's have a look at M'lord Edge."

They drove through pine-covered hills, turned from the main road through an open wooden gate, and followed a winding gravel road through the bluish-green brush to the grassy parking lot for the small beach of Port D'Alon.

It was Monday afternoon; the beach wasn't crowded, and Malta parked the Bentley in a secluded corner of the shady tree-edged parking lot. Sullivan took the suitcase from the trunk and got into the backseat. He opened the big suitcase and with a quiet pleasure looked over the contents.

There were two rifles (disassembled), one submachine gun, two pistols, and various special-purpose commando knives. The rifles were a Heckler & Koch FN-FAL semiautomatic assault rifle using 7.62mm ammunition, and an M-LA Match rifle; the Match rifle was a World War II-vintage semiautomatic, the more accurate of the two, with very close tolerances and sniper-scope attachment. Beneath the rifles were an Ingram

Mac 10 submachine gun, 9mm, not much bigger than a Colt .45, and the pistols, a Beretta Model 92, 9mm, and an AMT .22 backup pistol, so small he could hide it in the palm of his hand.

"So you even got the Beretta—great piece of iron. Flatter trajectory, better penetration, and it's got that extra round. Thanks. How'd you get everything so quickly?"

Malta grinned. "I already had most of it. I know what you go for, more or less. When she told me I was to hire you, I—"

"You were that damn confident I'd go along? One fool knows another, I guess. How about the special stuff?"

"The radar equipment and the night-seers will take longer. But here is the soundscope. The small belt-attachment variety."

"Okay. Let's go."

The beach was horseshoe-shaped, more pebbles than sand, cupped by two tree-thatched headlands; the water was translucent blue and fairly calm. There were about a hundred people scattered over the beach—so many innocent bystanders, if things turned out badly. A couple of cabin cruisers were anchored about forty yards out, and at the mouth of the little bay the *Essex Returns* rocked at anchor—about a hundred yards from where Malta and Sullivan sat on a boulder, in the shade of a viny cliff.

Sullivan peered through binoculars. "I see three guys on deck, two of them armed, looking like pros, one some sort of deckhand. No sign of Ottoowa or his wives." He passed the binoculars to Malta.

"They might well be ashore," mused Malta. "Or still asleep belowdecks—that's the biggest yacht I've ever seen."

Sullivan glanced at his watch. Nine-thirty A.M. "Yeah, they're probably late sleepers."

"What are you going to take with you?"

"Not much. Mask and snorkel—if that's Hayden on deck, he'll keep his eye on the water. If he sees something that looks like scuba bubbles, he'll get suspicious. . . . And there are lots of people swimming with snorkels here. So the guards are used to that. . . . How long they here for?"

"Perhaps another day. Then they go to Château Borne. A

small castle, really, on a hill overlooking the sea. A fortification—harder to get to Ottoowa there."

"Then I'll see if I can get to him here."

Sullivan stood, and strapped on a belt containing a commando knife and a small soundscope, a device for knowing what's on the other side of a wall—or a hull. He pulled on his mask, his fins, bit down on the snorkel, and slipped into the water.

He'd entered another world. It was cool and blue—four or five shades of blue—and shot through with shivering light shafts. The outcropping of volcanic rock was pitted, crusted with mussels and sea urchins, waving with purple and lime-green seaweed, flowery with sea anemones. Schools of yellow-striped fish grazed the seaweed; a cloud of purplish minnow-sized fish broke up the light like confetti.

Sullivan enjoyed the swim, skimming along near the surface, feeling almost as if he were flying, so effortlessly did he move through the balm-cool waters. There was nothing sinister here—except men. Two snorkelers swam side by side, with spearguns in hand, their skins ghostly blue-white underwater, about twenty yards off. But they were looking for fish—their spearguns weren't the big "industrial-sized" sort men use to hunt other men in the sea.

Sullivan swam with occasional kicks, strokes of his arms: he'd kick, stroke, and coast; kick, stroke, and coast. He moved through the grottoes, over patches of rock and spreads of white sand that rippled with the wave-shaped rainbow patterns refracted from the surface. Gradually the water got a little colder, a little more turbulent, as he passed the sheltering arms of the headlands. He could see a white fizzing above and left, where the surf smacked the rocks, marking the end of the bay water. A shadow loomed: the hull of the *Essex Returns*.

The boat was fairly new; there were only a few barnacles on the white-painted hull. He swam close, hoping he was right that the guards, if they spotted his snorkel tube, were used to seeing them. But maybe not this far out from shore. He shrugged off that worry and dived, holding his breath. He kicked to the rudder, held on there with one hand, with the other removing the soundscope from his belt and holding it on the hull. He pressed the button on the scope's side and moved forward to a position just under the tea deck, where he repeated the process. And again just under the bow. His lungs nearly bursting, he kicked off from the hull, heading toward shore. He tucked the scope into his belt.

Later, ashore, he'd read off the sonar signals recorded by the soundscope. They'd tell him how many rooms there were in the boat, about how thick the hull was—which he'd need to know if he decided to sink her—and how many people were belowdeck. The sound waves bounced around inside the boat, and some returned, altered; from the difference between the original send and the return signal, it was possible to calculate fairly closely what the sonar waves had come into contact with.

He swam to the surface about twenty yards from the boat, sputtered, and cleared his snorkel. Biting down on the mouthpiece, he kicked off once more toward shore, thinking: Maybe I'll blow a small hole in her, sink her, give it time so everyone can get safely in a boat. And then I can separate the innocents from the targets once they're ashore. Maybe tonight.

He paused in his swimming, floating to listen: he'd heard a sound he didn't like.

It took him a moment to identify it. He had to separate it from the various eerie undersea noises and the rasping, repetitive sound of his own breathing. There: the sound of an outboard motor, coming his way. From behind. From Ottoowa's yacht.

They'd seen his snorkel, and someone had become suspicious. Probably Hayden, who'd decided it was unlikely a snorkel swimmer would wander so far from shore. Maybe he'd recognized Sullivan through binoculars when he'd come to the surface to clear his lungs.

Sullivan looked over his shoulder—the boat was speeding toward him, just ten yards behind. He veered off sharply to the left. The boat changed course to intersect him. It was him they were after, all right.

Sullivan spat out the snorkel, took a deep breath, and dived. He swam furiously to the right, as deeply as he could bear it. He heard a *thud-shush* and looked up—the boat was nearly overhead, idling, and someone had dived overboard. The diver was an ominous silhouette against the scattered light of the surface. Whoever it was wore a scuba tank, flippers, face mask—and carried one of the special spearguns.

The sort used for hunting men.

Sullivan dived deeper, till the pressure brought a pounding in his temples, and found a turret-shaped outcropping of volcanic rock. He swam hastily, his lungs beginning to ache, to put the jutting pitted black rock between himself and the man with the speargun.

He looked up, spotted the diver making straight for him; the diver was just five yards off, coming from above at a forty-five-degree angle. Sullivan drew his commando knife and looked around, wondering if he could outswim the other man, and thinking: Three years out of action, doing calisthenics and working out at the karate clubs and keeping my hand in at the firing range and thinking it was enough. It wasn't.

Now the killer in the red bathing suit, speargun gleaming dully in his hand, was close enough so his face was visible through the glass of the diving mask. Sullivan knew him—he could see the scar that entirely closed the man's left eye, and he knew that scar. He had put it there with a broken bottle one night, when his other weapons had been taken. He'd thought he'd killed him. Red Marlow. Former Mafia hit man.

Marlow was only three yards off now, and raising the speargun to shoot past the rock. His red hair waved about his mask like an undersea flame. He knew Sullivan, and he probably looked forward to killing the man who'd taken his eye. He was grinning under the breathing apparatus.

Sullivan could see Marlow's finger twitching on the trigger—and the speargun spat bubbles and steel. Sullivan jerked aside, timing it. The spear hit the rock close beside him. With spears, unlike bullets, there was a moment for an artful man to dodge.

Sullivan snatched up the spear with one hand, his long commando knife in the other, and kicked off from the rock, lunging through the water at Marlow's torso.

Marlow's speargun carried three twenty-inch spears, and one had been shot. He cocked the gun to shoot the second, as Sullivan closed with him. Sullivan angled to come from Marlow's left, his blind side. A spear was pointing directly at his liver, from within arm's reach. Sullivan brought his knee up to deflect it, just as Marlow fired. He caught the spear mid-shaft with his knee, turning it aside, and up; it whizzed past his head in a plume of foam, and he felt a biting pain at his ear.

Sullivan—eyesight obscured by dark splotches as his brain

begged for oxygen, his lungs screaming—jabbed the captured spear at Marlow's side. It deflected from the scuba tank as Marlow twisted to get at him. Sullivan dropped the spear, swung the knife at Marlow's throat—but the water resistance prevented his moving swiftly. Marlow brought the speargun up to block the knife. They were too close now for the speargun to be useful for anything else.

Sullivan clawed at Marlow's breathing apparatus, got his fingers around the rubber tube, and yanked.

The rubber mouthpiece came free, vomiting bubbles. Marlow got hold of Sullivan's wrist, tried to bend it backward, and with his other arm brought the speargun in close, hoping to tilt it at a usable angle.

Sullivan was near blacking out from lack of air. He had to finish it now. He dragged his knife hand away from the speargun, giving Marlow an opportunity to point the spear at him. But before Marlow could find a shooting angle, Sullivan had driven his knife through the rubber fitting at the side of Marlow's face mask, digging the blade into the killer's remaining eye.

Sullivan thought he heard the man scream—in the water the scream was just a muffled whimper followed by an eruption of bubbles.

Instinctively Marlow dropped his speargun and let go of Sullivan to claw at his gore-spouting eye socket. The water in several shades of blue became, in a cloud around them, a single shade of red.

Sullivan withdrew the knife and plunged it once more—this time into Marlow's throat.

I won't make the mistake of leaving you alive a second time. This time I'm going to make sure, Sullivan thought.

Marlow thrashed, deepening the blood cloud's shade of red, and Sullivan kicked free of him, heading for the surface.

He broke from the water, gasping for air and watching out for the enemy boat.

Funny—he didn't see it. . . .

He swam toward shore. Behind him, Red Marlow's body bobbed to the surface, floating limply.

Sullivan swam quickly to the nearest outcropping of rocks beneath the headland's outermost cliff face. Breathing raggedly, he clambered up onto the boulders and made his way, slipping now and then, to the little path that led up into the trees, around to the right of the cliff.

Minutes later he was walking along the path in the shade of the pines, cursing himself. The *cigalles* seemed to chant raspily: You-blew-it, you-blew-it, you-blew-it.

Ottoowa would be warned now. He might leave the country entirely. Sullivan shrugged. Well, he'd follow.

He turned a bend in the trail, saw Malta jogging up toward him. Malta was carrying Sullivan's towel, and shaking his head. "Well, Sullivan, looks like somebody wanted to see how your ear tasted, *mon ami*."

Sullivan looked at Malta, was struck by the odd look on his dark face. Malta seemed to be looking at someone *behind* Sullivan—someone he wasn't happy to be seeing, judging by his expression.

Sullivan casually reached out and took the rolled towel from Malta. He tucked it unconcernedly under his left arm—and slipped his right hand into the towel, gripped the butt of the Beretta wrapped in it, thinking: The boat must have come ashore somewhere. Whoever was in it hid in the rocks, then followed me up the trail to look for a secluded spot . . .

They stood between high boulders in a copse of pines. A secluded spot.

Very slowly Sullivan turned till he found he was staring into the muzzle of a submachine gun in the capable hands of a professional murderer.

3

Looking into the Eyes of a Gun

Sullivan smiled, and he hoped it was a "disarming" smile. "Well, hello, Hayden," he said. "Good to see you. On the Mediterranean for a little R and R? Or . . ." He glanced at the submachine gun. It was a Czech M-61 Skorpion, ostensibly—but Hayden always customized his weapons. He'd probably reset the sights, updated the feeding mechanism. Sullivan had always admired Hayden's handiness as a gunsmith. "Or for a little target practice?"

He raised his eyes to meet Hayden's, and it wasn't much different from looking down the barrel of a gun. You felt, looking into Hayden's gunmetal-blue eyes, unwavering as steel, that you were looking down the double barrels of a shotgun. The rest of Hayden's face was less threatening. He had the features of an aging beachboy, deeply tanned, marked by weather, blond hair bleached by sun. Sullivan hadn't seen him in four years; he hadn't aged much. Must be about forty-five by now. Looked younger than Sullivan, though he was ten years older. He wore jeans, army boots, a T-shirt, and a windbreaker—over one shoulder he'd slung a canvas bag, in case he needed to conceal the machine gun. The only visible scars were on Hayden's knuckles.

"You know why I'm here," Hayden said softly. He stood about two yards from Sullivan. He was a head shorter, so the gun was tilted up: a twitch of his finger and it would stitch half a dozen holes across Sullivan's chest. His hands were rock-steady. He smiled faintly. His eyes flicked past Sullivan to Malta. "Your friend had better stand real still. If he thinks I'm going to miss him because I'm going to shoot you first . . ."

"He won't miss, Malta. No matter how fast you jump," Sullivan said calmly. He said it calmly, but his heart was pounding; he seemed to hear his blood sizzling in his veins. He had to stay externally cool—if he tensed, it might make Hayden nervous. And Hayden's gun was never on safety—he filed the safety mechanism off his guns. "I assure you," Sullivan went on, playing for time, "the guy can handle that thing. He taught me how to handle mine. Taught me most of what I know about guns and weapons. We fought side by side in Ethiopia more than once. And in Vietnam before that. Hayden here saved my life. Surprised the hell out of me."

"That's enough stalling, Sullivan," Hayden clipped.

"You're not going to blow me away, Sam. You're not that kind of mercenary. You're the soldier kind. Not the butcher kind." But Sullivan was no longer so sure of that. He'd heard that Hayden had gone sour on life, had stopped caring about whom he worked for or what he did for them. And the fact he worked for Magg Ottoowa now was proof.

"I could have killed you before you turned around," Hayden pointed out. "I would have. But Ottoowa wants you brought back alive, if possible. You pissed him off, killing Marlow. He valued Marlow."

"You ready for that, Sam? You know what Ottoowa wants. He's a torture freak. You want to listen to me scream? You save my life for that, man?" Maybe someone would come up the trail. Hayden wouldn't want to blow his boss's cover by killing in front of a crowd. Sooner or later the police would connect it with the big yacht.

But if no one came, Hayden might blow them away and then hide the bodies in the brush.

A flicker of doubt showed in Hayden's gunmetal eyes. He could ignore Ottoowa's torturings—until it came to listening to the guy torture old friends.

"I saved your life," Hayden said slowly, "because you were a good soldier and we needed you to get the job done."

"Risking the life of another good soldier—yourself? No, I don't think so. I think much as you hate to admit it, you and I were friends. We could still be friends—it must be a drag working with assholes like Marlow. Mafia punks. You could put that thing away. We could go somewhere and talk. You could change sides. I'd split my fee with you."

"Who hired you to go after Ottoowa?"

Sullivan smiled. "You expect me to tell you? Come *on*. You know me better than that. You know I wouldn't tell Ottoowa, even under his knives and corkscrews and—"

"You always were a pain in the ass about principles. Loyalty to the employer. Picking the right side to work for." Hayden snorted. "It's a lot of bullshit." He said it, Sullivan guessed, to convince himself. "Bullshit. Now: are you coming, or do I bring your head back to show him I got The Specialist for him?"

"So that's the way it is."

"That's right."

Sullivan dropped his smile. "Now, don't get jumpy—because I'm not going to use the gun unless you make me."

Hayden didn't ask: *What gun?* His eyes flicked to the rolled towel under Sullivan's arm and to Sullivan's right hand hidden in the folds of that towel.

"Now you're wondering if I'm bluffing," Sullivan began. "Well . . ."

"Now you mention it," Hayden said wearily, "I can see the outline of the gun in the towel. But it ain't pointed at me."

"No. But you used to make bets with people about my reflexes. Remember that little bet in Saigon? You bet a guy I could shoot three dimes with a .45 before they hit the ground. Remember? You tossed three dimes in the air over your head—you trusted me that much, because they weren't far over your head. And—"

"I remember." Hayden had to grin. "We took 'em for fifty bucks. They couldn't believe it."

"Wanta bet fifty bucks now that I couldn't whip this gun around and drill you before your little Skorpion puts an end to me? Sure, you'd hit me first—but I'm betting that in the two seconds before I died I'd plug you. What you say?" Sullivan's voice was dead soft. "Fifty bucks?"

Hayden's grip on the gun tightened; his knuckles went white; a muscle jumped in his cheek. The tension would have screamed if it had had a mouth.

Sullivan heard Malta shift uneasily. Dammit, Malta, Sullivan thought, stay still! Don't move or you'll make him go for it!

Very slowly, Hayden lowered the submachine gun.

He smiled crookedly. "Sullivan, you're a son of a bitch. I guess you know it goes the same both ways. You try to use that pistol . . ."

Sullivan nodded. "I know. You'd get me." He took a step backward. "You going to come with us, or not, Sam?"

Hayden hesitated. Then he shook his head. "I got one principle of my own, Jack. You know that."

"I remember: Finish the job you're paid for." Sullivan continued to back away. "But I sure wish you'd reconsider. You guarded Ottoowa for a while. That's enough. Forget it and jump ship. You don't have to sign on with me—but get out of it. I don't want to have to kill a guy who saved my life. Especially not you, Sam."

Hayden smiled grimly. "You think too mucha yourself."

And with that he backed behind a boulder and was gone from sight.

Sullivan and Malta hurried down the trail and were quickly among the crowd on the beach. Someone was shouting that there was a dead man floating in the surf. Marlow's body. How would Ottoowa explain that? Probably pretend the guy had never been with him.

They trudged back to the car, Malta looking nervously at the brush. "He could have skirted us, could be waiting for us at the car, Jack."

"I don't think so," Sullivan said. "It was sort of understood: a truce till we got back to our home camps. But that'll be the last truce. He won't give me a chance for another Mexican standoff. He'll tell Ottoowa I got away—and then he'll tell him all about me." Sullivan sighed. "So Ottoowa will be ready."

"He'll go to the château he's purchased," Malta said, nodding. "The Château Borne."

"It'd be smarter for him to leave the country."

"He's got an important meeting here. And he'll consider himself well-protected in a fortress like Château Borne. He'll hire a lot more men."

"The funny thing about a fortress," Sullivan said, getting into the Bentley, "is that it can trap you as well as protect you. And assaulting fortified positions is one of my specialties."

"Yes, indeed," Malta said, chuckling. "I've seen you at work with the reluctant ladies. They don't remain reluctant for long."

Sullivan grinned and thought about Edie. There was nothing reluctant about her. But there was lots of charm. She probably had some surprises in store for him. Women usually did.

"What's this meeting Ottoowa's waiting for?" Sullivan asked as Malta started the car.

"I haven't been able to find out—except that it involves people from his native country. So I am supposing he's trying to engineer a coup to retake power."

"That son of a bitch is never going to be in power anywhere, ever again," Sullivan said quietly.

Quietly—but as if he believed it. . . . Because Jack Sullivan never took a job he didn't believe in. He was psychologically incapable of it. He was a man of many talents—and he had a special capacity he didn't even know he had. But Malta knew about it. Malta had spoken about it to Madam Penn: Sullivan had the ability to throw himself *completely* into a just cause. He became a fanatic for whatever fight he took up, as long as it was a fight for revenge. It didn't matter that much of the time those against whom he took revenge had never done him, personally, any harm. If they'd done something to hurt the world, they had, in Sullivan's mind, attacked him too. He might have made an ideal cop—except that he was impatient with the laws the cops were forced to work around. The laws that evil men can use to shelter themselves.

As far as Sullivan was concerned, all Magg Ottoowa's rights had been canceled by his deeds. And Sullivan would fight in the cause of Julia Penn as if she were his own sister—though he pretended to insist on being paid to do it, for the sake of his professional pride. And because it takes money to kill efficiently.

The car tooled smoothly between the hills, whipping around ribboning curves on its way back to La Cigalle. Sullivan didn't say a word till they got there. He was brooding on strategy. He was completely caught up in the campaign against Ottoowa. He'd follow his quarry to the ends of the earth if he had to.

When they arrived at the motel, Sullivan said, "See that those goods are delivered to me tomorrow, Malta. And find out what you can about Ottoowa's movements—and that yacht."

"Okay. *Bon soir*, Jack."

Sullivan found Edie out back, beside the swimming pool. The smile melted from his face when he saw her expression. She looked as if she'd been forced to swallow something bitter. A great deal of something bitter. She sat in a deck chair, scowling.

"Hello, Edie. What's—?"

"There's a woman waiting for you in the bar, Monsieur Sullivan," she said icily. "A beautiful woman. Said you were *expecting* her."

"Yeah? Well, I'm not. But I'd better go see—"

"Yes," she said, fuming. "You'd better."

Sullivan shrugged and turned away. Funny how some women became possessive when they scarcely knew you.

The bar was an attempt to reproduce what the French thought of as "American-style cocktail bar," which meant it was dark and tackily furnished, with a small mirror ball throwing off shards of light as it rotated in the silence of the deserted dance floor. The bar was empty except for Julia Penn.

Sullivan knew it was Julia Penn, sitting on a stool with her back to the bar, watching him approach, because he'd seen a picture of her in a newspaper once, with an article about her sister's death at Ottoowa's hands.

The newspaper photo hadn't done her justice. His employer was more beautiful than he'd expected. She was model-thin, blond, pale; her short, boyish Parisian haircut worked nicely with the two white streaks at her temples. Odd that she didn't hide those white streaks with dye. That wasn't the only odd thing about her. She couldn't have been more than thirty, but there was something very old in her eyes. No age wrinkles, no yellowing—just a sort of deadness. As if something in her had been used up. She slid off her stool and moved languidly to meet him. Her smile, too, was odd. Her green silk dress clung to pointed, ice-cream-scoop breasts, as if it had been "shrink-wrapped" over her hard, round little ass; the dress was slit from hem to hip, showing soft milky skin up to her waist—no underwear.

All the life that was missing from her eyes was in her lips.

Her sinuous pink lips quivered invitingly. Her feline green eyes raked him. She nodded to herself as if confirming a suspicion. She wobbled a little on her transparent plastic high heels: she was tipsy. He judged her to be the gin-drinking type. She said, "I will be very disappointed if you're not Mr. Sullivan. You're the perfect Mr. Sullivan."

"I'm Sullivan. Let's have a drink—over there."

She nodded and followed him to a booth across the room from the bar. The soft-voiced bartender lit the candle between them on the table; Julia Penn, speaking French, ordered a gin and tonic for herself and a beer for Sullivan.

She looked like a predatory night animal in the flickering candlelight. Trying to read the expression on her face, Sullivan began to suspect she had come to see him for more than just business. She was drunk, and lonely—and maybe a little deranged. If she was deranged, then he was caught between two crazies—her and Ottoowa. He shrugged, remembering Vietnam. Everyone in Nam got a little nuts after a while. He was used to it.

"Well, Mr. Sullivan," she said after the waiter had brought their drinks, "welcome to the firm."

"Thanks." He sipped his beer. "You come here to call off the operation?"

"What? No!"

"Then what's the point? You plan to look over my shoulder? I can't let you in on it till it's over. You shouldn't even be seen with me. The operation isn't just illegal—it's the sort of thing the authorities would consider terrorism."

"I know I'm taking risks, Mr. Sullivan—I really should call you Jack, except I like the sound of 'Mr. Sullivan' . . . I like the way it feels on my tongue." She smiled impishly. "Anyway, I know I'm taking a risk meeting you in person. But I . . . I just want some kind of . . . of idea how it's going. I guess I need reassurance that what you call the 'operation' is real."

He nodded. "Fair enough. How much do you want to know?"

"I want to know everything, Mr. Sullivan." There was a little life in her eyes now—the glimmer of madness.

He shrugged. "I did some reconnaissance at the target's yacht today. Haven't had time to check my readings yet. But, bad news: they're onto me. I should have done it at night, but there were so many people around I thought I'd blend in with them."

"Oh, I suspect you don't quite blend in anywhere, Mr. Sullivan. . . . Are you . . . discouraged about finishing the operation now that they know about you?"

He shook his head. "They won't blow the whistle on me. And they won't find me. . . . When you were in Africa, in Maggia, was there a red-haired guy with a scar over one eye working for—?"

"Yes!" She tensed, her fingers gripping the glass so it squeaked. "He was one of the worst."

"I'm glad you didn't like him. I had to kill him."

Her nostrils flared, and even in the dim light he could see her cheeks flush. At first he thought she was angry. And then, with a mixture of anticipation and shock, he realized that she was aroused.

"Tell me exactly how it happened," she said.

He told her. She hung on every detail.

"Mr. Sullivan, this bar annoys me. It's so dark in here. And not private. Could we . . . talk somewhere in private? Your room, for example."

I shouldn't do it, he told himself. She's drunk, and a little nuts anyway. But . . .

"Okay," he said tonelessly.

He knocked back half his beer, and got up, carrying the rolled towel with the gun in it. The gun slid halfway out of the towel with his movement. For a moment, as he stood, its barrel was visible in the white folds of cloth.

Julia Penn's eyes locked on the gun barrel. Sullivan had never seen anyone look at a gun that way before. With lust.

Weirdly embarrassed, he pushed the gun back into the towel and led the way from the bar.

He hesitated at the door to his room. What the hell, he thought. She's paying for the room, after all. . . .

He unlocked the door, pushed it open, stepped inside, the gun now in his hand, glancing quickly around. Nothing had been disturbed. "Come on in," he called, tossing the gun on the bed.

"Have you got . . . ?"

"Right here. I'll make it." He made another gin and tonic for her from the bottles on the table beside the bed. He passed her the drink, and poured himself a neat whiskey, watching her firm curves ripple as she moved to sit on the bed. He sat beside her, swallowed half the whiskey, and asked, "How the hell did you get mixed up with Ottoowa?"

"My sister and I . . ." She broke off, and he could see she was making some kind of effort to control herself. She took a long pull on the gin, and continued, "My sister and I were traveling through Africa. Sightseeing. We were in Kenya at an embassy party. Ottoowa was there, he was in Kenya on some sort of diplomatic mission. Everyone was staring at him—they couldn't believe 'M'lord Edge' was there in the flesh. He was wearing some kind of absurd military costume. He was staring at us. I guess he made some inquiries. We took a train that passed through a corner of Maggia, about a week later. Soldiers stopped the train and 'took us into custody.' Said we were smuggling drugs. They planted hashish in our baggage. They took us in a jeep to the capital city, and we were told we had a choice between life in prison and 'cooperation' in the palace. We chose the palace. . . . That's all I want to say about it. Except: you know what he did to my sister."

"I know."

"Then . . . you'll kill him?"

"Naturally. And with pleasure."

"I . . . I know how this sounds, but . . . I want you to bring his head to me. On a plate." She closed her eyes and spoke between clenched teeth. A tic jumped in her cheek. Moving almost with a life of its own, her left hand caressed the inside of his bathing-suit fly. And began to work skillfully to open it.

He burned hard in her hand. Her caresses became more daring.

He took her by the shoulders, lifted her off her feet, swept her onto the bed. The breeze of the motion blew her skirt back. He'd been right: no underwear. A wet pink slit in a mound of creamy fur. She gasped, and opened her arms for him; he threw himself onto her, feeling her small and helpless under him, her legs entwining, her fingers feathery on the back of his neck, her lips parting under his. He forced his tongue into her mouth roughly, and she moaned.

She broke from the kiss and gasped in his ear, "Tell me how you'll kill him . . . and bring his head to me . . . on . . . on a . . ."

Revulsion uncoiled in him then. He rolled off her, stood, and went to find his pants, to hide his erection.

"Come back . . . Mr. Sullivan . . ." She lay on the bed, arms outstretched to him.

He tugged on his trousers, shaking his head. "Forget it. Doesn't come with the gig. Not that way. I'll kill him. Hell, I'll bring his head. But I'm not going to play twisted sex games on his corpse with you." He went to the door, but paused long enough to say, "Ottoowa did this to you. Twisted you this way. Maybe that's worse than what he did to your sister—it's like he reached in and screwed up your soul. I'll kill him for that, too."

And then he went to the motel's bar.

Edie, wearing a bathrobe, was sitting at the bar, arguing with the bartender. "I'm sorry, mademoiselle, but your father said you were to have no more than one drink a day from—"

She swore at him in French, and swung to face Sullivan, demanding, "Are you through with her already?"

"If I'd made it with her and was through already, I wouldn't be much good, would I?"

"I'm not so stupid, Mr. Sullivan, to believe—"

"I don't care if you believe it or not," Sullivan said, turning away. "You're just a kid anyway."

He heard her sharp intake of breath, and grinned on his way to the pool. He ordered a bottle of champagne and two glasses from the poolside waiter. As the waiter took his order, he saw Julia Penn walking tipsily through the lobby. She went into the parking lot and got into a waiting Rolls.

Edie strode past him to the pool, pointedly ignoring him. She dropped her bathrobe, preparing to dive in. They were alone at the pool except for a waiter.

"You want to take a glass of champagne with you into the swimming pool?" Sullivan said, holding a fizzing glass under her nose. She hesitated, then turned to him bright-eyed. "You didn't . . . ? With that horrible woman?"

"No." He didn't bother to add: I would have if she hadn't been so crazy.

She took the crystal champagne glass and drained it. "Mm. Come for a swim?"

"Okay."

They swam, and sunned, and talked. She was only twenty,

it turned out. She'd had two years in college but didn't want to go back—she wanted to be a performer. A singer and songwriter. She could play the guitar. She liked skiing. She'd taken second prize in an amateur photography competition—photos of French peasants seeming lost when they came to the big cities. She was proud of having twice been to New York. He told her a little about himself—only a little.

"Where's your guitar?" he asked as the evening came on.

"You'd like me to play for you? It wouldn't be a bore?"

"I don't know. I haven't heard you yet."

She laughed. "Okay. My dad's gone—I'll play for you in my room. I've got my own suite."

As she unlocked the door to her rooms, a thin blond teenage boy with bad skin passed them, carrying towels. He glared at Sullivan as he passed. "What's with the kid?" Sullivan asked, following her into the suite.

"Him? Oh, he's got an infatuation on me. Jean-Pierre. Such a child. He's not . . ." She shrugged and looked at him. "I prefer grown men."

They sat in candlelight drinking chilled white wine. She played the guitar and sang, and he was relieved to be able to say honestly, "You've got real talent." Three songs later she put the guitar aside and looked at him, waiting.

He took the cue.

She was very different from Madam Penn—and he needed that. He needed her to cleanse the bad taste of Julia Penn from his mouth. She was a bigger girl, not so fragile, and glowing with health. She pretended to wrestle with him for a while, giggling, playing as if she would try to throw him off; he let her nearly win free, and then he took her in a grip that bruised her shoulders—and took her, and took her.

She didn't whisper madness in his ear, as Julia Penn had.

She just moaned.

4

Flipping the Flat Rock: The Mafia

"Why should I risk your life just to satisfy your curiosity?" Sullivan said, sipping coffee. He glanced at Edie, was not surprised to see she was sulking. "Believe me, you'll read about it in the paper. Eventually." He put the coffee cup aside, got out of bed, and dressed himself.

"Where are you going?"

"To open some presents." He kissed her good-bye.

The "presents" were waiting for him in his room. Three large wooden crates. He used a screwdriver to prize them open, one by one, after inspecting them to see if they'd been tampered with—no, Malta's code seal was there, in wax at the joints.

In the first crate were grenades, flares, tracer ammunition, and—the real prize—a pair of night-seeing infrared field glasses with radar accessory. The glasses combined several functions; held by attachable grip, they became something like the radar gun used by highway patrolmen to check speeds. He could use them to know how far away a moving vehicle was, in precisely what direction it was going, and how fast—they were useful in calculating for antitank guns and other field weapons.

In the second crate were a portable missile launcher and four Eagle-Eye missiles. Very expensive prototype models—Malta might well have gotten them as "samples" from the USA. He had a gift for posing as a potential armaments buyer from obscure Arab countries. Sullivan was impressed. Each missile had a small TV camera mounted on the snout. After launching, the missile would transmit a picture back to a monitor screen on the back of the tracking unit; the screen would show just what a man would see if he could ride the missile. Using a remote-control unit, the missile could then be guided with great accuracy to the target; the operator would steer the missile to its target using a complex "joy-stick" and the TV screen. Each missile was no bigger than a yard high, and thick as his arm—and each one had enough explosive charge in it to blow a fatal hole in a battleship.

In the third crate: a mortar, a bazooka, and half a dozen land mines.

Sullivan meticulously examined the weapons. He'd have to field-test them later. Because atop the crates was a note from Malta, saying only: "The ship has gone to the castle."

So Ottoowa had dug in at Château Borne. That made it necessary for Sullivan to learn as much about Château Borne as possible.

He'd just closed the last crate when there was a light knocking at the door. He caught up his Beretta and barked, "Who is it?"

"Edie. Can I come in?"

He sighed. But he let her in.

"Sullivan?" she began, purring up against him. "Tell me what you're doing here—exactly. I want to help."

"I'll think about it. We'll do it this way: first you help, then I tell you. Maybe."

"I can help?" she asked eagerly. "What . . . what can I do?" She noticed the crates. "What's this?"

"That's how you can help. I need to hide these things—somewhere they won't be bothered."

"I know a place—my cousin's cottage. It's all overgrown with brambles. But there's a path through. He used to hide things in it—for smuggling. But he's in jail now. The police never found out about the cottage. It's in the woods, not far. About a half kilometer. I can get someone to move it there tonight—"

"Someone who won't open them. They're booby-trapped."

Her eyes widened. "I'll see no one opens them."

"One more thing: you know anything about Château Borne?"

"A little. It's down the coast a ways. All alone on a private road. No houses near it. An old castle, rebuilt to be modern. It's on a cliff by the sea. I heard it was sold to some foreigner. It used to be owned by a Mafia don in Marseilles. A man named Morlaine."

"Morlaine?" Sullivan smiled grimly. "I know Morlaine. And where to find him."

"But, Jack, why do you want to know about—?"

"I'll tell you later." He grinned. "Maybe. But now I've got to take a short trip to Marseilles. Probably be back tonight. With luck. See you then."

"But . . . *merde*, Jack—"

"Later." And, the Beretta cold and reassuringly solid in his jacket pocket, he went to the parking lot.

Morlaine's house was on the southern fringe of Marseilles, only a half-kilometer from the quays where his ships unloaded their heroin—hidden in bales of silk and rolls of Persian rugs. That, at least, was the sum of Morlaine's operation the last Sullivan had heard. Now, though Sullivan didn't know it, Morlaine had branched into an even more lucrative crime.

Sullivan parked the little Renault a short distance from Morlaine's mansion. He walked around the perimeter, getting the lay of the place.

It was set well apart from the others, its landscaped acreage bounded by a hurricane fence. It was a brick-fronted four-story structure, shielded by palm trees and hedges. A balcony at the third floor overlooked the courtyard. Two small cars and a limousine were parked in the courtyard at the end of a long drive. Sullivan saw a guard with a shotgun slung over his shoulder smoking a cigarette on the balcony. He was relaxed, had probably never had trouble at Morlaine's house.

There's a first time for everything.

Sullivan, leather satchel slung over his arm, climbed over a hurricane fence at one of the house's blind spots. He dropped to the ground inside, expecting a snarling attack dog or an alarm called by a nosy neighbor. There were only the chirping of birds, the breeze bringing the briny perfume of the sea. It was twilight; the shadows grew long under the trees, over the neatly cut grass.

He ran in a crouch to a front corner of the house; he heard two guards telling dirty stories in French at the rear-right corner. He listened. Their voices got softer—they were walking away from him. He bent and hid his satchel in the flowerbed around the corner from the front of the house. Then he retraced his steps to the fence, climbed over in less than three seconds, and sprinted back to the road. He took thirty seconds to light a cigarette and compose himself. And then he walked up to the front gate and rang the bell.

A spike-topped black iron gate closed off the driveway; it was electrically locked, between two high stone fenceposts capped with barbed wire.

Sullivan rang the bell again. Two thick-chested, dark-eyed men carrying sidearms—they'd stowed their shotguns when they heard the ring, for the sake of public appearances—wearing guard uniforms complete with badges, came from the house to the front gate.

"*Oui?*" one of the men asked with his best appearance of civility.

"Do you speak English?" Sullivan asked in French.

"I speak a little English. What you want?"

"Tell Morlaine a friend of his cousin Coretti is here," Sullivan said. He crushed the cigarette out on the driveway. "My name is Sullivan."

"You wait."

One of the guards went into the house; the other remained on the other side of the iron gate, glowering out through the metal bars. Sullivan chuckled.

"*Quelle droll?*" the guard snapped.

"What's funny? You look like you're behind bars, through the gate—and it's funny, because that's just where you ought to be. But then, I could be wrong about you. You might be the den mother of a troupe of cub scouts in your spare time."

"Eh?" The man didn't understand the words, but Sullivan's tone told him he was being mocked. His face clouded, and his fingers hovered near his gun. Sullivan grinned and turned his back on the man, showing utter unconcern.

He turned when he heard the crunch of the other guard's bootsteps on the gravel drive. The two men muttered together in French, and then one threw a switch. The gates hummed and swung inward. The two guards just behind him—one now carrying a shotgun—Sullivan walked up toward the house. Ornamental black iron buttresses divided the front of the house into three sections; the central section, containing the balcony, stuck out a little past the others. It would be easy to shinny up that ornamental metal buttress, then climb over to the balcony, if it worked out that he had to do it that way.

The guards escorted him into the house, stopped him in the anteroom for a weapons check—he was carrying none—and then took him into a black metal elevator cage. They stood behind him in the small elevator, literally breathing down his neck; he could smell their heavy cologne, their sweat, and, underlying, well-oiled gunmetal.

The elevator creaked up with annoying sluggishness, rising past two floors of antiques, yellowed oil paintings, spiral staircases with brass handles, marble steps. It was a big house, and, Sullivan reflected, would probably have a big basement. There were probably a great many things of interest to the police—the few uncorrupted police—in that basement.

The elevator made a lot of noise, and Sullivan took note of that.

They stopped at the third floor, went down the hall to dark-paneled double doors. One of the guards rapped on the door and gave a password. The door was opened from the inside—just a crack at first. A man with sagging white cheeks and blue sunglasses inspected Sullivan, grunted, and opened the door wider for them. They went in, Sullivan first. The man with the blue sunglasses stood to one side, shotgun in the crook of his arm, its muzzle pointed at Sullivan's feet. Two armed men stood behind Sullivan, and two faced him. One of these in front was the guard who'd stood on the balcony; the other was Morlaine. Morlaine was a barrel-shaped man with a squarish head, thinning hair combed in a poor attempt at covering his bald spots. There were deep lines around his black eyes. He smoked incessantly; the glass ashtray at his elbow was overflowing with butts. He sat behind a big antique wooden desk, leaning back in a leather swivel chair. He looked annoyed and mildly puzzled as Sullivan calmly lit a cigarette and looked around the room with casual interest, as if he were mildly curious about Morlaine's interior-decorating scheme. On the floor there was a locked wooden cabinet, a gray metal safe beside it, and on the blue velvet flower-patterned walls, a couple of badly executed seascapes. And a framed certificate from the Marseilles Lions Club for Public Service. Sullivan laughed.

Realizing what it was Sullivan was laughing at, Morlaine went red. "What the fuck you doing here, Sullivan? What's this bullshit about my cousin? You're no friend of Coretti's."

"Oh, that's a matter of perspective. We're not enemies. Why, I nearly took a job from him. He took me out to dinner—"

"Yeah, I know. Nearly took a job! You told him not only wouldn't you work for him, you couldn't even stomach eating with him. You left five minutes after you got there. Too big a man to take a hit job from an Italian, eh? But some pimp Jew pays you a few thousand bucks and you go out and blow away a few dozen Arabs, maybe. Eh? You're just a goddamn mercenary. And what's the difference, mercenary or hit man for the Brotherhood? We got respect, that's the difference. We got a family. What *you* got? You got nothing. You insulted my family, turning down that job. And then you come around here talking like you're a friend of my family? I ought to kill you. But you're an American, and the fucking American embassy gives me a headache when Americans get snuffed. So you can leave with your lily-pure high-minded mercenary ass intact."

Sullivan smiled coldly. "All through now? You want to know why I'm here, or you want to play godfather some more?"

Morlaine made a brisk gesture, and the two guards behind Sullivan seized his arms and held him; the white-faced man in the sunglasses stepped in close and gave Sullivan a crack across the chin with his shotgun-butt. Sullivan's head jerked, and then he looked calmly back at Morlaine. He smiled, blood running from a cut on his jaw. He made no move to break free.

"You talk to me respectfully, Sullivan," Morlaine said, crushing his cigarette out and lighting another. "Or I let these boys make you into a pâté. Now, what you want?"

"I came to buy something. The plans for Château Borne. You used to own it, and you had it rebuilt, rewired—you probably still have a copy of the plans. I need them. I'll give you five thousand dollars for them."

"Besson . . ." Morlaine addressed the man in the blue sunglasses. "Can you believe this guy?" He said something more in French Sullivan couldn't make out. Sullivan's French was pretty shaky.

Besson snorted and shook his head.

Morlaine blew smoke in Sullivan's face. "I'm an honest businessman: I sold the house to a man, he is now the owner, and I'd be dishonest and low . . ." He smiled sadly. "If I give to you this thing. Because I know what you want: you want it so you can kill this man. This man has done nothing to me—he has paid me well. He's good business. You, you're bad business. Get the fuck out of here." Morlaine was partly French, partly Italian-American—his accent was a strange blend. "Gedim outta here, Monsieur Besson."

Besson and the two guards shoved Sullivan into the hall; he pretended to stagger, and acted as if he were beaten and scared when they prodded him down the hallway to the elevator. He pretended to cringe after Besson slapped him when he was slow to get into the elevator, thinking: That's right, make me good and mad at you.

Besson said in French, "He's nothing. I'll take him out. You go back and see if the boss wants anything."

The two guards returned to the study. Besson, shotgun in hand, got into the elevator facing Sullivan.

Sullivan waited till the elevator had sunk almost to the first floor. He'd noticed it made a loud clattering noise in its flywheels as it approached the ground floor. He slumped against the metal cage of the elevator, waiting. When the clattering came, he snapped from a slump into attack position. There was less than a yard's space between him and Besson.

The Frenchman had the shotgun tilted upward. Sullivan seized it at the stock and slammed the barrel upward, crushing Besson's nose. He'd gotten the angle just right: bone splinters from the bridge of the nose were driven up and in, penetrating Besson's brain. The man slid to the floor, stone-cold dead. Sullivan had learned lethal handfighting in Nam. Special Forces.

Sullivan dragged Besson into the ground-floor hallway, then took the shotgun to the front door. He looked through the windows—no one in sight outside. The outdoor guards were in the back, probably. Sullivan quietly opened the door, glancing up at the balcony. It was unoccupied. The guard was still inside—probably Morlaine was instructing them to find out who had hired Sullivan to get at the owner of Château Borne.

Sullivan sprinted along the grassy fringe between the house

and the driveway, found his satchel in the bushes around the corner. He tossed the shotgun aside, opened the satchel, and fitted the three main parts of his 9mm submachine gun together. He stuck the Beretta in his waistband, slung the SMG over his shoulder, and took up a long, sharp commando knife. He went hunting for the guards out back. He saw them standing together by a bone-dry swimming pool, passing a joint back and forth; they stood with their backs to him, talking in low voices. Sullivan crept noiselessly toward them. It might be difficult to kill them both quietly. One would have a chance to shout, maybe get off a shot, warn Morlaine, when he saw the other one falling. . . .

But there was always a way.

Sullivan held the Beretta in his left hand, the commando knife in his right. In order to carry it off, he'd have to hit both men at once, and both accurately. He moved in a crouch through the hedges, onto the concrete around the pool, came within reach . . .

The taller of the two chose that moment to turn around, chuckling over some joke his companion had made. Sullivan was forced to strike. His right hand whipped out with the blade, making a silver arc in the air; his left hand was a half-second behind, whistling down overhand with the barrel of the Beretta; the heavy black pistol caught the shorter man between the eyes, poleaxing him; his eyes crossed and he crumpled; at the same moment, his friend was gurgling, trying to shout through the welter of blood gushing from his severed artery as Sullivan slashed through his windpipe, stopping the blade only at the spine. The guns dropped with a clatter to the concrete; the man with red-spurting throat spasmed, flopped, went glassy-eyed—and was still. Sullivan skirted the house to the right, checked the balcony—still empty—and began to climb the ornamental metal buttress. He'd jammed the gun back in his waistband. The knife, still bloody, was clenched in his teeth.

Morlaine was indeed discussing Sullivan's interest in Château Borne. When one of his men suggested the simplest thing to do would have been to *ask* Sullivan about it—after a suitable period of softening up—Morlaine replied that he'd heard a lot of stories about Sullivan, and by all accounts he had an inhuman resistance to torture. Sullivan had been tortured by the Viet Cong, as a young man, and had revealed nothing. And the Viet Cong knew all the tricks. The Specialist, Morlaine informed them, was deranged. A crazy man, a fanatic who got so deeply involved in whatever cause he chose to fight for that he'd die before betraying it. Which was crazy, for a mercenary, in Morlaine's opinion. The guy was . . .

Morlaine broke off, staring at one of his guards. The guard had said that Sullivan was whimpering when they dragged him down the hall. Sullivan had behaved as if he were scared and beaten.

That just didn't fit. It wasn't like the Jack Sullivan who had laughed in Coretti's face. It wasn't like the Jack Sullivan who, it was said, had led raids of half-starved Afghanistani guerrillas against overwhelming Russian forces—had led them to victory after improbable victory.

So Sullivan had been pretending to be weak. Why?

And . . . where was Besson?

Morlaine froze, hearing a noise on the balcony behind him. He snatched up his .45 and spun in his seat.

The doors to the balcony were wide open. Beyond the trees, the sun was setting, turning the sky blood-red. And Jack Sullivan stood on the balcony, a gun in each hand and a gore-dripping knife clenched in his teeth, blood smeared around his lips, his eyes bright with the fire of fanaticism—he stood silhouetted against the red sky, laughing around the blade.

That was the last sight three of the four men in the room ever saw.

The fire in Sullivan's eyes transferred to his hands. The small submachine gun and the pistol flamed; the 9mm chattered and the Beretta roared. Sullivan cut down the two on his right before they had turned all the way to face him, taking them out with two bursts from the submachine gun in his right hand; his arm bucked with the firing, wrenching the muscles of his forearm—the gun was meant to be fired with both hands. With two shots, the Beretta in Sullivan's left hand brought down the third guard and blew a messy hole in Morlaine's right wrist—the Mafia boss's gun fell from limp fingers. Morlaine howled and clutched the wounded hand to his overripe belly. At the same moment, the third guard's shotgun roared as the man fell, triggered by a death spasm in his hand. Sullivan staggered and grunted—he'd caught some of the buckshot across the outside of his left hip. It made Swiss cheese of his pants, but he wasn't badly hit—most of the blast had been absorbed by the desk.

Sullivan spat out the knife. He pumped three slugs into the fallen men, just to be sure. Thrusting the pistol in his hip pocket, he yanked Morlaine to his feet with his left hand by the simple expedient of taking him by the throat.

"You were making a speech about my defects a few minutes ago, Morlaine," Sullivan said.

"Tough guy," Morlaine hissed. His face was purple; spittle trailed from the corner of his mouth. He glared defiance at Sullivan. "You think you're the only tough guy around? Go on, do your worst."

"Do your worst!" Sullivan laughed. He made that laugh as crazy-sounding as possible—the looks in their faces when they'd seen him laughing with a bloody mouth, knife clenched in his teeth, had given him an idea. Make people think you're crazy, and they're scared of you. They panic, and you've got them on the run.

Sullivan wondered: How come I can play the part so well? Maybe I *am* a little crazy.

"My worst," Sullivan was saying, "would turn you inside out and make you a squealing baby again."

Morlaine went pale.

"But I'm not gonna do my worst to you, Morlaine. I want you coherent enough to give me the information I need. Like: where's the plan for Château Borne?"

Morlaine screwed up his courage and spat, "Fuck off!"

Sullivan lifted him off his feet by his throat, and held him there, suspended, feeting kicking, choking to death. Sullivan had become a human gallows.

"You know, Morlaine, I risked my neck coming after you and your pet assholes. One of you might have got off a lucky shot. And I risked my neck like that . . ." All the time he spoke, Morlaine's face swelled purple, his limbs thrashed more desperately. ". . . for free. No one paid me to get down on *you*; I could've got the château's plans another way—maybe bribed the people who rebuilt the place for you. But I've been hearing stories about you, and . . . well, frankly, Morlaine, I was revolted. The way I'm revolted when I see a cockroach in my kitchen. I see it, I squash it."

Morlaine had almost lost consciousness, so Sullivan threw him across the room.

It was funny about strength, Sullivan thought, walking over to where Morlaine sprawled, gagging, across one of his dead henchmen. Sure, Sullivan worked out hard every day, but normally he wouldn't be strong enough to toss Morlaine across the room with one hand. It was like those stories of people lifting overturned cars off their loved ones, displaying superhuman strength in a moment of desperation. That kind of strength was something Sullivan had always been able to tap into, but it wasn't desperation that gave it to him. It was anger. And maybe a touch of madness. Just a touch.

Sullivan let that madness shine through as he grinned down at Morlaine. "Maybe I *will* do my worst to you—for fun."

"Okay," Morlaine gasped. "It's in the safe." He was crying now; his teardrops fell on his shattered, blood-caked wrist; splinters of pink-white bone showed in the wound. Some tough guy, Sullivan thought. Crying like a baby. Maybe making a play for my pity. How many people had begged Morlaine for mercy—just before he had them killed?

"Open the safe, then, big shot."

"I can't. My hand . . ."

Sullivan picked up the commando knife and used its point to tap the bone splinters protruding from Morlaine's wound.

Morlaine's scream was ear-splitting.

Sobbing, he got to his knees and hobbled to the safe. Fumbling, he opened it—it took him four tries.

Sullivan shoved him aside and inspected the contents of the safe. A strongbox filled with American money—hundred dollar bills. Something that looked like a brick wrapped in plastic. Various rolled papers, real-estate deeds—and a blueprint. He held the blueprint up to the light and nodded to himself. That was it. He folded it, zipped it into a jacket pocket, then took the money and the "brick" to the balcony.

Morlaine, wide-eyed, finding strength in the sight of his cash, got to his feet and, one arm hanging limp, staggered onto the balcony. "Sullivan . . . what you doing?"

Sullivan unwrapped the "brick"—which, as he'd guessed, turned out to be two kilos of heroin. "I'm surprised at you, Morlaine, keeping heroin here in your house. And so much. You must be in real close with the local cops, to be this confident about them. Maybe you got it here to give as a sample of a larger load to a prospective buyer?''

Morlaine said nothing. He simply swayed, his eyes fixed on the money.

It was almost dark on the balcony; a few stars were beginning to glimmer above the palm trees. The only light came from the lamp at the gate.

A light breeze rustled the curtains at the open doors behind them.

Sullivan opened the packages of dope—a fortune in heroin—and tossed the contents into the breeze; some fell in chunks to the white-gravel driveway, some was lifted like smoke on the wind, dispersed through the grass. Morlaine moaned. Sullivan turned to look at him. The man looked delirious. He'd fixed his eyes on the cashbox.

Sullivan smiled.

He snapped the small lock on the cashbox with his knife, opened it, and began to toss handfuls of crisp green bills into the air. ''American money,'' Sullivan mused aloud. ''So much of it. I'd guess you were planning a trip to the States. To buy something. But what?'' The bills were caught on the breeze, lifted a little, and then fluttered like emerald butterflies to the ground three stories below. Sullivan took up a great wad of money and suspended it in the air beyond the railing. ''Tell you what—you can have this much, Morlaine, if you come and get it.'' Morlaine lurched forward, clutching at the money; he flailed blindly at it, leaning half over the balcony railing trying to reach it. Sullivan let the money go, so it drifted in a green cloud to the ground, and then, with a single swift kick, he sent Morlaine after it. Morlaine turned end over end, falling—and struck headfirst. He lay in shadow, an untidy outline, forever still; his blood ran to mix with the small brown heaps of heroin and handfuls of hundred-dollar bills.

Sullivan surveyed the grounds and what he could see of the street. No one around. Morlaine's body would be hidden by the gathering darkness. Still, he'd better hurry—the gunshots might attract the police.

He stowed the rest of the money in his satchel—he'd pick it up later. It would be useful.

Sullivan retrieved his knife and went to the locked cabinet beside the safe. He prized it open and took a step back, surprised at its contents. On hooks inside were chains, handcuffs, leather restraints, leather gags. This was heavy-duty stuff, not the sort S&M people used for kinky kicks. Hanging on a hook, alone, was a key ring with seven magnetic keys.

Key ring in his left hand, submachine gun in his right, Sullivan went to check the other rooms. Bedrooms, bathrooms, all empty and unremarkable. No one in the kitchen, no gardener outside. Sullivan was surprised at the absence of servants. Apparently Morlaine had been planning some kind of incriminating activity on the grounds, something even faithful servants couldn't be trusted to see.

On a hunch, Sullivan went to the basement door. The heavy oak door, reinforced with bands of steel, was double-locked. Sullivan unlocked it with two of the keys on the ring, and, taking a flashlight from a kitchen cupboard, gun at the ready in his right hand, went down the steep, winding stone stairs. At the bottom there was a wine cellar; at the far end of the cellar, another locked door. He approached the door, unlocked it—and froze, just before opening it. He'd heard someone cough on the other side. Probably a guard who hadn't heard the gunshots through all the intervening floors and thick doors. Sullivan shrugged. He flattened himself against the wall to the left of the door and then shoved it open with the flat of his hand.

"Who's there?" someone called gruffly in French from inside.

Sullivan simply waited.

A man stepped through the door—a bull-heavy man with a black handlebar mustache and a knit cap—a Luger in his hand.

Sullivan stood a little behind the man, to his left; he squeezed the trigger on his submachine gun. Nothing. He'd forgotten to put in a fresh clip. Cursing himself for this unprofessional slip—blaming the years out of action—he dropped the SMG and grabbed the guard's gun hand at the wrist as the man spun to face him. They grappled—the guard was strong, and he outweighed Sullivan. Sullivan felt himself forced back; his bones creaked under the pressure. The guard had Sullivan's left wrist; Sullivan had the guard by *his* left.

Stupid, Sullivan told himself, realizing he was losing ground. Stupid to let yourself get taken this way—by one man.

Thinking that, he got mad.

Strength surged up in him, and he laughed—the guard looked scared, hearing that laugh, seeing the blood on Sullivan's teeth. Unnerved by the bloody-mouthed laughing madman, the guard hesitated—and Sullivan used the opportunity to drive him back, slamming him viciously against the stone wall. The guard grunted, stunned. Sullivan broke free, stepped back, and kicked, catching the big man squarely on the chin. The henchman blinked, and staggered. Enraged by the man's reluctance to give up, Sullivan leaped at him, took his head in his hands, and cracked it with all his strength against the stone wall. There was a sickening *crunch* sound, and then blood sprayed over the damp gray stone. The man went limp and slid to the dirt floor. Sullivan turned him over—the skull was broken open, brains dashed to pudding. This one would be no more trouble.

Sullivan stood, and shuddered, feeling dizzy. He picked up his gun, fed a fresh clip into it, and went through the door the guard had come out of.

He was in a small semicircular room, empty except for a wooden chair, a table, a naked bulb overhead. A game of solitaire was laid out next to a half-empty wine bottle and a pack of cigarettes on the table. Beyond the table, another door. This one was open, onto a dark corridor. Sullivan shone the light down the corridor. Concrete floor, concrete walls, metal doors set in the walls at intervals, a small barred window in each door. Cell doors.

Seeing the cell doors, Sullivan shivered.

He took up the key ring and went into the narrow corridor to open the first cell. Inside, a thin, pale, rumpled blond girl of about sixteen was huddled on a bed. A tray of food lay uneaten on the floor; the only light was from a small electric lamp on a wooden bedstand. The room was not much bigger than a walk-in closet. There was a chamber pot under the bed.

She wore a dingy blue dress, torn at the shoulder; there was a bruise over one of her large brown eyes.

"Stay away from me!" she rasped, backing up against the wall.

"You're American?" Sullivan asked.

"Don't come near me!"

"Hey, it's okay. I . . ." He felt himself at a loss for

words. "I'm an enemy of the men who put you in here. I'm here to let you go."

"You . . . you're a cop?"

"No. You might say I'm a concerned citizen. How many others are there?"

"I don't know. . . . They . . . I was in New York and they pushed me in a van and kept me in a room, and then this man Morlaine came and bought me from the people and they put me on a boat and . . ."

She broke off, sobbing.

Sullivan thought: So that was Morlaine's latest fund raiser. White slavery.

Probably that was what Morlaine had all the American cash for—to buy more white slaves. And then he'd sell them at a profit, maybe to back-country sheikhs, maybe to . . .

Maybe to Magg Ottoowa.

"Okay." Sullivan tried to smile reassuringly, now regretting the blood around his mouth. "Okay, come on out. I'm gonna see you get home. . . . You got a passport? Probably not."

"No passport."

"Then you'll have to go to the American embassy."

He turned away, leaving the door open, to give her a chance to collect herself, and opened the other cells. There were another girl and two boys, all of them wan and half-crazed from confinement. None of them older than sixteen. All very attractive, prime white-slavery commodities.

Sullivan felt a little sick to his stomach. How many others had Morlaine sold? What had happened to them?

"Do you know the name of the people who kidnapped you in New York?" he asked the girl he'd found first.

"I . . . I heard someone call the man Heinrich."

"Van Kleef," one of the boys said, shaking with anger at the memory. "I heard one of his creeps call him Mr. Van Kleef."

"Heinrich Van Kleef? Okay." After this assignment was done, he might just do a little free-lance work in New York. He might just try to locate Mr. Van Kleef.

"Okay, kids—here." He took out his wallet and divided all his cash up with them. It came to about three thousand francs apiece. "That's all I've got on me. That's for an emergency. But you probably won't need it. The embassy will take care of you. I'm gonna take you out of here personally, in case any of Morlaine's friends come around. And I don't trust the local cops. I'll drop you off at the embassy. But you've got to do me a favor, okay?"

"Anything!" "Whatever you say!" "You got it!" That was the response from three of them. The fourth one, sobbing with relief, could only nod.

"Lie to the cops about me. Don't describe me—tell them a friendly guard got soft and let you go after a gang war offed all his pals. Okay? You can work out the details and get it straight. See, I had to kill Morlaine and his boys to get you out. And the French police don't like people who take the law into their own hands. . . . Now, you're going to see some bodies out here. So if you want to shut your eyes . . ."

"No," the blond girl said. "I want to see them dead."

5

Some Guns Listen, Other Guns Speak

Early afternoon on the following day, Sullivan inspected the fittings on his cabin cruiser. He'd bought it that morning with the money Julia Penn had advanced him. It was secondhand, and certain braces were tired; the engine would have to be souped up—no, best he replace it with the most powerful engine the boat could hold. He'd need all the horsepower he could get, once he'd had the boat armored. Altogether, another twenty to thirty thousand dollars' work. Maybe more. But it had to be done, to make the plan work.

Sullivan tinkered with the engine, frowning as he listened to it idle. Sounded as if the rods were cracked. Yeah, he'd need a whole new engine.

"Hello, Jack," said someone standing on the wooden dock.

Sullivan looked up into Malta's bright grin. "Hi. You bring those things for me?"

"I did, yes." Malta lifted two large boxes onto the boat and climbed on after them. The cabin cruiser was big, and scarcely rocked at all as he came aboard.

"You have bought yourself another toy, I see, Jack."

"The boat? Well, it needs some work. I've got a crew going to start on it this evening, work straight through till they finish. Got to pay overtime, bribes, pay for their wine, maybe for girls too, if they think of that."

Malta laughed. "You think you can armor this boat, my friend? That will make it heavy in the water."

"I'm going to try to get the new silico-aluminum armor.

It's lighter than the rest. And I'm going to put a new engine in here. A *big* mother. But this boat's built for speed. Good wind-cutting lines, shallow draft . . ." As he spoke, he cast off the mooring line and steered the boat into the sea lane between rows of sailboats, fishing boats, cabin cruisers, and small yachts in the Bandol Marina. Around them rose a thicket of naked masts like a forest after a forest fire.

They putted out of the marina, then went into higher gears on the open sea. It was a fine day. The azure sky was flecked with small clouds, and the waves hardly lifted at all. The sea might have been asleep. It was a bad day for sailboats, but a good day for motorboats.

They cut a white wake across the bay, rounded the headlands, and swung to parallel the coastline, heading roughly north.

They sat in the bucket seats on the top deck behind the windshield, Sullivan steering. "How long it take you to put in the remote-control steering, Jack?" Malta had to shout over the roar of the engine.

"Hope to get it installed in maybe two days. Then we play seriously with Magg Ottoowa." Sullivan consulted a map, then scanned the coast for landmarks. He spotted a diamond-shaped inlet which was marked on the map, and knew he was close to Château Borne.

The coast grew rockier, less crowded with beachhouses and private docks, until there was no sign of humanity at all—only shallow inlets sandwiched between rugged cliffs. Above the inlets were steep pine-covered hills. Here and there the pine was broken up by stands of bamboo or palm trees.

They ran alongside the coastline another quarter-mile, rounded a gray-bouldered outthrust of land, and came into sight of Magg Ottoowa's cliffside fortress.

From this angle the château looked almost like a medieval castle; it had a turret at either side—towers of weathered, moss-patched gray stone—and a number of the old-fashioned slit windows. But between the two towers was a tar roof over the house's main body, topped with an aluminum chimney. Sullivan saw no skylights—too bad, a skylight could be useful in an assault. One of the towers showed a telltale shortwave radio antenna.

The grim gray face of the château was built on a clifftop two hundred yards above the churning blue-green sea. A staircase cut into the stone zigzagged down the cliff from the high barbed-wire-bristling stone wall at the north side of the château. The staircase met a jetty of asphalt overlaid on boulders. The *Essex Returns* was anchored at the jetty, its sails packed away, its hatches battened with canvas. A single guard sat in a deck chair on the yacht, rifle across his lap, sleepily listening to a transistor radio.

Just beneath the tar roof was a balcony which looked as if it had been recently added on; its stone and concrete were a different shade from the rest. Three men sat on the balcony around a white metal table. They were too far away for Sullivan to be sure, but he thought one of the men was Hayden. The other two were black. The shorter, thicker black was probably Ottoowa, judging from his coat. It *had* to be Ottoowa. "Who else," Sullivan mused aloud as he cut the engine and let the boat drift, "would be wearing an old-fashioned military parade jacket on a hot day like this? Christ! On the coast of France, too!"

"He is crazy," Malta admitted, "but that doesn't make him less dangerous, Jack. . . . Don't you think they'll notice us out here after a while?"

"Oh, I *want* them to notice us! The boat, anyway. That's part of the strategy, Malta." Sullivan grinned, enjoying Malta's discomfort. Malta had realized that someone at the château could check them out through binoculars, and, identifying Sullivan, might start shooting at them. "Hey, don't worry, Malta, my man. A lot of boats like this one go up and down the coast. They won't start shooting till they're pretty sure it's me. They don't want to attract attention to the château."

Sullivan went below, and returned with navy field glasses. He adjusted the filter for glare, then focused the glasses on the balcony. "That's Ottoowa, all right. Ugly brute. Big lump of a face . . . yellow teeth . . . even at this distance he looks brain-damaged. . . . And the white guy is Hayden. I wonder—"

"Jack!" Malta interrupted hastily. "Put this idea you are making from your mind, please, my friend—you are thinking about taking out a sniper's rifle and killing Ottoowa from here, yes? But if you do, the others will return fire, probably sink us before we could get out of range. And the boat is rocking, so you'd probably miss."

"I wouldn't miss. But it's true they might blow us away before we got clear. And anyway, I promised Julia Penn—

stupid promise—I'd bring her Ottoowa's head. So I've gotta do it the hard way." Sullivan put aside the field glasses. "Break out the directional mike, Malta, will you?"

Sullivan started the boat, moved in slowly, as close as he dared. He cut the engine, dropped anchor, and went to help Malta put the surveillance mike together.

It was a long gray instrument, looking almost like a loaded antitank gun. "You know how to use the thing, Malta?"

"*Oui*. The CIA taught me." The mike attached by a wire to a black box. Two sets of earphones were jacked into the box. It was a powerful microphone, capable of picking up a man speaking in a whisper across the length of a football field, if the mike was pointed directly at that man. Malta pointed it at the balcony, twiddled some knobs, listening on the earphones, and then nodded. "I've got it, Jack."

Sullivan put the earphones on. The conditions for long-distance electronic eavesdropping were perfect: sound comes easily over water, and the wind was low, the sea quiet. They lost some of the conversation in the occasional scream of a gull or the rumble of a passing motorboat, but most of it came through with such spooky clarity that Sullivan felt he was standing at that white metal table at Hayden's elbow.

Hayden's voice: "M'lord Edge, you've asked me for my recommendation. When I gave it to you, you ignored it. I realize it would be an inconvenience to leave the area, but it would be smarter. The meetings could be postponed and rescheduled some other place, right? We could—"

"*Inconvenience,* you call it?" Ottoowa, probably. A low, grating voice. "It's not an inconvenience!" The voice rose in pitch. "It's an insult! I've been pushed out enough! Enough! It was a great shame to run from Maggia, a great shame to run from Libya! This is all for running! The Lord of the Dark Lands takes a stand!"

Hayden sighed. "Yes, of course. And you spent a great deal on this place. But you don't know the guy like I do. All your fortification isn't gonna scare him off."

"He is just another punk-boy like you. A servant. I am not afraid of servants!"

There was a rustling, muffled words, then the clack as a servant set a tray of drinks on the table. Sullivan thought: How can Hayden let the bastard talk to him that way? Ottoowa calling him a punk and a servant! Hayden having to call

Ottoowa "M'lord"! It must be that Ottoowa impresses people as someone to be careful with. You put up with things, with him, because he's so dangerous.

Maybe Hayden would put up with it. Not Sullivan.

"M'lord"—Hayden's voice again—"you . . . you said yourself that it would be five or six years before you could get enough backing to stage the coup in Maggia. So a few weeks' delay won't—"

"We stay!"

"Okay. Okay. . . . Then you got to hire more men."

"More? But you said this man works alone! He is only one! We have six already!"

"Yeah. Well, with *luck* I could take him myself, but . . . I've fought beside him. I've seen him work. He's not like other mercenaries. He's *smart*. And he's a fanatic. He sinks his teeth into something and he won't let go. He's—"

"How many more men?"

"At least ten."

"Ten! That will make sixteen!"

"You just don't take chances with Sullivan. The guy's a maniac. But he's careful, too, and he's probably the most dangerous guy I ever saw in action."

"No one is that dangerous except *me*! We will hire *four* more."

Sullivan grinned. That's right, Ottoowa. Be sensible. Keep the odds down for me.

"When is the meeting?" the third man asked.

"Two days," Ottoowa said. "Unless we have trouble. But I don't think we will. You say this Sullivan sinks his teeth in and holds on? Well, I have pulled his teeth! I have found out where he lives! Morlaine recommended a detective agency in Marseilles—these people don't care who they work for—and they took this Sullivan's description through all the villages in the area, you understand? I got a phone call an hour ago—they located the motel he is in. They say he has a girlfriend there. If we take *her* . . ."

Sullivan swore, and tore the earphones off his head.

He ran to the anchor, cranked it up, then started the engine.

The sudden roar of the engine made the men on the balcony look toward the boat.

"They've spotted you!" Malta shouted, tossing the earphones aside.

Sullivan swung the boat in a tight arc and headed it back to the marina. Someone there would take it over and move it to the private drydock where—safely hidden in a boathouse—it would be overhauled. But . . .

The bastards might already have gotten Edie.

He pressed the accelerator to the floor. The boat leaped up and sprayed brine as it shot away from the château.

The right half of the windshield exploded, glass spraying like the seawater under the prow. He heard, a second later, the gunshot rolling across the waters. They were being fired on.

Malta, shouting, "*Merde*! I dislike being forced to exert myself in this way!" returned fire with a rifle he'd taken from the cabin. Bullets dug into the deck, spitting splinters, and dented the hood; one whined off the engine cover.

Then they were out of range.

"You get any of them?" Sullivan shouted.

"No—I'm not the marksman you are, Jack. Fortunately it was someone besides your friend Hayden shooting at us—he seemed to be busy arguing with Ottoowa. What now?"

"Yeah," Sullivan growled. "That's the question. What now?"

Now—find Edie. *Fast*.

6

"Should Have" Isn't Good Enough

Even driving recklessly fast, it was almost five before Sullivan drove up to La Cigalle. The parking lot was almost empty—he was nearly the only guest at the moment—so it didn't take him long to determine that Edie's little white convertible wasn't there. Maybe . . . Maybe she was okay, was away somewhere, swimming or sailing. Maybe they hadn't gotten her.

Or maybe they'd gotten into her car with her and made her drive it away from the motel so they'd be less noticeable when they took her.

Maybe she was dead now. Like Lily.

"Shit," Sullivan muttered, hastily parking the Renault. He ran into the motel, thinking: I should have used another place as home base—maybe rented a cabin somewhere. Shouldn't have spent so much time with her. Should have told her I couldn't see her till after the job was done. Should have realized she might be in danger. Should have . . .

He pushed the regrets from his mind and asked the little man at the front desk, "You seen Edie—Edvige?"

"Yes, sir. She went to the village about an hour ago. Said she wanted to pick up something." He smiled knowingly. "Probably champagne. Here they won't . . ."

But Sullivan had turned and bolted out the door. He leaped into the Renault, gunned the tired engine to life, and burned rubber.

He roared down the narrow country road, thinking: The village, she's gone into the village. Try the wine seller first.

Find her and take her somewhere safe. So it won't happen again. Not again—not like Lily. Sullivan refused to consider that. . . .

The Beretta was a friendly weight against his ribs under his left arm, and in the unzipped leather satchel on the seat beside him was the Ingram Mack 10 submachine gun. Loaded and ready.

The olive groves whipped past, the curves screaming warnings at his burning wheels as he took them without slowing. He swerved in and out of the occasional knots of traffic—and then, on a long deserted stretch of road, he saw Edie's car. It was coming toward him. He could see her at the wheel, the top down so that the wind picked up her hair and streamed it behind her. For a moment he felt deeply relieved—till he saw the big blue sedan.

The sedan was behind her, quickly catching up.

She was only a few hundred yards from him and the distance was closing. But in the intervening seconds the blue sedan leaped ahead of her, passed—and then forced her over. Her car swerved into the ditch. For a sickening instant he thought it would turn over. But it stopped, half-nosed into the ditch, right-rear wheel off the ground spinning. The engine gave off blue smoke.

He had to jerk the Renault wrenchingly to keep from slamming headfirst into the blue sedan. There were two men in the sedan—that's all he could make out as he screeched past them. He brought the Renault to a whiplash-making stop, then spun it in an abrupt U-turn and gunned it full at the enemy vehicle.

The sedan was a few yards past the ditched convertible, swinging around to face him like a bull turning to charge a matador. "You sons of bitches," Sullivan muttered. He braced himself, and as he came abreast the sedan, jerked the steering wheel hard, plowing his left-front fender into the blue sedan's driver-side door. The impact almost threw him into the windshield. He grunted, taking a slam in the chest from the steering wheel.

Both cars were stopped, stalled and locked together in twisted steel.

Seeing the flash of a gun from the corner of his eye, Sullivan threw himself to the right and down, below the level of the dashboard. Glass from the bullet-shattered window rained on him.

Sullivan quickly reached up and restarted the Renault, twisting the key with one hand, tapping the gas with the other. He shifted into reverse and slammed his fist onto the gas pedal. The car whined. Then, with the sound of metal creaking, it tore loose from the sedan and backed away. That gave Sullivan the seconds he needed to slide to the right-hand door, open it, and shoulder-roll out onto the tarmac. He was up in a crouch in one more second, Beretta in one hand and and Ingram grease gun in the other.

Both men had gotten out of their car. The driver, a tall man with a drooping lower lip and a dangling, shattered left arm—thanks to Sullivan—was just on the other side of the hood, angling an old Thompson burpgun at him. The Thompson belched fire and lead—but Sullivan had already moved aside, was running around the back of his car, trying to get between the killers and Edie.

He heard a second burst from the Thompson blow out the Renault's windshield and rip through the seats and then he saw Edie climbing from her convertible. "Get down!" he shouted at her. "Get . . ." He was distracted by the second killer, a blocky red-faced man with a potbelly and thick tattooed arms, coming face to face with him behind the Renault. There was no time to think. The man fired three times—but Sullivan was not an easy target. He dived, rolled, came up with the Ingram chattering and the Beretta barking. The little submachine gun sliced the stumpy man's potbelly open; the Beretta shot the tits out of a mermaid on the screaming killer's biceps. Blood spurted over the chrome of the blue sedan as the man fell back, turning to clutch at the car, his entrails slithering from the wound in his belly like a nest of slimy multicolored snakes. Sullivan, getting to his feet, heard the crunch of footsteps on the gravel beside the road, and spun, firing. The tall driver had tried to slip around behind Sullivan—and had been surprised by Sullivan's instantaneous reflexes. He didn't get off a shot. He simply sank to his knees, gaped for a moment at the three big red holes Sullivan had punched through his chest, and fell forward, twitching in death.

Two cars had come down the road in the course of the gun battle—both of them had stopped at the curve and begun to back away. They'd send for the cops, probably, Sullivan reflected. He'd have them to contend with, as well as Ottoowa.

Sullivan stowed his weapons in his satchel and went to check on Edie. She was bruised, and she had a small cut on her right cheek, but except for being shaken up, she had gotten off easily. She came into Sullivan's arms, and he said, "I'm sorry. This is my fault."

She shook her head. Her tears fell hot and wet on his arm. "Just get me out of here."

He'd rented the Renault under a false name. It would take the police a while to trace him—and maybe they never would. Her convertible was still running. He pushed it out of the ditch—Edie at the wheel, gunning the engine in reverse—and got in beside her. "Let's get out of here before the police come," he said, lighting a cigarette. "I'm going to explain to you—because you're involved now—but I don't want to have to explain to every goddamn cop in France."

"You sure no one but your uncle knows you hid my toys in this place?" Sullivan asked as they entered the cottage.

"Toys!" Edie exclaimed. "Don't talk about them like that. They're for killing and . . ." She winced. She hadn't quite adjusted to the violence she'd witnessed on the highway. There was awe and a little fear in her eyes when she looked at Sullivan now. He regretted that.

"You're right," he said. "They're far from being toys. But after you've been in this profession for a while you talk about things . . . uh . . . lightheartedly. You make a joke of it. Maybe so you can live with it. . . . I'm not ashamed of what I do. I know, somehow—in my gut, intuitively, whatever—I *know* I never killed a man who didn't deserve it. Unless maybe in Nam. In war, people get killed, right or wrong, good or bad. There are a lot of innocent bystanders, and you have to kill some guys you know might not be so bad, really—a lot of the VC had homes and kids. They were fighting for something they believed in. What they believed in was a lie, but . . ." He shrugged. "You didn't answer my question about . . ." He kicked the crates in the middle of the dusty wooden floor—a mouse scampered into a hole in the wall, frightened by the noise.

"No one knows about them. Except my uncle." She smiled weakly. "He thinks it's my own store of champagne because my dad won't let them give me much. I wrecked a car and broke my leg once when I was drunk, and ever since then . . ." She sighed. But she brightened a moment later, saying, "Oh, I've *got* some champagne!" She patted the canvas bag over her shoulder. "I went to get it in the village before . . ." Her face crumpled, tears welled in her eyes, and she began to sob. "I'm . . . sorry. I've been trying not to think about it, but . . ."

He took her in his arms. "I know it was ugly. But believe me, those guys were gonna kill you. Maybe they'd take you prisoner first, but eventually Ottoowa would've gotten his hands on you. You've heard about him. You know what he's like. Maybe you don't believe me, but . . ."

She took a long rattling breath and said, "I believe you. My uncle mentioned a rumor about a man living at the Château Borne—no one sees him except when they go by on boats. They say he's a big black man who wears a strange military coat. They think he must be crazy. No one has seen him up close . . ."

Sullivan scowled. "That's Ottoowa: cunning and stupid at the same time, like all crazies. Smart enough to escape assassins half a dozen times, stupid enough to wear a military uniform that might identify him if the wrong people see him. I hope the cops don't find out about him before I get to him. They take him into custody, it would make things tough for me. . . . Stupid, wearing that coat. Proves he's crazy. Probably the story about his syphilis is true: after a while it eats away at the brain." He took Edie's shoulders in his big hands and held her a little distance from him so he could look in her eyes. "I'm not gonna let the guy get to you. You're safe. Okay?"

"Okay, Jack." She smiled, and looked as if she believed him.

He wished he were as sure of it as she was.

Sullivan looked around appraisingly. It was a two-room cottage—a main room with a kitchen, and bathroom. It was empty except for the crates, thick with dust and cobwebs, but apart from a few mouse holes it was intact. There was a fireplace opposite the doorway. Probably no running water, but they could be comfortable for the night. They'd stopped at the motel to get sleeping bags and a few other things. They couldn't stay at La Cigalle—Ottoowa would send a follow-up crew there, and soon. They'd hide out here for the night, till Sullivan could think of someplace that would be both comfortable and safe. The best thing would be to send Edie away—but then Ottoowa might trace her, and Sullivan wouldn't be around to protect her. Maybe Malta could arrange something. Tomorrow.

Sullivan went to the window. The late-afternoon sunlight came through the glass a sort of sickly yellow-green—they were down in a hollow, surrounded by brambles, with an encircling copse of pine trees on the slopes above. Not a very defensible position, Sullivan thought. The sunlight grew redder as he watched, tinged with green because it was filtered through the sea of blackberry vines that almost engulfed the cottage. The vines were higher than the cottage roof in some places, some of them thick as a boy's wrist. The only access to the cottage, unless you cut through the bramble vines, was by the narrow dirt footpath winding up the middle of the hollow to the front porch. But Hayden could lob grenades on the place from above, or riddle it with high-powered-rifle fire from the ridge crest—Hayden would have the best equipment.

Still, Hayden would have to find them first.

Sullivan turned, was a little startled to see Edie staring at his left leg. "You told me the bandages on your leg were there because you scraped yourself on some rocks, swimming," she said.

"Sorry I lied to you about that. I was trying to protect you."

"Is . . . is it bad?"

"No. A little buckshot from one of Morlaine's punks. I was lucky—missed out on most of the shot. Stings a little, is all." She continued to stare at his leg. He thought she would cry again. "Hey, Edie, you going to break down on me? You gave me the big lecture about how women are tough too, and I shouldn't assume they're a burden, right? Then—"

"I'm okay." She said it a touch defensively. She went to the only closet, found a broom, and began to sweep the carpet of dust away from the floor in front of the fireplace. Clearing a place for them to sleep.

"I'll get some wood." There was a stack of pinelogs on the front porch. Sullivan brought an armful inside and started a fire. They'd brought cheese and bread and pâté from La

Cigalle. They sat cross-legged on their sleeping bags in front of the fire, eating and staring into the flames.

Edie's mood softened. Sullivan wished he could feel as romantic about it as he ought to—alone with a beautiful girl in a cottage, eating cheese and bread, drinking champagne on the floor in front of a roaring fire—but his thoughts kept drifting to Hayden. Would Hayden come after him, or wait for Sullivan's attack?

After a while—after they'd drunk half the champagne directly from the bottle—Edie bent over and kissed his hand. She ran her tongue over his scarred knuckles, then took two of his fingers between her lips, began to suck on them softly and suggestively, in a way that made him forget about fighting strategies for a while.

She nuzzled up his arm, down his chest, all the time her hand working to unzip his pants. She ducked her head over his hips, murmured, "No, I can't, it's too big . . . too . . . big . . ." But she did. He shuddered, and almost gave way in her mouth. Then he withdrew, feeling her lips slide tightly over his iron-hard masculinity, and pressed her onto the sleeping bags. He slid his hand under her dress.

"Tear them off," she whispered. "My panties. Just . . ."

His fingers closed over the precious silk and he twisted it, wrenching his hand back. The silk tore like tissue paper under Sullivan's fingers. With his other hand he tore her halter top away so her big breasts bobbed with sudden release. The firelight fell in flickering fingers over those buoyant golden swells; it was like tiger stripes on her brown skin. Her nipples wrinkled, then stiffened to stand up as he ran the tip of his tongue over them, like berries becoming ripe and sweet in seconds. He sank his teeth in them—not hard enough to draw blood—and she moaned, writhing in the ecstatic mix of small pains and large pleasures. She spread her legs in invitation, and he rammed himself home. . . .

A strange mixture of pictures—like the mixture of pleasure and pain—flashed through his mind as he impaled her womanhood on his manhood: pictures of himself, in Nam, surprising a machine-gun nest in a stand of bamboo, watching their bodies fly apart under the impact at close range of the slugs from his heavy automatic weapon—his weapon hard in his hands. . . . He pictured Lily, shuddering underneath him, raising her hips to meet his. . . . He pictured a firefight in

Afghanistan: turbaned barefoot warriors at his side as they charged up the mountainside through a terrain of hard-edged black boulders into the teeth of Soviet machine-gun fire; saw the astonished faces of the Soviets—so pale and blue-eyed—as he outflanked them and tossed hot grenades in their midst, their bodies leaping in the air with the explosions, pieces of men and rubble and helmets all mixed up in the air. . . . He opened his eyes to see Edie undulating beneath him, her pink tongue running over her lips, panting now and then, murmuring, "Harder . . . harder . . . *oh, oui, oui, très forte, ah oui* . . ."

Afterward, after they'd each come twice, as they lay steeped in relaxation, listening to the diminishing crackle of the fire, she said, "Jack, you have a funny way to make love."

"Funny?" He pretended, humorously, to be offended. "What's so *funny* about it?"

She laughed. "I mean . . . different. Because it's very *aggressif*, almost brutal, but . . . but very tender at the same time. Very kind. You never really hurt me—only just enough. Most men are either too rough or too tender."

"If you're trying to say I do it good—thanks. You inspire me, I guess."

"Really? You . . . you really like me?"

"Sure. But I wouldn't blame you if you never wanted to see me again, Edie. It might be better. Safer for you. I mean, my kind of life . . ." He shrugged. "It's not pretty."

"I don't care what you do. You have a good soul. I can feel that. You are here in this world for a reason, Jack Sullivan. I know that—I have always had a strong second sense. And . . ." She nestled against him.

"And what?"

"And . . . *Je t'aime*. I love you."

When he didn't respond, she said, "And you—how do you feel about me?"

For answer, he kissed her. It was a kiss that said a lot. He hoped it was enough. But for women, there is never enough.

Hayden and Benny "Quickfingers" Strickland watched through the window of the bar as the last police car pulled away from La Cigalle. "You think they found out anything we didn't find out?" Strickland asked. It was a question typical of Strickland. He was a tall, bony, dark-eyed man whose eyebrows grew together and who always needed a shave. He smoked incessantly, his nervous fingers shaking as he lit the cigarettes. Hayden suspected Strickland took speed. And he was always asking useless questions. Hayden wished Ottoowa hadn't teamed them up together. More than once Hayden had wished he'd never taken on the job with Ottoowa—but a job was a job, and once taken on, it had to be finished. Finished to the bitter end. That was Hayden's philosophy in a nutshell.

"How do I know what they found out, Strickland?" Hayden said, sipping his Perrier. He never drank alcohol "in the field."

"You think they'll come back?" Strickland asked, knocking back a whiskey.

"I dunno. But Sullivan's little rumble on the highway attracted a lot of attention. They're not sure who he is, the way I figure it, but they'll find out. I doubt they'll find him, though."

"So listen . . ." Strickland bent near Hayden to whisper, "Who were those greasers that paid off the desk clerk? Whatsa story on that? I mean, they got to be working for Ottoowa, but who the hell *are* they? I thought I met everybody working for—"

"Shut up!" Hayden hissed, glancing at the bartender. "Don't say his name, no matter how goddamn softly. Just 'the boss,' all right?"

"Yeah, yeah, okay, I just—"

"Strickland, you talk too much. But against my better judgment I'm gonna ask you a question. *What* 'greasers that paid off the desk clerk' are you talking about?"

"You don't know 'em? I thought—"

"Strickland!"

"They're sitting in that Citroën over there. Rented-car sticker on it, so maybe that means they're from outta the country, right?"

"Where . . . ?" Hayden peered through the window. "In the parking lot?" Then he saw them, about twenty yards away, talking earnestly in the immobile car. "I see 'em. Damn. Why didn't you tell me before? I know one of those guys. Italian-American—real scum. Mafioso name of Coretti. Tried to hire me and Sullivan once. We laughed in his face. I figure he's here for Morlaine's family. Vendetta against Sullivan—I guessed that was Sullivan that offed Morlaine, soon as they said in the news it was 'commando style' with the use of 'military weapons.' And because whoever it was left all that heroin on the ground for the cops to find. No rival gang would waste the shit—not that much. So Morlaine's people are after Sullivan too."

"But, hey, tha's great, right? Means we let 'em do our job for us—"

"Shut up, Strickland," Hayden clipped. "Stop talking crap. First of all, those assholes are no match for Sullivan. He cleaned out a whole nest of them single-handed in Marseilles." He smiled grimly, feeling a touch of pride. Sullivan had been his student once. "No, Sullivan will get them first—unless they get lucky. That's a possibility. But even if they get Sullivan, they got a way of hiding the bodies they snuff over here in Europe—they cram them in with legit corpses just before regular burials. Lots of doubled-up bodies like that in graves all over Italy."

"You think they might kill him and we'd never know for sure?"

"That's right."

"What you think they found out from that desk clerk?"

Hayden sighed. "Now, how the hell should I know that? You're always asking—"

"But maybe he, like, saw the girl'n this Specialist, Sullivan, saw where they went—maybe he *knows*! Only we can't find him, this desk clerk, and ask him. He left! I saw him go off-shift and leave."

"Shit. Then we'll have to ask the mafioso. And here's our chance." He nodded toward the parking lot. One of the mafiosi, the smaller man, round-shouldered and wearing a slouch hat, was walking toward the bar. "Looks like he needs to use the john."

They watched as the rat-eyed little man came into the bar and walked across it to the men's room. Hayden nudged Strickland and said, "Back me up outside the john."

Strickland nodded. Hayden got up from the stool and strolled toward the men's room. The bar was nearly empty—the motel was too far out in the country, and not doing well. It was eight P.M., and the thickening darkness outside would serve Hayden's purposes. He always felt better, working in the night.

He pushed through the door that said "Hommes." The

little mafioso stood at the urinal, his back to Hayden, trying to read the graffiti on the wall, muttering, "Why don't they write it in English?" The man had a Bronx accent. Probably he wasn't Italian-American—which meant he couldn't be an important man in the Mafia. Not heavily built enough to be a "soldier"—maybe a driver.

Hayden let him finish pissing.

But he didn't let him zip his pants up. "Leave it out," Hayden said, pressing the snout of a .45 to the mafioso's head from behind. "Leave it dangling outside your pants, because I might want to cut it off if you don't tell me what I want to know."

The man made a gargling sound. After a moment he managed to say, "Who . . . who . . . ?"

"You an owl, buddy? Never fucking mind who I am." He slapped the man's hat off with his gun barrel. "Who are *you*?"

"Man . . . Mandrell. Bucky Mandrell."

"And you work for Coretti? Doin' what?"

"Uh, you know, sorta . . ." He swallowed.

"Sorta *what*?" Hayden dug the gun snout into the little man's ear. Mandrell's whole body was shaking now.

"Sorta . . . everything. Everything he needs. Like, like a secretary. Driver. You know. Assistant."

"Uh-huh. Coretti paid off the guy at the motel desk. Found out something the police didn't get. What?"

"No, no, you got it wrong. He was paying him . . . uh . . . he owed him some bread."

Hayden sighed. He didn't like beating up on guys smaller than himself—but that didn't mean Hayden was soft: Hayden liked beating up on guys *bigger* than himself. Liked it a lot. Still, it seemed he'd have to play cat to Mandrell's mouse.

Outside the john, Strickland stood against the wall opposite the door in the little hallway, smoking, listening to the choked-off yelps, the whimpers, the thumps, the banging sounds coming from the bathroom as Hayden worked Mandrell over. Once, a tubby tourist in a damp bathing suit and sweaty T-shirt tried to press past Strickland with a nervous, "*Ah, bon soir, monsieur*," to go into the men's room. Strickland stopped him with a clammy, shaking hand—a hand that could grip like a talon when it wanted to. "Nah, you can't go in, Frenchie, it's broken. Okay?"

"*C'est marche pas?*" the little man asked, jumping when he heard a frightened squeak from inside the bathroom.

"Yeah. Yeah, Say-Marsh-Paw, whatever that means."

"*Ah. Merci . . .*" He scuttled away.

The men's-room door opened. Hayden paused in the open door and said over his shoulder, "And, Mandrell, put that thing in your pants and zip 'em up. Disgusting, you letting it hang out that way." Then he went out the back way, into the night.

"You bust him up bad?" Strickland asked. They walked past the placid swimming pool and around behind the motel, coming up to the parking lot from another angle so Coretti wouldn't see them come out of the bar. Hayden hadn't let Mandrell see his face—which was easy, since Mandrell had kept his eyes squeezed shut during the beating. Better that Coretti and friends not know for sure who did the number on Mandrell.

"No," Hayden replied, yawning. "He's still kickin'. But . . . uh . . . maybe a little the worse for wear. Found out where Sullivan is. Some kid at the motel that's crazy about Sullivan's girl followed them, out of jealousy. Came back and complained to the desk clerk. They're in some cottage out in the woods. I got directions from Mandrell. But I told him I'd go and collect the body later, after they finished with Sullivan."

"But before, you said—"

"I know, I know. Christ, I gotta explain everything? I'm gonna let them take Sullivan on—and keep him busy till I get what I came for. They'll keep him distracted. Maybe, with luck, they'll get him. He'll probably leave the cottage and outflank them. So the girl will be left all alone. That's the orders: we get the girl for sure. If we can get Sullivan too, that's great. But if we can't, well . . . once we got the girl, Sullivan's neutralized. At least"—he spat at the ground—"that's what Ottoowa thinks."

Sullivan opened the door softly and stepped into the cottage. He stood in the darkness for a moment, listening. The only sounds were the scurry of mice, the faint pop from dying embers in the fireplace, and Edie's regular breathing. Good, she was still asleep. Quietly as he could, he set his tools down on the floor, then began assembling one of the weapons from a crate he'd opened earlier. He did it quietly—he'd had long practice in that. He did it in the dark, by touch. He knew that weapon.

It was a USA Smith & Wesson M76 submachine gun, 9X19mm caliber. It weighed about nine pounds. Seventeen-inch barrel, the whole weapon just thirty inches with stock extended. Muzzle velocity 1300fps. Air-cooled and blowback-operated. Sullivan's was a silenced version customized for him by a certain manufacturer of automatic weapons for "collectors" in New Mexico. It was a heavier SMG than the Ingram, capable at close range of sawing a man in three pieces. At night, without the aid of flares, it was more practical, to Sullivan's mind, than a more accurately on-target weapon. True, the SMG's weren't much for long-range target shooting, and as they say in the Marines, no matter where you are there's always "more air than meat" to hit. But at night, when you couldn't see for precision shooting, a sprayer was the best policy.

Sullivan had no definite reason to expect trouble—and that's why he kept watch for it. That's why he'd set alarms and traps along the path to the cottage. Because it's when you least expect it that you'd better watch your ass.

That's why Sullivan had assembled the Smith & Wesson M76 and had brought out his infrared field glasses. That's why he intended to stay awake, tired though he was, all night long, to guard Edie. Foolish, loyal, golden-bodied Edie.

Sullivan bent over Edie and looked at her; her face was only partly visible, even more golden than usual in the glimmer from the dying embers; her lips were slightly parted; one breast showed at the opening of the sleeping bag; she slept on her side, head on her arm.

Sullivan smiled.

He went to the canvas bag of odds and ends, rummaged for a flashlight and the thermos of coffee. It could be a long night.

He stepped softly to the open window, sat on the floor below it, legs crossed Indian style, the lower sill just below eye level. There was a faint wash of moonlight, just enough to see the snail-track of the winding footpath between the high banks of thornbushes. The brambles rising to either side of the path looked, in the dimness, like ocean waves held in suspension, forever about to crash down.

Sullivan sipped black coffee, listening to the insects and the rustle of small animals in the bush. And listening for noises that didn't belong. About forty-five minutes after midnight, he heard one of those noises.

A man cursing.

The faint ripping as someone's coat sleeve caught on a bramble. Another curse. A voice telling the first one to shut up—in Italian.

Italian? What the hell?

Sullivan scowled. Associates of Morlaine, maybe. He'd better check it out before they came nearer—it could also be someone friendly. And that crossbow trap would be an unpleasant way to greet a friend.

Italian friends? Malta had a few. Or . . . He shrugged, and raised the infrared glasses to his eyes, pressed the switch. The scene outside was transformed into a negative image of reds and yellows and blues. He saw the silhouettes of four men, like bloody ghosts, glowing red, about fifty yards away, at the bend in the trail. They carried shotguns, pistols—and one of them had an old-fashioned submachine gun, a French MAT-49, judging by its outline, a rugged weapon with a thirty-round capacity. Looked like his visitors might be a mixture—considering the presence of this weapon and the Italian voices he'd heard—of French and American-Italian mafia. Not friends—not the way they were crouching, swinging their guns around at every slight noise. There might be two or three more on the ridge above the house.

Sullivan sighed. Too bad: the noise would wake Edie.

It was better if he woke her, he decided. He padded to the fireplace and crouched beside her. "Hey, babe." He shook her shoulder.

"Mm?"

"Better wake up quick. Here, take some coffee. Sorry."

"What?" She sat up, accepted the coffee cup. "What's going on, *chéri*?"

"Unfriendly visitors. I think I can handle them. But . . . here."

He gave her the Beretta.

"You know how to use it?" he asked.

"Yes. My uncle showed me how to use pistols. I'm not very good with a gun, but I can make it shoot."

"I hope you won't have to. Get dressed and go into the

bathroom. If the door can be barricaded, do it. There's a little window onto the back from the bathroom. If the place catches fire or they get me and they come in after you, go out the window."

"But it's all thorns out there!"

"I know. That's why they won't be coming from that way. But in an emergency, do it. Take along the sleeping bag and this stick—use them to keep most of the brambles off. It won't be fun, but you might slip past that way. If you crawl on the ground under these berry bushes, sometimes there are tunnels, like archways made out of vines." He grinned. "I found that out when I was a kid. And—"

He was interrupted by a jangling noise and a shrill scream. Someone had walked into his alarm and crossbow trap. One less in the enemy assault force.

Vince Coretti shone the flashlight on his cousin Sonny's chest—and winced. There was a finger-thick wooden shaft protruding from Sonny's sternum. Sonny was lying on his back, gasping, eyes wide, staring up through the thorns. After a minute or two he stopped gasping. His eyes iced over. Coretti reached out and closed the lids.

Get angry, he told himself. The bastard has killed another member of your family. Get angry so you can get moving and kill the goddamn mercenary maniac.

But the anger was smothered under an icy blanket of fear.

This Sullivan wasn't human. How did he know they were coming? How did he rig up a goddamn arrow-shooter? By the look of the arrow, Sullivan had carved it himself. One of these Special Forces guys.

Coretti shivered, remembering the look on Sullivan's face when, years before, he tried to hire him to hit someone for the Mafia. He'd sat across from Sullivan in a café, talking it over, outlining the proposition, all businesslike, and then Sullivan had given him a look that said: I'd like to tear your head off and stuff it up your ass, you scum.

And then that story in the paper about what the cops had found in Morlaine's mansion. The work of a crazy man. Why else had he done it, besides craziness? No one had paid him. The whole operation blown wide open—those kids yapping to the reporters in the American embassy. One of 'em had told Coretti's paid contact in the embassy the real story, told him just what the man looked like who'd rescued them. The man who'd blown away all those pros.

We're fools to come down here with just seven men, Coretti realized. To kill the Specialist, he'd need—

What was that?

"Hey, Vince, someone's—"

"I heard it, and shut up," Coretti hissed. He switched off his flashlight, and crouched, listening. He heard nothing more, but there'd been that telltale rustle of someone big moving through the brambles.

Through the brambles?

Not possible! The guy'd be snagged, tangled, cut to pieces! Was this Sullivan a ghost?

Come on, he told himself. Get a hold on yourself. Take command. Kill the bastard.

Sullivan lay on his belly under an arch of brambles, a dozen yards west of the footpath.

He'd left the field glasses behind, because they were too clumsy to crawl through bushes with, but he could see the three men on the path, crouching shapes in the moonlight, the faint gleam of gunmetal in their hands.

The big man with the pale face and the hawk nose—Sullivan could see it in profile—an SMG in his hands, would be Coretti.

Sullivan considered firing a burst into them immediately, since they were knotted together. But at this range he couldn't be sure of getting them all; they might see his muzzle flash and return fire; and one of them could get away and bring the backup soldiers down on him. Sullivan preferred to take the backups out in his own good time, his way.

As he watched, one of the men, running in a crouch, began moving up the path toward the cottage.

Sullivan frowned. That wouldn't do. He had to keep them away from the cottage. And Edie.

He tugged sharply on the piece of twine he held in his left hand, causing the bramble to which the string was attached to quiver, a safe distance to his left, between him and the cottage.

The rustling was answered by the *whap whap whap* of a .44 magnum, fired by the lead mafioso on the trail.

Sullivan smiled and tugged the vine again. Again the

"soldiers" fired at it, wasting ammunition and deluding themselves as to Sullivan's whereabouts.

Sullivan's Smith & Wesson SMG was slung over his shoulder. In his right hand was a commando knife. He wore a pair of goggles to protect his eyes from thorns. On his back was a small pack containing a flashlight and one other piece of equipment.

Sullivan had more experience working in thorny terrain than his childhood forays into blackberry bushes—he'd had a mercenary assignment in South America once, fighting mountain bandits, and he'd set up ambushes twice using thorn foliage for cover. There were methods for getting through the stuff, besides cutting it, with the least amount of snagging. You went with the "grain" of the bushes where possible; you wormed on your belly through the natural tunnels formed by the curves of the bramble vines; you stayed close to the main stem of each bush, where the thorns were fewer. And disentangling yourself once you were caught was a fine art learned by painful experience. He smiled, thinking that the Mafia punks would get that experience.

Coretti, Bartley, and Larouche turned almost simultaneously to stare at the brambles. The bushes had rustled about five yards down the path and a few yards into the morass of greenery.

"Larouche," Coretti breathed, "you're going in after him. I'll soften him up first. Maybe we'll get lucky and plug him." He raised his submachine gun and fired four long bursts into the brambles at the place where the rustling had been. Bullets zipped through leaves, and the muzzle-flashes lit up his face eerily from beneath.

There was no return fire.

Larouche edged into the brambles, muttering, "*Merde, merde . . .*" when he was snagged. And he was snagged again and again. The vines seemed almost to seek him out, slithering around his ankles and arms like snakes, digging thorns into him like fangs. "*Merde, merde, merde.*" Shit, shit, shit.

After about ten minutes, he'd penetrated only a few yards into the brush, and he realized he was going about it wrong. He dropped to his belly, began worming through the vines, dragging his gun, and soon found the going easier. Still, his skin felt like it was on fire where the thorns raked him. He squinted to see through the blue-gray darkness; here and there, pale shafts of light outlined sheaves of viny main stems. The ground was soft, giving off a rich scent of rot and humus. The surface gradually sloped upward. He saw nothing like a man. But . . .

A light. A moving light, there, to his left. It was up the slope from him, deeper in the brambles.

He began to inch toward it, .44 magnum in hand, cocked and ready.

Sullivan used his elbows to pull himself along, slowly circling Coretti's position, to come from behind.

In his right hand was a second piece of string—this one was attached to a flashlight about twenty yards behind him. He'd dug a shallow hole in the humus, dropped in the flashlight, switched it on, quickly covered it with leaves. Then he'd crawled on. The line had grown taut and pulled the light from its concealment. It dragged along behind him, giving another false indication of his position. He heard two *whup* sounds, glimpsed a muzzle flash out of the corner of his eye, some distance down the slope from him. He smiled. Someone was shooting at his flashlight. He crawled on, pulling the shining decoy through the brambles, tugging it loose now and then when it was snagged on vines. He paused, took a land mine from the pack on his back, buried it under a thin layer of humus just behind him. He set it to detonate on a slight pressure, and then crawled on, dragging the string close by the land mine. He'd have to be careful the flashlight didn't move over the land mine and set it off too soon. It would be a shame to waste it.

Coretti started and spun when he heard the explosion. It was a low *crump* sound, and a crackle, followed by a man's scream. Was that Larouche who'd screamed—or Sullivan?

It must have been Larouche.

What the hell was it? A hand grenade? The guy was equipped like an army.

He could see a flickering red light in the brambles—the explosion had started a small fire.

"Yeah, he's out there," Coretti whispered to the gaping

Bartley. "I got a feeling he just took out Larouche. This Specialist guy is crazy."

As if to confirm this, a low, throaty laughter floated out of the jungle of bushes.

"Oh, shit, that laugh—that sounds weird!" Bartley whined.

"Shut up! He's tryin' to scare you!"

"How'd he make that fucking explosion out there? He—"

Coretti backhanded Bartley sharply. "I told ya, shut up. Listen: you go back up the trail, get help. I'm gonna go on to the cottage, find that bitch he's supposed to be hangin' out with. Maybe we can use her for a hostage. Go on."

"Sure, sure!" Bartley was more than glad to take that order. He turned, and tightening his sweaty grip on his shotgun, moved up the trail. There were two other guys up top, in the trees, keeping an eye on the cottage and the trail. Two Italian guys, who didn't speak much English. He hoped he could explain what the boss needed. What were their names? Lambretto and Gambini. That was it. They—

"Drop it, pigface," said a voice close to his ear. He felt a gun pressed into the small of his back. He dropped his gun. He went cold inside when the man gave that low, throaty, crazy-sounding laugh again. The man was behind him, but the laugh seemed to float out of the shadows all around, from everywhere, as if the darkness itself were laughing. Maybe it was. Maybe this guy was the devil.

"Call those boys on the ridge," the steely voice ordered. "Get 'em down here or I blow your kidneys out through your fat belly."

"Lam . . . Lambretto!" he called. "Gambini!"

His voice echoed up the hollow. Then, faintly: "*Si?*" came floating down in reply.

"Come on . . . uh . . . come on down here! We . . . we got him—he's dead!"

"We . . . Come . . ."

"I'm going to move a little bit away from you, pigface," came Sullivan's voice. "But not far. I've got a Smith & Wesson submachine gun pointed at your back. Don't fuck around."

"Sure, sure." Maybe Coretti would come back.

Sullivan crouched in the bushes, watching Bartley, waiting and worrying: Where is Coretti?

Then he heard bootsteps, two men talking softly in Italian as they came down the trail. The fat guy stood between him and the backup "soldiers." There was something pathetic about the fat guy that made Sullivan want to spare the man's life—provided he was no threat. And sparing his life might be useful in the long run. That night—and in his campaign against Morlaine—Sullivan had learned something about psychological warfare. Unnerve them, and half the battle's done. He'd seen the blood-freezing effect his "crazy" laugh had had on Bartley.

"Okay, pigface," Sullivan whispered. "I might let you live if you do what I say. When they're within arm's reach, you throw yourself on the ground."

"Sure, sure, you bet, hey—"

"Shut up."

He heard the Italians rounding the curve in the trail.

"Hey, uh, guys," Bartley said, "Coretti wants to see you. Come on over here . . ." And then he threw himself flat.

Sullivan leaped onto the trail, Smith & Wesson spitting steel-jacketed murder.

The silencer-fitted submachine gun bucked in his hand, every part working smoothly with every other just the way a good army works. The gun made a hissing sound, silenced, flame licking like the tongue of a cobra.

The two hit men raised their shotguns—and that's all they had time to do. The slugs caught them at three yards' distance, lifting them off their feet, playing havoc with all the neat arrangement of their anatomies, rearranging their inner organs, jerking them around, spilling their insides out . . . Sullivan firing at their silhouettes in short bursts was zigzagging across the midsections.

And then it was done.

The two bodies, complete strangers to Sullivan, lay jerking in the reflex action of death's finish.

"Get up," Sullivan told the quaking Bartley. "What's your name?"

"B-Bartley."

"Listen, Bartley. What do you dream about when you're homesick?"

"Huh? Uh . . . I guess I think about my hometown. Yonkers. And Dullen's Bar. A cool scotch. . . . They called us over here to do a hit, but . . . uh . . . I never did a hit before, I got the job because my brother-in-law—"

Sullivan interrupted him with soft laughter. "What a bunch of bozos. Okay, you go home to Yonkers. Get on the first plane and don't report to anyone. Or I'll find out and kill you. You believe I can do it?"

"Sure." Judging from his voice, he really believed it.

"You go home to New York, and you quit the mob. Real politely, you quit it. And you tell 'em that there's a man who'll kill any Mafia asshole who stands in his way. His name is Sullivan and he's got a second sense that always warns him. And he dies three or four times a year and always comes back to life to kill whoever made him die. And he's ready to eat his enemies alive. You tell them all about tonight. Okay?"

"Sure!"

"Now, run! And don't stop till you get to the airport!"

Bartley turned tail and was soon gone from sight.

Sullivan turned toward the cottage—and froze.

Gunshots, coming from the direction of the cottage.

He ran, submachine gun at the ready, teeth clenched. When he was in sight of the cottage, he kept to the shadows, darting back and forth across the trail, moving up as quickly as he dared.

He moved silently onto the porch, looked through a window.

Coretti was there. Dead.

He was lying facedown in his own blood. Judging by the red-cratered ruin of his belly and back, he'd been sawed at close range by automatic-weapon fire.

Hayden?

The bathroom door was open. Sullivan—recklessly—ran into the cottage.

The bathroom was empty. The bathroom window was open. He looked through the window. There was a wide swath cut through the brambles behind the cottage. Someone had used a machete to get through. Yeah, Hayden.

There was a blood-soaked white skirt on the floor in a corner of the bathroom. Written on the wall, in blood, shown up by a patch of moonlight coming through the window, was a message: "WE GOT HER."

7

M'lord Edge

A peacock's tail of blue and green sparks shot out from the armor plating on the cabin cruiser as Alain, Sullivan's foreman for the refitting operation, used a power tool to smooth out the last of the welds. The power tool screamed like a banshee, then trailed out with a disappointed-sounding whir as Alain switched it off. "*C'est fini*," he announced, getting to his feet and pushing his goggles back on his forehead. His dusty, dark Algerian face was creased with the lines of middle age and a lifetime of hard work.

"Okay," Sullivan said, nodding. He glanced at his watch. It was ten P.M., the night after Edie had been captured—or killed—and Sullivan was impatient to begin taking his vengeance. "If Malta doesn't need you anymore, I'll pay you off and you can go. . . . Malta!"

"Yes, Jack?" Malta emerged from below deck, a wrench in his hand.

"You need Alain to help you finish that remote-control-steering mount or . . . ?"

"No, no, I am finished. He can go."

Sullivan paid Alain and his two assistants in cash—he paid them generously, very generously, so that their eyes widened, and then he put his finger to his lips and nodded toward the boat, to tell them: The extra cash is for your silence.

They nodded understanding, shook his hand, and left.

Malta and Sullivan were alone on the boat. It was moored in a sort of wooden garage over water, reminding Sullivan of an incident in his boyhood. He'd grown up in Missouri, near the Mississippi River. More than once their house had been flooded; their garage, on lower ground, a ramshackle wooden outbuilding much like this one, was often in three feet of water—it finally floated away one year. His father had been a carpenter, and Sullivan remembered him out helping the neighbors rebuild their flood-ravaged property, grimly pretending he was going to send them a bill for it, and then somehow always "forgetting" to bill those who couldn't afford it. "The world is kept from falling apart only by people who help other people without being told to," his father had informed him one day. "Though it's best you pretend you're doing it for profit—otherwise people try to take advantage of you, some of them." Sullivan's father, a joke-cracking, whiskey-drinking Irishman who liked to pinch his wife just to watch her pretend anger, died by the side of the road because no one would stop to help. He and the young Jack Sullivan had been driving into Kansas City to buy ammunition—they were going to do some target practice together—when the steering went out and they slammed into a steel pylon. Young Jack hadn't been hurt much, but his father had bled to death as passing motorists ignored the boy's frantic signals for help. . . .

"You look like you are somewhere far away, *mon ami*," said Malta, sitting across from Sullivan on a tool chest.

Jerked back to present time, Sullivan looked up and smiled wearily. "Guess I was. . . . Was wondering why I live the way I do, do the things I do—hell, it ain't for money, not really—and then I remembered something my dad said to me once. Something that has a lot to do with . . . with why I do the job I do." He shrugged. "Silly, I guess. Try to wipe out a human blight like Ottoowa and end up by hurting an innocent girl."

"She insisted on getting involved, Jack. And, *bien sûr*, Ottoowa will keep her alive, to keep you at a distance."

"But what's he do with her in the meantime? He's a torture freak. No, I can't take the chance he'll keep his hands off her. I've got to find a way to go after him, to get her out without endangering her."

"But he might kill her out of anger if you attack him, Jack. I know it was I who got you into this job, but—"

"I know Ottoowa's reputation—he'll kill her anyway, sooner or later. Still, there might be a way to hit him hard without giving him any certain idea what's happening to him. If I simply peel his men away, one by one, wear down his force by attrition, he might think they're deserting, or that they got themselves busted, if he doesn't find their bodies around. There might must be a way . . ."

"But Ottoowa is not the only one you have to contend with."

"The late Morlaine's family? It'll take them a long time to mobilize another hit on me. By that time I'll be well away, with the job done—or dead."

"I was thinking of the police. You've left a trail of bodies. They're not sure who you are yet—but the Mafia may well tip them off."

"I'll have to risk it. I'll be sleeping here on the boat from now on. Can you get me another car?"

"Of course. Jack, my 'ears' inform me that Ottoowa has hired ten more men. Your escapades impressed him—"

"So that's about eighteen men at Château Borne. And Hayden—Hayden is a match for any twenty men." He shrugged. "I probably won't come out of this alive."

Hayden stood looking down at the girl, shaking his head sadly. A damn shame. But you take a job, you got to finish it. That was all the meaning there was in life for Sam Hayden. The years of killing, of losing loved ones who couldn't handle his life-style, of loneliness, had stripped away anything more from him. All he had left was pride in his craft.

But still . . .

She was beautiful. Probably a sweet kid. A damn shame.

She lay on the big double bed, an ornate wooden-framed bed with a blue lace canopy. She was still out cold, lying between silk sheets pulled up to her neck, her auburn-honey hair fanning over the white-silk pillowcase. Hayden hoped the sap he'd hit her with hadn't given her a concussion. He bent and patted her cheek, saying, "Hey . . . uh . . . lady, you better wake up." She moaned but didn't open her eyes.

He went to the window, threw open the shutters onto the night. The hiss and rumble of the sea came in, the breeze humming a little as it passed between the black iron bars over the window. That black iron was ivy-patterned and decorative—but it was still bars. And even if Edie could saw through it somehow, she'd find herself on a window ledge alone in the middle of a stone wall, nothing handy to climb to freedom with—and below, only sea and jagged rocks. Way, way below.

Hayden walked across the Turkish rug to the bed, hoping the sea breeze coming through the window would wake her. She began to stir and her eyes fluttered.

She wore only a halter top and shorts. She'd had a skirt on over the shorts when they'd found her, but that had gotten torn off in the struggle to subdue her. She'd shot that fool Strickland in the arm, and he'd bled all over her skirt—they'd used Strickland's blood to leave the message on the wall.

Thinking about it now, Hayden wondered why he'd left such an ambiguous message—it had almost hinted that the girl was dead. And if Sullivan thought the girl was dead, nothing would stop him from coming at them. It was almost as if he'd *wanted* Sullivan to . . .

He shook the idea away. Crazy thought.

Groaning, the girl sat up, holding her head, looking around with a wince. "*Où suis je*?" she murmured.

"I think that means 'Where am I?' in French, right? *Parle anglais*?" Hayden tried to smile reassuringly.

"Yes. Oh! You're the . . ." She broke off, backing away from him.

"Be cool, babe. I'm sorry I had to hit you. You're okay now. At least, if Sullivan doesn't make Ottoowa too mad, you're okay. I woke you up because M'lord Edge is gonna come and look in on you. Maybe slobber on you a little. But he knows you're valuable to him intact, so I don't think he'll hurt you as long as you don't piss him off and as long as you cooperate with him."

"What . . . cooperation?"

"I can't say how far he'll go . . ." He looked away from her. "But at least he's going to ask you to write a letter to Sullivan, telling him you're okay but in danger unless he stays away, et cetera." He liked her, seeing the game look of defiance on her face. "Look, at least pretend you're going to cooperate—the guy is crazy. Ottoowa. He's . . . he's dangerous. It's too easy to set him off. We all humor him. We got to call him 'M'lord' and . . . it's a lot of bullshit but we do it because he's paying us so much we could all retire after this job. So . . ."

He broke off, listening, looking at the thick metal-banded wooden door. He heard Ottoowa coming.

Edie's eyes widened as she heard the same thing: a brass band. It sounded like a whole brass band coming down the hall to the door, playing military marching music.

Hayden sighed. If it was anyone but a homicidal maniac insisting on the marching music, it would be a big joke. But no one laughed at Ottoowa and lived.

The knob turned, and Hayden snapped to attention. The door opened. Two men in army-fatigue uniforms came into the room and took up positions facing each other on either side of the door, standing rigidly at attention. And then Ottoowa came in, followed by a sheepish little man carrying a large tape deck that played the music from a cassette.

Black as midnight, gorilla-faced, yellow-eyed, with a mouth that nearly split his head in half, Ottoowa was, even without his gaudy uniform, a man people stared at. He was a barrel-thick man with short arms, stumpy fingers almost always clenched into fists. He wore a bright red nineteenth-century military dress jacket with gold epaulets and gold braid on the sleeves. The chest was bedecked with medals, and his belt—wide black patent leather—bristled with pistols and ammunition pouches. He wore black patent-leather knee boots; his fingers glimmered with jewelry. There was a diamond inset on the front of one of his incisors which sparkled when he opened his mouth. The diamond looked out of place on his stumpy yellow teeth. His grin was lopsided. So far as Hayden knew, Ottoowa had only three clearly distinct expressions. That lopsided, demented grin; a look of fierce, intense concentration; and an animal expression of rage.

Now, to Hayden's relief, Ottoowa was grinning.

Ottoowa gestured briskly at the man with the tape deck; the little man shut the sound off. Two more men came into the room when Ottoowa moved away from the door. They were silent, doggedly loyal blacks, Ottoowa's personal bodyguards. They stood just behind him, their submachine guns gripped at the ready.

Ottoowa paced back and forth, cracking his knuckles. His gaze fixed on Edie and never left her, no matter which direction he turned. She shrank under that gaze.

Hayden found himself hating Ottoowa then. Hayden was no racist. He'd worked beside a great many black and brown and yellow men, and respected them. He'd been commanded by them too, and knew they could be good officers. His hatred for Ottoowa was of a different order: sheer revulsion. But a job once begun . . .

Ottoowa spoke, as he paced, in a disarmingly polite, even soothing tone. "Good evening. You have been asleep a long time, young lady. Your name is Edie, I think. Yes? I am Brigadier General Magg Ottoowa, emperor of Maggia." He paused in his strutting to bow.

She just stared at him.

When he saw she wasn't going to acknowledge his title, he grunted, and the grin faded from his face, replaced by his look of deep concentration. His round forehead wrinkled; his eyes burned with tiny red fires. He resumed pacing, continued to speak congenially. "I am concerned for your health, young lady. I hope the accommodations are acceptable. Are you hungry?"

"*Oui,*" she admitted reluctantly. "But I have such a headache I'm afraid to chew."

"We shall fetch you aspirin and some dinner." He nodded toward the little servant with the tape deck. "Go see to it."

"Very good, M'lord," the man chirped. He left the room.

"It's very kind of you to speak English with me," Ottoowa went on. "English is a second language in my country—we were colonized by the British once. It is traditional to despise the nation which was sovereign over your own, after it has been driven out, but I rather admire the British. Yes, I do, and when I am *their* sovereign, they will come to admire *me*. I think—"

Edie interrupted, looking at the door, "I suppose it would do me no good to demand that you let me go?"

He stopped in the center of the rug, surprised at being interrupted. "Your intuition has informed you correctly, my dear." All the warmth had drained out of his voice.

"I . . . my family is an influential one, monsieur. And Monsieur Sullivan knows you've got me. He will go to the police."

"Not at all. He knows I'd kill you if he did. As for your family—they don't know where you are. And there is nothing they could do in any event. . . . Ah, here is the tray with your dinner, a little cold, as it has been waiting for you to wake. *Where is the aspirin*?" This last he roared at the servant.

"It is coming, M'lord!" The servant, hands shaking, set the tray down.

"Quickly!"

"Yes, M'lord!" The little man—balding, pasty-faced, with a slight British accent—dashed like a frightened rabbit into the hall.

Ottoowa's good humor returned. "He gives me great pleasure. He was, years ago, the chief government administrator for the British in the little corner of Maggia where I grew up. He was the oppressor of my family. After the revolution, it took me years and a great deal of money to have him found and kidnapped, brought back to me, to be my servant. . . . Well, now, enjoy your dinner, my dear. Filet of salmon, I think. Nothing poisoned, I assure you. Eventually I will decide how to use you to bait Mr. Sullivan into our hands. Or if we can find a way to get a message to him, I will ask you to write a short letter for me. Mr. Sullivan has made me very angry. Very angry. Very angry. Very . . ." He scowled, and Hayden tensed, fearing one of Ottoowa's homicidal rages. But Ottoowa's grin returned as he finished, "When I have Sullivan here, I intend to strangle him to death with his own entrails. Good night, my dear."

Midnight. Sullivan was in a black commando's outfit, complete with boots and black knit cap, his face blacked out, the Smith & Wesson SMG in his right hand. He had tied up the cabin cruiser, just behind, at the little cove a short distance south of Château Borne. There was a steep, rocky ridge, fledged with scrub and small pine trees, between Sullivan and the château. He carried a small pack of equipment on his back, everything in it secured so as not to clack when he moved. Strapped to his right calf was a long commando knife.

He began to work his way up the ridge, doing his best to keep from dislodging stones. The hiss of the sea covered much of the noise, but if there were guards on the ridgetop, he didn't want to arouse their suspicions by making even a small noise.

He soon hit on a well-worn trail, and climbed along it

silently, grateful that there was a cloud cover tonight to blot out the moonlight.

He had just reached the spiny ridgeback when he heard low voices murmuring in French: someone coming down the trail to the east, hidden by a bend. He climbed hastily onto a boulder, concealing himself on the far side from the trail. Peering through a crevice in the rock, Sullivan watched as four men, coming two at a time, strolled down the trail. Two of them were speaking English; the others whispered together in French. They were big, rangy men wearing fatigues and bulky shirts under which the outlines of bulletproof vests were clearly visible. Sullivan's combat-trained eyes picked out details in the darkness that untrained men would've missed.

One of the men carried a submachine gun in a shortened version of the M16 semiautomatic. The other three carried M16's and pistols. They darted glances at the brush. As the English-speaking guards passed beneath, Sullivan heard:

"You'd think being around Ottoowa would make you used to crazy guys, so you wouldn't be shook up about this Sullivan nut. But from what I hear, the guy's a bloodthirsty wacko. The way Hayden talked about him . . ."

"I know what you mean. Being around Ottoowa doesn't make me *used* to crazy guys—it makes me *more* scared of 'em. I—"

One of the French gunmen, evidently in command, stopped and hissed at the Yankees, "You will please be quieting down. Not so loud, Ottoowa say we quiet, no? Now, we split up—you two that way, one on right trail, one on the left."

"Hey, look, I'd feel better if we stayed toge—"

"Do as you are told or we get someone else, understand?"

"Yeah, yeah. Fucking frogs."

"What?"

"I said okay, I'm going."

Sullivan smiled. From his sniper's roost not far over their heads he could waste them all now if he wanted to, with a judicial use of the Smith & Wesson. But that would alert Ottoowa. Better stick to the alternative plan.

He waited till they'd gone in their respective patrol directions—split up to cover four parts of the ridge—and then moved into position on an adjacent boulder. The boulder was shaped like a half-moon, hooking one of its horns over the trail. He lay in the deep shadow atop the rock on his left side, quietly taking a few "working tools" out of his pack.

He worked a noose into one end of a rope, secured the other end on a spur of granite. He coiled the rope and waited.

As he'd anticipated, one of the Yankees passed down the trail beneath his boulder. The clouds broke, pouring moonlight onto the man's face. Sullivan recognized him from wanted posters he'd seen during a brief trip to New York a year before: a man named Carter, a convicted murderer who'd escaped from the New Orleans penitentiary. Typical of Ottoowa's employees.

Carter had a puggish face, one of his eyes noticeably higher than the other. He looked down the slope, away from the boulder on which Sullivan lay. Sullivan let him pass beneath, emerge on the other side—and then he whipped the noose down, so it settled gracefully over the man's head. Carter had time only to say "Whuh?" before Sullivan jerked the rope taut, closing the noose around the man's throat.

Grunting—Carter was heavy—Sullivan leaned back, pulling hand over hand to lift the hired killer off his feet.

Carter's gun clattered down the slope, lost among the bushes. His feet kicked. Sullivan hung on grimly—it was almost like using a fishing pole. Five minutes later, Carter hung limp at the end of the rope, his head bent unnaturally over his left shoulder, his face bloated and red, tongue protruding swollen and black. Sullivan lifted the corpse onto the boulder about six yards above the trail. He slung it over a conical rock, its contorted face hanging down in the shadows; it lay cooling, blood dripping from the horribly grinning mouth.

He moved back into position on the big half-moon boulder, and waited, now and then flexing his muscles to keep them from going to sleep. He might have to move quickly if someone spotted him.

The second American strolled along the trail. He was humming, and seemed strangely unconcerned. And then Sullivan smelled the reason: the man was smoking pot. Good—that would confuse him and slow his reaction time.

Just before the man—a big blond cowboy type with a leather vest—walked beneath the overhanging boulder, Sullivan kicked the corpse still attached to the rope so it slid off the rock and swung like a meaty pendulum back and forth under the boulder directly in front of the cowboy. The cowboy spat out his reefer and backed up, gagging, fumbling for his weapon.

But he became statue-still when Sullivan, atop the boulder, shone a flashlight in his eyes and hissed, "Don't move or worse things will happen to you than what happened to your friend here." And then Sullivan gave his low, insane laugh.

The man stared at the corpse of his friend, swinging on the creaking rope, its face contorted—and then nodded. "Sure, okay. You . . . you got the drop on me."

"Throw your rifle into the bushes. The pistol too."

The cowboy did as he was told.

"Good," Sullivan growled. "Now get off the trail and lie down just under me, facedown, hands behind your head."

"Okay, just don't get trigger-happy."

"I was trigger-happy years ago. . . . Good." Sullivan hauled the corpse up on its rope and dragged it into the shadows of a crevice. "Don't you move, cowboy," he said while he was doing this. "I've got one hand free, and it's pointing a gun at you."

"Look, buddy, I never had nothing against you. I—"

"Cut the bullshit and keep your voice down." Sullivan dropped from the overhang and stood over the cowboy, SMG in hand. "Get to your feet and walk straight ahead—you see that crevice? Go on in there."

"Uh . . . okay. But, listen, don't—"

"Quiet. Now, call to your French boss. Tell him you're deserting. You're fed up and you're leaving—you and Carter."

The cowboy's eyes widened when he heard his friend's name. "How did you know his—"

"I know all about you and your friend." It was true—in a sense.

"You know all about me? Look, I got a bum rap on that arson-homicide conviction. How was I to know there was little kids asleep in—?"

"Christ," Sullivan muttered, "Ottoowa sure picks the beauts. . . . Somebody's coming. Yeah, it's your C.O. Tell him what I told you. Tell him not to come near or you'll fire at him—because you know Ottoowa doesn't allow deserters."

The cowboy cleared his throat—and hesitated. Sullivan, standing close behind him, drew his commando knife and laid it against the man's throat. That was motivation: the cowboy shouted, "Hey . . . uh . . . Jacques!"

"*Oui?* Keep your voice down, fool, or the—"

"Fuck off! Me'n Larry, we're takin' off. This guy Sullivan is too weird. I don't wanna fuck with 'im. Tell Ottoowa I'll send him the advance back. We're leaving! Don't try'n follow us or we'll blow you away! Now, beat it, I got my gun aimed atcha!"

Swearing, the Frenchman backed away down the trail, then turned and ran, going—probably—to report to Ottoowa.

"You . . . you gonna let me go now?"

"You?" Sullivan snorted. "You, the guy who burned down an apartment building in some slum so the landlord could collect on the insurance? Burned up some little kids, right? That was it, wasn't it?" Sullivan was just guessing—but it was a popular scam among slumlords in New York and L.A. and Chicago. It seemed likely that's what the cowboy had been referring to.

"Yeah, but I thought everybody was out of the building."

It was clear that he was lying; Sullivan could hear it. He had an uncanny talent for detecting lies. "I don't know how you slipped the law, cowboy—maybe they got you off on a technicality. But you're paying for it here and now. Eat death, cowboy."

The cowboy did just as Sullivan had anticipated—he tried to break free, lurching forward so all Sullivan had to do was hold the knife steadily. The man ran right into the razor-sharp steel edge, executing himself in his panic. Blood, thick and warm, spurted onto Sullivan's wrist and ran down his arm. The man sank to his knees, gurgling, jerking as he bled to death. He slumped over and lay still.

Sullivan wiped the blood from his arm with the dead man's shirt. He carefully cleaned his blade, sheathed it, dragged the body into the crevice, and dumped it on the other.

Then he went prowling. He expected to get at least one more that night.

Thirty minutes later he was moving low to the ground along the edge of the cliff. He was a dizzying distance over the toothy rocks and frothing breakers below. To his left a screen of brush hid him from the trail. There was at least one other guard on this ridge, and Sullivan guessed he'd be on the promontory ahead of him.

Sullivan was wrong. The man was behind him.

He knew it when a bullet smacked into the stone beside his cheek, stinging the left side of his face with tiny bits of rock. Cursing, Sullivan whirled and ducked at the same time; a burst of bullets sang just over his head.

He cut loose with the Smith & Wesson submachine gun without having time to aim it. The hired killer fell back against the cliff edge, groaning. Sullivan's own weapon was silenced, so it made only a sharp hissing as it spat bullets. But the other man's gun had spoken loud—Sullivan hoped the sound of the breakers would drown out the gun noise. He preferred that Ottoowa think his men had simply deserted him.

Worrying about this, his mind a little distracted, Sullivan went to make sure the man who'd tried to ambush him was dead.

But the guard was playing possum. As soon as Sullivan bent over him, the man brought his M16 up and squeezed the trigger.

Reflex action saved Sullivan. He straightened and kicked at the gun, catching it at the breech with the toe of his boot. The kick struck the barrel back so that the gun roared over Sullivan's shoulder, but so close his cheek was burned by its muzzle flash and his ears rang.

Sullivan jumped a step back, kicked again, this time balancing and aiming in a karate move, to get the maximum impact. The kick connected and the gun went spinning over the edge, onto the rocks. The guard rolled aside, leaving a glistening patch of red on the rock where he'd lain—Sullivan had wounded him with his SMG burst.

Sullivan swung the Smith & Wesson around to finish the job.

But even a wounded man can move quickly when he knows he's about to be executed. The clouds broke again, and moonlight poured down on them. The man was an experienced fighter, a true mercenary, Sullivan guessed—he was a brawny, black-eyed man with an old bullet scar creasing his right cheek, his hair clipped in a military crewcut. He grinned at Sullivan to show he wasn't afraid, and was up in a crouch, within the reach of Sullivan's gun barrel. He shouldered the Smith & Wesson aside and slammed Sullivan in the pit of the stomach with a ham-sized fist.

Sullivan felt like the world had turned inside out. He gasped, and staggered backward, trying to bring the gun muzzle between him and his assailant.

The man continued to bull Sullivan back till he had him pinned against the rock. Sullivan, still gasping for air, found himself cheek to grizzled cheek with the mercenary. The man favored his left shoulder—that would be where Sullivan had hit him, then. Sullivan snapped his forehead down hard, like the head of a hammer, onto the bullet wound in the man's shoulder.

The big man howled and his grip loosened for a moment. Sullivan brought his knee up sharply into the man's groin. The mercenary staggered back—but caught hold of Sullivan's gun barrel with his right hand, forcing it up and away from him.

Sullivan reached for his commando knife and got it clear of the sheath just as the big iron-muscled thug rammed him again with his right shoulder, striking Sullivan squarely in the sternum. Sullivan shivered with pain. Points of light flickered before his eyes. But he wrenched free and slashed at the other with the commando knife in his left hand. The man let go of his gun barrel to block the knife thrust. Sullivan swung the gun between them and squeezed the trigger but once more the big man, though wounded and battered, leaped aside with almost supernatural speed, a split second before the Smith & Wesson hissed steel-jacketed slugs.

He stepped in, knocked the gun aside with his left fist, and caught the wrist of Sullivan's knife hand with his right. The man kicked with his right foot—and caught the SMG squarely in the magazine, knocking it from Sullivan's grip. But that kick exposed his ribs—and Sullivan aimed a vicious kick at them, heard them crack as he connected. The man wrenched loose, and fell, grunting, rolling to Sullivan's right, dangerously near the cliff edge—and near the machine gun. It had fallen close beside the rim of the precipice.

Shouting with triumph, the mercenary snatched up the gun, leaped to his feet, braced himself to fire . . .

Sullivan had a split second to make a decision. He stood with his back against a wall of rock, just two yards from a man who had a machine gun pointed at him. If he jumped to the right or left, the man—an experienced gunman—would compensate and swing to cut him to pieces. If he threw his knife, it would never reach its mark in time. But if he leaped forward and down, at the big man's ankles—the man had the gun tilted upward, so *that* might give him the moment he needed.

All this Sullivan considered in that fraction of a heartbeat as the mercenary was drawing a bead on him.

Sullivan leaped—and as he went, he realized that his momentum would carry them both over the cliff.

The submachine gun hissed, sizzling the air near Sullivan's right ear with bullets. Then Sullivan connected with the mercenary's knees, taking him off his feet in a football tackle.

They went sailing over the cliff edge into space.

Sullivan felt unreal, turning end over end, still gripping the man's knees, and it was as if time had slowed—they seemed to fall through syrup, though this was an illusion created by his frantically racing brain. He saw the submachine gun whirl past him, a spinning blur of metal. The other man had let go of it, and Sullivan had lost his knife. He moved instinctively—though his mind told him: *That's it, you were overconfident and now you're dead*—to force the bigger man beneath him as they turned, holding him now by the biceps. . . .

They struck. The mercenary struck the rock first, and Sullivan fell atop him, his fall cushioned a little by the man's broken body. Even so—and though they'd struck the rock only glancingly—Sullivan felt like he'd been crumpled up and thrown away. Forces mightier than him had taken over—the immense gravitational suck of the earth, the murderously hard sheer mass of those jagged rocks, the thundering waves crashing down on him. The sea closing over his head.

All the wind had been knocked from Sullivan, and his chest ached where he'd taken the brunt of the blow when they hit the rock—it hurt like an explosion that wouldn't stop exploding. The water—surprisingly cold, dark as the depths of a tar pit—surged around him, oblivious of the pain its wrenching cost him. It lifted him, seemed to raise him the way a baseball batter poises a bat, then slammed him against the rocks again and again, while his brain screamed for oxygen and his limbs turned to lead. Death closed in on him, and he seemed to see the laughing, bestial face of Magg Ottoowa mocking him, telling him: You were overconfident and now you're dead, you were overconfident and now you're dead, you were overconfident . . .

No!

Sullivan found the inner tap for the strength that came to him when he was sufficiently enraged. He turned on the tap, and strength flowed through him.

Once more a wave threw him against the rock, but this time he clung, though the flinty edges cut his fingers and his limbs felt as if they were ripping, the suction of the wave's receding trying to tear him loose.

But he held on, and at last the wave fell away from him. He sputtered, spat salt water, and drank in the open air.

Every movement hurt, but he forced himself to climb higher on the rock, out of reach of the sea. His throat burned with salt water, his ears rang, his head pounded with ache, but he felt a singing sense of triumph. He'd lived through it.

The mercenary's limp, shattered body—the cushion that had saved Sullivan's life—floated like so much flotsam in the water, facedown, spinning as the eddies caught it, then dragged out to sea. . . .

Sullivan watched it go and felt a pang of regret. The man had been a formidable fighter.

Jack Sullivan coughed, and dragging limbs that seemed weighed down by invisible anchor chains, he made his way by the dim moonlight to the tumble of boulders at the base of the cliff. From there he could sidle around to a beach—with luck. He sighed. He'd have to go up and get those bodies and bury them. It would be a long night.

8

The Sea of Blood

"Looks like a painting of a sunset," Sullivan muttered, gazing at himself in the mirror. He was naked from the waist up. On his chest was a bruise bigger than a football, over the right pectoral and spreading down onto the ribs. It was bright red in the center, spreading out from there into rays of violet and purple. "A *bad* painting," Sullivan added.

He shrugged—and regretted it, since even that much movement of his shoulders hurt—and turned away from the mirror to the cabin cruiser's washbasin. He had to stand a little bent over in the cramped cabin. He dabbed antiseptic on the lacerations along his gut, then taped a pressure bandage on to hold his four cracked ribs in place.

He'd just finished his wound-dressing and pulled on his jersey when he heard the door to the boat garage open. He checked the Beretta, found it in order, loaded and ready to kill, and moved to peer from the edge of the little porthole.

All he could see was a pair of white trousers moving past on the dock beside the boat, a little above the porthole.

He moved to the door, prepared to shoot through it. He heard the creak as someone dropped onto the boat, then footsteps as the person moved to the door. He cocked the gun—

"Sullivan! Jack, are you . . . ?"

Sullivan relaxed, shaking his head, and opened the door. Malta came in. "Dammit, Malta, why don't you give the signal, man? I almost blew you away."

Malta slapped his forehead, said apologetically, "Ah, *excusez moi, je—*"

"In English."

"You see? I am not myself today. I am being forgetful from worry, Jack." He sat down on the bunk. "I'm afraid I have taken a sort of paternal interest in this little girlfriend of yours. I brought you into this job, and that led to her involvement—and to her situation now, yes? And the bad news this morning . . . I am simply not—"

"What bad news?" Sullivan asked, taking a pot of espresso off the mini-stove. He poured out two cups, and glanced at his watch. It was nearly eleven A.M. Well, he'd needed that rest. He wouldn't get many more till it was over.

"The French police. They know about Ottoowa. They know he's here. I'm afraid they may have someone watching his château."

Sullivan sipped his espresso, and sighed. Bad news and bad coffee. Great combination. "Yeah, that's . . ." He shook his head. "Ottoowa will kill her if they move in on him. He'll think I put them onto him."

"Perhaps. But I have a friend in the ministry who told me about this. He told me that they are not yet ready to arrest Ottoowa. There's some debate about Ottoowa's legal status. And they are a little worried about all those men he hired. So they are taking their time, planning, acting like rabbits—which is lucky for us. It might give us time."

"*Us?*" Sullivan looked at Malta.

"I . . ." Malta looked sheepish. "I feel foolish letting my feelings get the better of my common sense. But I want to help you save the girl. I will feel bad if you are both killed."

"Malta, you astonish me. I never knew you had a conscience. Are you actually proposing to take up a gun and storm the enemy's position with me?"

Malta looked unhappy. "*Oui*. Stupid of me. But, yes."

Sullivan grinned. "I'll find a use for you."

"So, Jack . . ." Malta chuckled. "I have heard something: that Ottoowa is trying to hire more men. It seems three of his men 'deserted.' "

"Did they? Yeah, they deserted the whole damn world. You think he'll replace them?"

"No. He was lucky to get the fighters he has—it is not easy to find men one can trust, men with no shred of scruples, in France."

"It's tough anywhere to find men you can *trust* who have

no scruples!'' Sullivan laughed. ''Ottoowa's got a problem, all right. He'll try to get bona-fide mercenaries, but that takes time. You have to find them, interview them, screen them, brief them—the finding alone could take weeks.''

Malta nodded. ''Still, there is the problem of the police surveillance of Château Borne. . . .''

Sullivan lit a cigarette, blew smoke at the porthole, and said thoughtfully, ''Maybe a little baksheesh.''

''Not a little, I am afraid. A lot.''

''How much?''

''I think I can bribe them to be gone on a specific night for forty thousand dollars.''

Sullivan whistled.

''*Oui*—a lot of money for turning the back. But these men will be risking their careers.''

''Okay. Take it out of my—''

''I already have. May I have a cigarette?''

''I would've thought you *already* took one.'' He tossed him the pack.

Malta chuckled. Then his expression became grave. ''You move stiffly, Jack—you are hurt?''

''Just a little bruised. Well, a lot bruised. I was lucky, considering. I'll be okay once I get moving.''

''When do we hit him, Jack?''

''When the time's right. When my instinct tells me. Soon. I think it'd be best to peel away a few more 'deserters.' ''

''Then you will have an opportunity today—Ottoowa has set sail in his yacht.''

Sullivan stiffened. ''*What?*''

Malta held up a hand in a gesture that said: Keep calm. ''He's not going for long. My friends among the police say he took along your friend and a few guards, and took the yacht out to sea—they think he's got a rendezvous, maybe on an atoll somewhere. He has a meeting, it seems, with someone afraid to come to France even in secret. Or afraid to be seen there with Ottoowa. Probably his secret financial backers for the coup. Maybe men with business interests in Maggia who prefer a dictatorship which will give them forced labor—the government currently in power is democratically elected, and they are not willing to force their people to work on plantations for nothing. Ottoowa had no regrets about doing that.''

"But how do you know he's coming back?"

"Most of his guards stayed at the château. He took on no supplies. There are signs."

"I hope you're right. Hey, if we could find that yacht . . ."

"No, I fear not. I found out about it hours after the yacht left this morning. It's too late to follow him. I expect he will come back tonight."

"Yeah? Then it's time for you and me to take a boat ride."

The *Essex Returns* sat an anchor near a small island.

Sam Hayden stood at the rail of the immense white yacht, watching the horizon sink and rise and sickeningly sink again as the vessel rocked in the waves. It made him ill—but the scene going on behind him was equally nauseating. Or worse. Finally he shrugged and turned to watch Ottoowa's "evening entertainment," as he'd called it.

Ottoowa's idea of entertainment was making two men fight to the death with ordinary kitchen forks.

Hayden leaned back against the rail, blinking in the sunlight. The noonday sun washed over the decks and chased all the shadows under the deck chairs.

Two men, facing each other, stood on the wooden white-painted deck between Hayden and Ottoowa. "M'lord Edge" sat in an intricately carved wooden throne he'd brought from Africa—an heirloom made of mahogany inlaid with ivory and precious stones. Once, Ottoowa had caught a servant trying to pry one of those rubies loose—the man's screams had been heard for two days afterward.

Edie, in a simple white shift, sat in a canvas chair beside Ottoowa. She looked more tired than scared. Sure had a nice shape on her, that girl. Hayden let his eyes linger on her long, shapely brown legs, her smooth shoulders, her almost swollen breasts. But the glow of lust in him changed to sadness when he looked at her face. Almost a little girl's face. With her hair mussed and that bruise over her eye, she looked to Hayden like a lost little girl.

Dammit, he told himself, push thoughts like that out and keep 'em out.

She sat with her hands in her lap, fingers opening and closing nervously. She tried to keep her eyes on the horizon, but now and then Ottoowa would lean over and hiss through his hideous grin, "Watch my little entertainment, my dear! Watch! It is most amusing!"

Afraid to anger him, she'd force herself to watch.

The son of a bitch, Hayden thought. If I hadn't taken this job and committed myself, I might just apply for a job helping Sullivan waste him. Ottoowa's an insult to all the good black men, the smart, strong black men I used to know. If Sullivan were here, he'd say—what was it he used to say?—yeah: "It isn't the color of a man's skin that matters, it's the color of his soul."

Ottoowa's insides were blacker than his skin.

Ottoowa watched greedily as the two men, clad only in their shorts, each with a silver fork in his right hand, circled each other, now and then making clumsy, halfhearted jabs. The two black bodyguards, expressionless, stood just behind Ottoowa, their submachine guns pointing over his shoulders at the men with forks.

Ottoowa sat restlessly in his squat, demon-carved throne, shifting his weight from side to side, his hands clutching his knees, then moving to slap the armrests when he was pleased with a particularly vicious jab. There weren't enough vicious jabs in the "entertainment" to suit Ottoowa; he drew one of his pistols and fired twice at the deck near the feet of the two "fork gladiators," pocking the wood and kicking up splinters. "*Attack him* or next time I shoot you! Stop playing children's games!" Ottoowa roared.

The "entertainment" consisted of two men who'd annoyed Ottoowa. One was the little prune-faced baldheaded man—pallid and flabby in his undershorts, sweating, gasping with effort—who must have been near sixty. The other was a middle-aged black man with a hangdog expression, a look of resignation; he was skinny and sweating even more than his opponent. The black man had been the yacht's cook—he'd cooked an egg wrong that morning—and the other, Ottoowa's personal servant (the former colonial administrator whom Ottoowa had kidnapped), had annoyed Ottoowa simply by "boring" him.

Ottoowa was careful not to try to mount "entertainments" using his mercenary force; despite his doggedly loyal bodyguards, there was too much chance a man like Hayden would put a bullet through Ottoowa's forehead before those submachine guns brought him down. Sometimes Hayden wished

Ottoowa would try something of the kind. Hayden was tired of living, and it would be a pleasure to kill the man. . . .

But Ottoowa was as cunning as he was crazy.

Goaded by the gunshots, the little men with the forks charged each other, raking the absurd weapons down overhand. The black man scored a hit on the erstwhile colonial administrator, sinking the tines into the meat of his thigh.

Ottoowa clapped his hands with delight. He turned to one of his bodyguards and spoke in his native language, a phrase that Hayden had learned, which meant, "Bring my wives to me." The man nodded and went below deck.

Meanwhile, the man with the fork in his thigh was screaming, backing away, the fork wagging in the wound with his movements. The man who'd stuck it there stared at it as if he couldn't believe what he'd done. The little white man backed against a mast—and came to himself. He plucked the fork from his thigh, and armed with one in each hand, a thin stream of blood running down his leg, ran shouting at the other.

"In his eyes!" Ottoowa shouted. "In his eyes!" He pounded the lion's-claw arms of his throne with excitement, his yellow grin flashing, the diamond in his tooth catching the sunlight, wraparound sunglasses making him a sinister enigma. "Stab him in the eyes!"

The black man had slumped, almost to the point of falling. He swayed on his feet. He closed his eyes and waited. He knew Ottoowa, Hayden guessed. He knew it didn't matter whether he died this way or another.

The pale-fleshed man with the skinny, flab-waggling arms brought the forks down hard, overhand, and drove them simultaneously into the black man's eyes.

Edie screamed and covered her face with her hands.

The little black man gave a faint moan and sank to his knees. He looked like some strange form of insect, the fork handles sticking from his eye sockets like antennae. He shuddered and fell, clawing at his face, beginning to flop about, his moaning becoming a sound of deep-throated anguish.

Hayden's gun spoke.

He'd drawn his .45 pistol and neatly shot the little black man through the head, ending his misery.

Ottoowa leaped to his feet, his grin becoming a snarl. His bodyguard brought the submachine gun to bear on Hayden.

Hayden stood with his gun arm hanging limply at his side, looking completely relaxed. He smiled faintly. "The noise annoyed me," he said. "All that screaming. I've got a headache. Do you mind very much . . . M'lord?"

Ottoowa looked at the gun in Hayden's hand. He sank back onto his throne. And shrugged. His grin came back. "Very good, Mr. Hayden. But please remember that, next time, it is Edge who is the referee for these little games. Not you."

Hayden nodded and replaced his gun in its holster.

The bodyguard slowly lowered the submachine gun, with an air of mild disappointment.

The balding little man, the "victor" in the "entertainment," stood panting, his lips cracked, staring at the shattered head, the disfigured eyes, of his former opponent. Without a sound, he began to cry. His chest heaved; tears rolled down his cheeks.

Ottoowa laughed raspily. "My servant!" he called.

The little man turned to face Ottoowa.

"You think you are victorious. So you might have been. I might have been lenient because you have pleased me. But you are showing weakness that shames us all. Crying for the enemy. Disgusting. A bad example. I now make a different kind of example of you."

He drew a pistol from his belt, and aiming carefully, shot the man through the left kneecap. The .45 made an explosion in the flesh of the knee as if a small bomb had gone off inside it: the skin folded back in ragged petals, the bone splinters flying out from the round red hole, followed by a drool of blood. The wounded man was knocked from his feet, fell forward, wailing, pounding the deck, howling, "No it's not bloody fair, it's not—"

And then suddenly he clawed at his chest, quivered, gulped air, and lay still. He began to turn blue. He'd escaped Ottoowa at the last moment—with a heart attack.

Enraged, Ottoowa rushed from his throne and began to kick the corpse, fracturing ribs, denting the skull so that blood sprayed across the deck from the torn scalp.

Hayden watched moodily. He'd seen worse.

Ottoowa snarled an order at his bodyguard. The man slung the SMG over his shoulder, went to the corpse, carried it to the rail—holding it almost at arm's length so the blood wouldn't drip on him—and pitched it over the side.

They were well out into the Mediterranean, far from land, except for the deserted atoll off to the starboard. There was no one around to link the drifting body, if it were found, with the yacht. And probably, Hayden reflected, the fish would nibble it away soon enough.

Ottoowa shouted for a steward to clean away the blood, and returned to his throne.

Edie sat beside him, weeping.

The second bodyguard had returned to the deck with two handsome black women dressed in leaf-patterned wraparound dresses, golden circlets holding their hair in place. They looked frightened and nervous.

Hayden had heard that Ottoowa was unhappy with his wives—he'd had some forty wives and had become "unhappy" with each of them in turn. And each had disappeared. There was no mystery about Ottoowa's bad luck with women. Even the most cunning woman couldn't conceal her loathing, at certain times. It was said there'd been one woman who *hadn't* loathed Ottoowa, who had admired him. But she'd nearly succeeded in pulling off a successful coup against him, and he'd reluctantly had to shoot her.

The steward, stone-faced, had cleaned up the blood with a mop. He brought Ottoowa a cold drink. Hayden accepted a daiquiri. Edie drank a whiskey. She had stopped crying, but she looked wrung out and empty. In a toneless voice she asked, "Excuse me, M'lord, may I go to the bathroom?"

"Hm?" He turned to look at her. "Yes, yes, go. You are a great bore, with all your sniffling. Go."

Ottoowa turned to his wives, and spoke to them in his native tongue. They nodded and sat at his feet, one to either side, knees drawn up, obediently listening to some bitter harangue that Hayden was grateful he couldn't understand.

Edie went to the hatchway. One of the bodyguards started to follow her, to keep an eye on her, but Hayden made a gesture that said: I'll do it. The man shrugged and went to stand behind his master. He stood in the hot sun, beads of sweat standing out on his black forehead, looking wistfully at Ottoowa's ice-clinking drink.

Hayden went to the hatchway and waited. When he heard the bathroom door open and Edie come out, he started back to his post at the rail. But he stopped in his tracks, hearing something that scared him. He was not a man easily scared, but this time he was scared by a woman's whisper. He'd been afraid this moment would come. She whispered from behind him, "Wait . . . I want to talk to you."

He knew she was going to ask him for help. He knew he would have to say no to her. But he knew he was going to hate having to say no. The smart thing to do would be to ignore her. But he turned back, and stood in the shade of the hatchway.

She stood just inside the door, a few steps down from him. "You're not a bad person," she said. "I know you're not. You didn't shoot that man to make him quiet. You shot him to save him from misery."

"Only because it wasn't risking my ass or my job."

"But it *was* a risk—you knew Ottoowa wouldn't like it. *Oui*? You knew he might do anything, he might order his men to shoot you. But you did it anyway. It was an act of kindness."

Hayden ground his teeth together. "Bullshit," he hissed. "I did it to spite Ottoowa. I agreed to work for him. But I don't got to like him."

"But why do you have to work for him? Not really for money, is it? A man like you could—"

"You wanna know why?" He laughed softly. "It's funny. Real funny. I figured it out the other day. I work for him because I hate him so much. See, a few years ago I decided that nothing matters. Not the way people just go up like smoke in this world. We're nothing, see? So nothing matters. So what's the point of living when nothing matters—and when all the good stuff in life has gone out of it? I don't know why, but I can't enjoy nothin' no more. So I figure the only thing that matters is what you make up *for yourself* to be important. With me, it's a job. I decided, see, whatever job I got, that's important and nothing else is. Keeping busy with work. But to prove it to myself, prove that the only important thing is the job, I got to take one I don't like. Workin' for an asshole. I found the king of the assholes."

"Monsieur . . ." There was desperation in her voice. "Monsieur, I . . . I think you are a sad, lonely man. That is why you say these things. If you can help me . . . I can help you. I can help you find good things again."

"Look, I'm sorry. That's the only time I'm gonna say it. I was the one who bagged you, right? I hit you on the head. Did I show you what a nice guy I was then? I ain't no nice guy, lady, so—"

Her soft sobbing interrupted him. "Please . . . I can't go on. It is too ugly, the things he makes me see. Please, I can't stay here."

He swallowed. "Look, if you hang on, I'll see that . . . that he doesn't do nothin' crazy to you. If I can. That's all I can promise. Now, don't talk to me no more."

He strode to the rail and called to the steward for another drink.

The sea's choppiness had lessened; the boat sat motionless at anchor, just off the almost featureless crag of rock-and-pebble beach, no more than an acre, that was to be their rendezvous point with the business cartel's representatives. He saw another yacht approaching, a smaller blue boat coming from the southeast. That would be them.

Ottoowa was speaking more and more loudly in his native tongue. The excitement in his voice made Hayden turn. It wasn't smart to keep your back turned to Ottoowa when he was in one of those moods. Come to think of it, it wasn't smart *ever* to turn your back to him.

Ottoowa, in his excitement, burst into English. "You think I don't know? But I know, woman! I know your thoughts! I am a god, and a god can read minds! And I know the things you think about *me*!" He had jumped to his feet, stood quivering, pointing a shaking finger at the end of a ramrod-straight arm at one of his cowering wives. He had chosen the smaller of the two as being the "conspirator."

She shook her head wildly and babbled denials.

He turned to the larger woman. "You can show me your loyalty!" He drew both pistols from his belt. He gripped one in his right hand; the other he gave to the bigger woman. He pointed to the smaller, then shouted an order in his native language.

The bigger woman shook her head, tears filling her eyes. Hayden felt a surge of admiration for her: at the cost of her life, she'd refused to execute the other woman.

Hayden was almost tempted to interfere.

But he told himself: It's just exactly moments like this that you prove to yourself you live according to what you believe in: the job is everything.

So he forced himself to watch when Ottoowa shot the bigger woman at point-blank range through the belly. The small of her back erupted outward, the torn flesh and torn dress all mixed together in blood and shreds of entrails. It didn't take her long to die.

But it took the other one a long time to die, because Ottoowa killed her a different way. With a dull knife.

And that was something Hayden couldn't watch.

He went to the rail and grimly tried to ignore the blood-chilling screams. He saw the yacht getting closer, and he scanned the horizon for another boat.

He didn't know it, but he was hoping he'd see The Specialist's boat.

Sullivan's boat, however, was a long way away. It was speeding north along the coast, cutting waves with a deep white wake as he rounded the headlands. He didn't slow till he came in sight of the château.

His every movement hurt, because of the enormous bruise on his chest and the cracked ribs, but he piloted the boat in toward the château, the pain swept away in an almost narcotic flow of fury.

There was a cabin cruiser tied up at the jetty below the château. Sullivan cut the engines and let the boat drift. He examined the jetty through field glasses. The other boat was smaller than his, and possibly faster. There was a good chance it was at least partly armored.

A dark man, probably a Palestinian, judging by the cut of his burnoose, sat in the cabin cruiser with an M16 across his knees. He was gazing out to sea. After a moment he noticed Sullivan's boat. There was a flare of light reflected from glass as he raised binoculars to check out the stranger. He must have recognized Sullivan, for he went immediately to his boat's radiophone and made a call—probably to the château; the yacht would be too far away to raise on light radio equipment.

Sullivan had guessed right: three men came bounding down the stone stairs from the château. In three minutes they'd joined their fellow on the smaller cruiser.

"Ottoowa must have offered a fat bonus for your head," Malta observed.

Sullivan nodded. He watched as the men in the boat cast off and turned the boat seaward. It coughed blue smoke, and then the rumble of its engines came to them, rising in pitch as it picked up speed. It was dull silver, the color of a polished knife, and it slashed toward them as if it wanted to cut them in half with its prow.

Sullivan smiled. "That's it," he said. "Come and get it, boys."

He pressed the ignition switch. The engine turned over—and sputtered, and died.

"Shit," Sullivan muttered. He tried again. The engine whined but wouldn't turn over.

He glanced at the knife-colored cruiser speeding toward them. He had maybe thirty seconds before it was within machine-gun range. They could hold it off for a while, but he didn't have the heavier weapons necessary to sink it—not with him. When the enemy saw the boat was stalled, they'd circle, firing continuously, and, outgunning them, would cut them to pieces.

Malta was working over the engine. He cursed in French. Then he cursed in an Algerian dialect of French. He worked through curses in two more languages, shouting between times, "I think it's the points—they are rusted on the spark plugs!"

He was scraping at the spark plugs with a knife.

The speeding cruiser was nearly upon them. Sullivan could see two men on either side of the windshield, leveling M16's to fire. He twisted the ignition switch.

The engine groaned and turned over, roaring into life. Sullivan threw the boat into gear and twisted the steering wheel, turning a tight circle, throwing up a circular skirt of spray. Bullets zipped into the water behind them and ricocheted from the armored cabin door. They ground into high gear, and as if startled by the bullets rebounding from its hide, Sullivan's heavier cruiser reared back in the water with a sudden burst of speed.

Sullivan piloted the boat in evasive action, zigzagging, doubling back when the enemy gained on him, and swerving to put the occasional outcroppings of rock between him and his pursuers. Once they were out of sight of the château, Malta knelt beside the engine casing and opened fire on the other boat. The shooting was difficult for both sides as the boats leaped and fishtailed in the water, kicking up great tails of spray, sometimes jouncing like flat rocks skipped by a skillful boy, leaping entirely out of the water, coming down with a *whump* that sent the crews clutching for support.

Both boats made looping ribbons of wake on the sea. Under such conditions the best Malta could do was force the enemy to keep their heads down, taking potshots when the boat was momentarily steady.

They had begun to encounter other craft, and it wouldn't be long before reports of gunfire at sea would bring the French equivalent of the Coast Guard down on them.

The setup would have to be soon, Sullivan decided. He scanned the coastline for the proper location. . . . So many swimmers, sailboats, motorboats now, it would be difficult to find a spot secluded enough.

"Malta!" he shouted over the roar of the engine and the hiss of the sea. "Take the wheel!"

Malta dropped the M16 and took over. Sullivan went below to consult a map. There—a stretch of coast fairly deserted because there were so many shoals and outcroppings, dangerous for boats. Dangerous for his, too, but he'd have to risk that.

Too bad he hadn't had time to find the ideal spot for the setup earlier. That would have been better tactics, but he'd had to act quickly, before the return of Ottoowa's yacht.

He went topside and took the wheel, piloting now in a beeline for the little lagoon he wanted, and trying to outdistance the enemy craft.

Sailboat sailors cursed at him as he rocketed so close to them they nearly overturned in his backwash. Consulting the chart with quick glances, he worked his way toward the rocky cliffs, moving in as close as he dared. He was only a few yards from the churning breakers on their right. He was forced to slow, five minutes later, when they came to a maze of jagged outcroppings. Seabirds rose shrieking from the rocks as they wove between them. Now and then the hull scraped bottom, and Sullivan knew they'd lose their screws if they hit a particularly hard jut of rock.

The enemy craft had slowed to a crawl, was working its way cautiously between the rocks. Malta and Ottoowa's men exchanged shots when the intervening rocks parted to allow it, resulting only in scratches on bulletproof windshields and dents in the deck. Still, a well-placed shot could put the engine out of commission—or take Malta between the eyes. Sullivan decided that the risk wasn't necessary at this point in the campaign. "Malta!" he shouted over his shoulder. "Take cover—go below and get the equipment ready!"

"Aye, aye, sir!"

Sullivan grinned, and gunned the engine to greater speed, seeing the maze of rocks open up for the lagoon he was looking for. He needed to put a little "operating time" between him and his pursuers.

It was a small lagoon, comma-shaped, the tail of the comma pointing out to sea. He swung the boat into the wider area of the lagoon and sharply to the left, so it was hidden from his pursuers by a tumble of boulders on the shore. He left it in first gear, then engaged the automatic pilot to make the cruiser nose in to the shore. He snatched up his Belgian FN-FAL, the automatic rifle he'd come to prefer for short-range sniping, and leaped from the boat into the knee-deep water. He sloshed to shore and took up a concealed firing position between two wedge-shaped red boulders. He lay on his belly, legs in a V behind, adjusting the rifle's sights for estimated range.

At the same time, Malta, as prearranged, carrying only a pistol and a small black box, leaped ashore and ran into the scrub ringing the beach. The box he carried was bare except for one face, which contained two dials, an antenna, and a miniature stick shift and steering wheel. He concealed himself behind a fallen log overgrown with creeping vines. Chuckling, he threw a switch on the black box—which was no bigger than a family-size cereal box—and threw the gear knob into reverse. The boat responded, backing away from shore just as the enemy cabin cruiser hove into the lagoon.

The silvery cabin cruiser made a throat-clearing sound as it shifted down, slackening speed to cautiously assess the situation. The men in the boat were still some thirty yards away, but Sullivan could see that their eyes were fixed on his own cabin cruiser. So far, they hadn't detected the setup. The door to the pilot's cabin in Sullivan's boat was shut, and Malta kept the boat moving so that the enemy got no clear look through the windshields—with luck, they wouldn't see that no one was standing at the wheel.

Malta kept the boat circling in the lagoon, always at the far side from the enemy. The two boats circled like wary knife fighters going round and round a central point, looking for an opening.

Sullivan sighted in on the back of the enemy boat. Three men were crouched there, taking a bead on his decoy; a fourth stood pilot.

He regretted he hadn't been able to be certain of the range ahead of time—he might have reset the sights properly. Still, it was a good three-power scope, and the enemy, when Malta brought them into position, should be well within effective range. The automatic rifle used 7.62 × 51 mm NATO ammunition. It was gas-operated, with a thirty-round capacity in its detachable box magazine. Sullivan had two such ammo magazines at his elbow; the third was already in the rifle. The twenty-one-inch (533mm) barrel rested on an extended tripod; the butt fit neatly against his right shoulder. The Israelis had made good use of this rifle, and an Israeli infantry captain, as a personal favor, had shown Sullivan how to use it on the range. But this was his first opportunity to try it out on live, moving targets. For Sullivan, every field operation was also an educational exercise. Soldiers who kept learning kept living.

Sullivan squinted through the sights, centering his cross hairs on the man who held the M16 with that ease of familiarity that showed long experience—the man who'd be most dangerous.

But the boat was at that instant on the far side of the lagoon. The tripod, while increasing muzzle stability and therefore accuracy, restricted his ability to move the sights to follow a moving target. So he let the boat slide out of his sights, waiting till it came around again, beneath him.

There was a moment or two of deceptive quiet. The birds, frightened into silence by the arrival of the boats, began to call again. The cicadas resumed their sawing song. The lagoon was almost mirror flat, reflecting the pine trees and groups of palms overhanging the narrow pebble beach. The boats puttered around in low gear, quiet and sedate as swans.

And then the enemy opened up on Sullivan's decoy. The lagoon echoed with the thuds and cracks of rifle fire, the stuttering of automatic weapons. Blue-gray gunsmoke rose in a veil from the silver cruiser—frightened birds rose, too, from the trees behind.

Sullivan smiled and held his fire.

The enemy boat had picked up speed, was pulling up alongside the decoy. The gunmen paused, jabbering at one another, apparently puzzled at the lack of response.

"Come on, Malta," Sullivan muttered. "Get it moving."

As if Malta had heard him—though he was well out of earshot—the bigger cabin cruiser suddenly spun in a tight circle and drove directly at the silver boat. The enemy corrected course just in time, swerving to avoid the collision. Spray from the decoy boat spattered the men in the other. They took up the chase, their boat nosing around to follow the decoy.

Malta led them on a wild-goose chase around the lagoon, inducing them to use up their ammunition, piloting evasively so that few of their shots connected. After repeated impacts, one of the so-called bulletproof windshields on the port side of Sullivan's craft shattered inward. The wooden fiberboard concealing the armoring on the rear bulkheads began to be shot away, revealing the blue metal beneath. It wouldn't be long before some random shot knocked out the remote-control reception antenna or put the engine out of order. That would ruin the setup. It was time to bring the sitting ducks into the shooting gallery.

Malta realized this at almost the same moment Sullivan did. He reduced the decoy boat's speed so it was just ahead of the enemy's prow, and moved it to the port or starboard to block the way whenever the smaller boat tried to overtake it. In this way he led them directly beneath Sullivan's sniping position, as close to the shore as possible. Sullivan could hear the hulls scraping on the rocks. His own boat passed beneath his firing position, and a second later the enemy boat hove into his sights, just ten yards away from him.

He had already lowered the tripod to compensate for his higher elevation—the rifle barrel pointed downward from his position, since the surface on which he lay was sloped toward the lagoon, his feet slightly higher than his head.

The boat slid into his sights—and nearly stopped dead. For Malta had abruptly changed gears, throwing the decoy boat into reverse—it backed into the prow of the boat behind. The enemy craft's pilot angled to port to avoid a direct head-to-tail collision, and the boats cracked together glancingly, rocking from the impact and rebounding. Two of the men in the rear of the enemy craft were thrown from firing position, falling back on their asses. The boat was effectively contained, for a few precious seconds, directly beneath Sullivan's firing position.

He centered the fine red cross hairs on the big man with the M16 and squeezed the trigger three times.

An automatic weapon fires more effectively, and is less likely to jam, if fired in short bursts of at least three rounds but not more than fifteen—or so some claim. Sullivan belonged to this school of thought, and squeezed off three five-round bursts into the rear of the enemy boat. His first target shouted and threw back his head, as if in exaltation—and fell back twitching, the M16 still clutched across his chest, his throat torn to a few rags with the first burst.

The second burst stitched the man with the burnoose across the chest so that he tossed his semiautomatic into the air like a parade baton as he staggered backward, doing a strange jerky dance as he went. He tumbled over the low rail, and splashed into the water, floating facedown behind the boat, a red stain spreading from his midsection to surround him like an aura.

The third burst was too high, and completely missed Sullivan's third target; Sullivan decided that the FN-FAL automatic rifle jerked its muzzle up a bit more than he'd expected, maybe because after several bursts the heat in the chamber increased the expansion of its escaping detonation gases. He shifted his position slightly to compensate.

The man he had missed, a short, squat man in fatigues, was on his knees now, trying to take cover behind the railing, and spraying the rocks at random with his submachine gun. One burst rattled off the rock just over Sullivan's head, stinging the back of his neck with minute rock chips. The enemy gunman spotted Sullivan and shouted something at the pilot as he tried to bring his SMG to bear on Sullivan's position, at the same time backing toward the cabin door and better cover. But the submachine gun is less effective at that range, and difficult to direct into a narrow sniper's roost with any accuracy. Bullets screamed off the rock around Sullivan, but none of them found their mark.

Sullivan was at a more advantageous angle, and had the more appropriate weapon—Hayden had always told him that selecting the proper weapon for an anticipated encounter situation was half the battle—and he exploited that advantage. He fired two quick bursts into the man, carving a connect-the-dots X of half-dollar-size craters in his torso. The gunman fell back against the cabin door and slid lifeless to the deck, submachine gun falling between his knees.

The pilot desperately tried to take the boat out of firing range, but Malta, at the remote-control box, kept the decoy always in the way, blocking the escape route and pushing the smaller, less powerful boat back into the lagoon and into Sullivan's firing line.

Sullivan removed the tripod from the rifle, pocketed the extra ammo, and cradling the weapon in his arms, got to his feet. He braced himself and clambered over the rocks to the water's edge, all the time pounding at the bulletproof rear windows over the pilot's cabin with a steady hail of steel-jacketed slugs, firing from the hip. The rifle bucked hard in his hands—it was too heavy to be fired from the hip, for most men—making his wrists ache.

But it felt good. It felt like an extension of him, as if it had grown out of him, a part of his arms, and all the machinery in it—the firing pin detonating bullets, the expanding gas from the discharged cartridge providing the force to push the automatic machinery into recocking and setting up another bullet—might have been a part of him, like his heart and his muscle. He felt good the way a man does when he's swimming hard, enjoying the exercise, feeling each part of his body work smoothly with all the others. Sullivan was part of that killing machine, hammering away at the boat, and he was expressing himself through it, expressing his fury—because the man in the boat was one of those who had signed on to help Ottoowa. Ottoowa, who'd decapitated Julia Penn's sister, who'd driven Julia Penn half-mad before she'd lucked into an escape—who'd left her twisted inside because of the things he'd made her see. He was cutting loose with his fury at Ottoowa, and all the men like Ottoowa, the ones who made the world ugly.

"Jack! Stop, *mon ami!* Stop firing!"

Sullivan shuddered, and realized it was Malta shouting in his ear. He took his finger from the trigger and looked down at the hot, smoking rifle. He was startled when he realized that, without thinking, he'd ejected the first clip and inserted the second and third, using up nearly a hundred rounds on the boat. He'd finally hammered through the back window—a crust of glass around the edges was all that remained of the window. "Bulletproof!" he snorted contemptuously.

"I surrender!" came a voice from inside the boat. "I give up!"

"I thought we might be able to use him," Malta said. "I heard him shout to give up, so . . ."

"You did the right thing to stop me. He'll be useful," Sullivan muttered. He shouted at the boat, drifting just a few yards away, at idle, "Come on out with your hands behind your head!"

A man with a face so gnarled it might have been made out of wood knots came out through the shattered door, hands clasped behind his neck. Malta splashed through the water and climbed onto the boat. He stepped over the dead men and frisked the captured gunman. "If he's got a gun, he's keeping it under his tongue!" Malta called.

Sullivan grinned. "Keep an eye on him, I'm coming aboard!"

Malta covered the prisoner with a pistol while Sullivan waded to the boat. The prisoner was a stocky, red-faced man, a pug-ugly with an Irish accent and rust-colored hair. Sullivan thought he knew him. "You're Rusty Spike," he said, though he wasn't sure. He knew him only by reputation. But a face like that marked a man.

"And what if I am, now?"

Sullivan nodded. It was him. A former IRA man, kicked out for brutalizing his subordinates. Sullivan shook his head in amazement: here was a man too brutal even for the IRA! He must have done something indescribably horrible. "Spike," Sullivan said, "pick up those bodies. I'll do you a favor: you can carry them one at a time. Carry them ashore. Burial detail."

Spike spat on the deck and, muttering a hundred Irish curses, dragged the bodies to the rail and heaved them over. Sullivan and Malta, guns in hand, supervised as he towed them onto the shore, and grunting, dragged them into the brush. Sullivan stood over him as he dug a shallow grave with a shovel cadged from the bigger cabin cruiser, then rolled the bodies into the pit and covered them. There was one left drifting in the lagoon. Malta took Sullivan's boat out to it, and weighted the body with pieces of scrap iron. It sank from sight.

They hosed the blood from the deck of the smaller boat, removed the glass fragments from the window frame, and did their best to conceal any other evidences of the carnage.

"Okay, Spike," Sullivan ordered, "take the wheel. I'm standing right behind you with a fat .45. Hair trigger, this pistol."

"No need for the drama. I follow you."

"Good. Malta," Sullivan called to the other boat, "take her back to the garage. You think the cops'll be out looking for us?"

"Yes. But I don't think they'll find us, my friend. *Au revoir*."

"See you."

Sullivan sat in the copilot's seat and said, "Take her out, Spike. Back to Château Borne."

Sam Hayden glanced at his watch. Six P.M. The sun off to port was already bloating in the band of haze near the horizon. The sea was becoming coppery in the reddening light. Soon it would be dark.

Ottoowa's yacht was returning to the château. They were still at least an hour away, unless Ottoowa ordered the coxswain to pile on the horsepower. But they were puttering along, sails packed away, engine in low gear. Ottoowa wanted a slow, smooth ride—probably because he was drunk, and prone to seasickness at such times, though he wouldn't admit as much.

But Hayden would have preferred they pour on the speed. He was nervous about having left too few men to guard the château. And without him there to guide them, they might commit any insane bungle. If Sullivan knew the yacht was gone, he might take advantage of its absence to attack the château. He might be there waiting when they got back.

Hayden doubted that holding Edie hostage would keep Sullivan at bay for long. He had pretended to accept the report about the three sentries deserting, but privately he suspected that it hadn't been desertion at all.

Hayden half-dreaded Sullivan—and half-hoped he'd be there at the château, gun in hand, ready to fight. Hayden was looking forward to that confrontation.

He stood leaning against the mainmast, one foot on a coil of rigging, watching the black coxswain—who was also a fighting man, a former lieutenant of Maggia's Marine Force—at the wheel, and smoking cigarette after cigarette. He heard Ottoowa raging below deck. His meeting had turned out badly—his would-be supporters had offered only a fourth of the necessary money. Ottoowa was furious—he'd nearly drawn guns on them. He'd stormed off the other yacht, where the meeting had taken place, and ordered his crew to cast off. He would seek other supporters. And then he'd begun to get drunk. Hayden suspected Ottoowa was taking drugs, too, which—added to his insanity and drunkenness—made for a dangerous unpredictability.

And the man had killed four people already that day, chiefly for his own amusement.

So Hayden's blood ran cold when he heard Edie scream. The scream was followed by a roar from Ottoowa, and then a banging, all of these sounds filtering up from the hatchway.

Hayden turned and, acting instinctively, sprinted across the deck and plunged down the narrow stairs into the corridor leading between the cabins.

Ottoowa's cabin door was open. There was a broken bottle of absinthe on the floor, and a half-empty bottle of gin on the table. The furniture had been overturned, holes kicked in panels. Ottoowa wasn't there.

Hayden turned the corner, came to the cabin assigned to Edie. One of Ottoowa's bodyguards stood in front of it, submachine gun in hand. When he saw Hayden, he glowered and snapped the machine gun around so its muzzle pointed at Hayden's belly.

From beyond the closed cabin door came a woman's wailing. Then an ugly smacking sound and a short shriek. Ottoowa's voice. Edie shouting angrily. Another smack. Silence.

Hayden looked at the submachine gun—and turned away. There was nothing he could do, unless he killed the bodyguard. If he managed to kill the man, the job working for Ottoowa would be finished—and he'd probably get himself killed. The important thing, though, would be losing the job. That would mean losing the meaning in his life.

Hayden walked heavily down the corridor and slowly climbed the stairs. He paused for a moment, and almost turned back, when he heard Edie scream again.

But then he forced himself to go on.

He went topside and told the coxswain to go to all-ahead-full.

And he tried not to hear the ugly sounds from below.

9

Defectors to the Army of the Dead

Sullivan was tired. He was hungry. He had a headache, and the massive bruise on his chest hurt like the devil.

But the fury burned in him still, the fuel for the engine of vengeance.

He sat in the pilot's cabin with his back to the starboard bulkhead, the automatic rifle across his lap, the Beretta in his hand, its muzzle pointed unwaveringly at Rusty Spike, the hijacked cabin cruiser's coxswain.

He glanced through the windshield at the sky. It was deepening its blue to the east, to the west tingeing red. Sunset. The yacht would probably be coming back soon. But how soon? There might be time. . . . This might be an opportunity. . . .

Suppose he were to penetrate the château while the yacht was still at sea? He might attack it, secure it, and wait there, hidden inside, till the yacht returned. But it was unlikely he could break into the château without alerting the men inside. He might get in, and past them for *a while*—but there would be someone doing radio watch. Eventually the radio-watch detail would realize the château was under attack, because Sullivan couldn't kill *every* man in the château in silence, and sooner or later there'd be an alarm. The radio watch would put in a call to Ottoowa. Ottoowa would kill Edie immediately and then set off for another hideout. He might escape Sullivan indefinitely. Maybe for years.

No, Sullivan would have to wait till Ottoowa was back in the château. He couldn't risk frightening him out of reach.

Sullivan was going to have to do it the hard way.

Still, there was a way to whittle the odds down a little more. . . .

Strickland popped another "black beauty" and nervously changed the channel on the château's big-screen color TV. A Frenchman babbled at him on this channel too. And on the last channel there was ol' John Wayne, wearing a cowboy outfit and looking like he could punch in a wall—and they had overdubbed him with some Frenchie. A guy with a high-pitched voice, too, and we're supposed to believe that's the Duke. An insult to his memory, by God. Making John Wayne speak a faggy-sounding language like French!

Disgusted, Strickland switched off the TV and got up, began to pace, propelled from one corner of the room to the other by the speed he'd been taking all day.

"Quit that bleedin' pacing," said Tolliver, the limey. He was sitting in a corner chair, looking over a stack of men's magazines. He skipped the stories and went right to the foldouts.

"Can't help it," Strickland said breathlessly. "I'm nervous."

"You wouldn't be so gord-orful nervous if you stopped eatin' them bleedin' leapers," Tolliver said, opening a can of beer.

"It's not the speed," Strickland insisted. "It's this Sullivan. And 'M'lord Edge.' " There was mockery in his voice when he used Ottoowa's title; at least, when Ottoowa was away. "We're caught betwixt the two of 'em. The way Hayden talks about Sullivan—"

"Hayden? He's got an obsession, 'e does, worryin' all the time about this Sullivan."

"You think so? Then why haven't Spike and the others come back?"

"Why?" Tolliver laughed. "Soon as they drove the bastard off, they went into the town to get themselves a little T&A, maybe. And I don't believe that was Sullivan."

"Does seem crazy, him coming at us in full daylight like that. In a boat. You'd think a guy with his experience would try commando tactics. Night assault. That's what worries me: it don't fit."

Strickland rubbed his sore left arm, which was in a sling. That Edie broad had creased him with a bullet there. Not a bad wound, but demoralizing. Everyone had ragged him about it. *Let the little girl put a bullet in you, Strickland? Next time take her gun away before you make a pass at her!*

She was a looker, all right. But M'lord Edge wouldn't let anybody go near her. Greedy bastard.

Strickland wished Hayden would come back. He had a bad feeling . . .

There was a loud crackling sound from the next room. The radio speaker. "Laforgue, here," said the man on radio watch, into the mike. "Who is calling, please?"

Strickland went into the radio room to stand at the heavyset Frenchman's elbow. Laforgue was a big, round-bellied man forever smoking small crooked cigars. He had a reddish beard and thin, graying brown hair. Strickland hadn't taken him seriously till, at target practice, he'd seen him use a weapon. He was fast and accurate.

The stainless-steel shortwave, just small enough to be carried in a backpack if necessary, sat on a wooden table beside one of the deep, narrow stone windows. The window had gone red with the sunset. It looked out on the sea.

Laforgue sat at the table, blowing cigar smoke toward the window and waiting with pen poised over a pad to write down the radio message.

The speaker crackled, and a tinny voice said, "Spike here. I'm just off the ridge that sticks out by the château. The other boys are in town. They sent me to ask you do you wanta come with us? We've got us a job, pays twice this one, with half the risks. Can't tell you all by radio, lads. Come on down the dock and we'll talk. Ottoowa might be listening. That's it, then."

Laforgue turned to Strickland, his jowly face dark with confusion and irritation. He said something in French, and then at Strickland's look of exasperation asked, "What is that he said?"

"You didn't understand? He says he's got another job for us. Wants us to think about giving this one the heave."

"Another job?"

"Bigger money, less risk."

"Ottoowa . . ." Laforgue shook his head. "Ottoowa would kill us."

"If he found us. But I dunno, maybe a new job's a good idea, maybe that's what I need. I get sicka bein' shut up in this fuckin' dump. Fuckin' place gets on my nerves. Wonder what the new job is? Maybe it's a job in Tahiti! I had a job in Tahiti once! Bodyguard. Nothin' to it. We hadda beat up a few guys, and we got to screw the guy's girlfriend. That was all right. Tahiti, man, that's the best. Babes everywhere. Soak up the sun, soak up the liquor, soak up the dope. Easy street. I bet that's it, I bet it's Tahiti. I got a feeling for these things. Time for a change. Like, you ever see *Mutiny on the 'Bounty'?* They deserted that Captain Bligh for Tahiti. And what's Ottoowa? Captain Bligh! I say we—"

Laforgue shook his head and stood, pushing Strickland aside. He hadn't understood much of Strickland's speed-rap. He went to the window, took a pair of binoculars from the table, and scanned the sea. It was hard to see against the glare of the sunset. He could make out the little boat, and a figure at the wheel that could be Spike. Nothing more. No sign of the yacht, so far. "I'll talk to him," he announced. "To make him come back here. We need the men. Six men guarding this place is not enough."

He went to the telephone and put in a call to the ground floor. He spoke in French to another French mercenary, telling him to come and take over radio watch.

Instinctively Laforgue picked up his M16 on the way out.

Strickland excitedly told Tolliver what was happening.

Tolliver muttered, "Another job? What the hell—what's the hurt of askin' about it? . . . Funny, though, a bleeder like Spike comin' back just to do us a favor like—"

"A favor?" Strickland broke in, laughing. "The hell it is! Whoever the new boss is, he's offering a bonus if Spike brings in new men. That's what I figure. Sure. That's what I—"

"All right, all right, can it, then." Tolliver strapped on his .38 and followed Laforgue to the armored outer door. They waited while the Frenchman unlocked the iron door—there were three locks and a bar—and opened it wide. Then they started down the stone steps to the dock. The sentry stopped them at the fence.

Laforgue, who was in charge while Ottoowa was gone, explained in French that he wanted to talk to Spike on the dock, and pushed gruffly past. Laforgue was a bearlike man, and the hired guns thought twice before arguing with him.

Following Laforgue and Tolliver down the zigging stone

steps, Strickland began to have second thoughts about the new job offer. He began to yearn for the safety of the château.

Maybe he should go back. . . .

No, speed made you paranoid, that's all. He'd heard Spike's voice on the radio. No mistaking that voice. Sure, the guy was a son of a bitch. Sure, he'd sell his own mother for ten cents. But he wouldn't be crazy enough to hire on with someone else *against* Ottoowa. Would he?

No, that's paranoia. It's that Sullivan guy: Got everyone jumping.

Sullivan . . .

Strickland looked at the cabin cruiser rumbling slowly in toward the dock to meet them. It was just a silhouette against the sunset-bloody sea. But that looked like Ottoowa's extra boat, all right.

Nevertheless, there was something eerie about it, coming at them so quietly, against that field of blood-red. It was just a blade-shaped blackness, coming closer. Damned sinister-looking.

Strickland would have liked to turn back. But he was afraid of looking cowardly in the others' eyes. They already thought he was flaky.

His heart raced, and he put his hand on the butt of his .45 in its hip holster.

"Sure darker down here, under the cliffs," he muttered as they stepped onto the asphalt dock. They walked out toward the end, where the square end of the dock broke off suddenly onto the sea. The sun sank a little more, and the sea turned a darker red and then began to shade gray-black, as if the blood on the sea were congealing. The shadows thickened, and Strickland watched his feet carefully, afraid of tripping and falling off the dock into the sea. Not much chance one of these cold-blooded bastards he worked with would jump in to save him. Strickland couldn't swim.

The boat nosed in, then swung around so it was pointing out to sea before it edged up to the dock.

Its engine made a soft pock-pock noise as it slowed, then stopped, nudging the dock, idling. The three men clambered onto the boat's rear deck.

Strickland realized that it was running without lights, even though now it was genuinely dark out. What the hell? And where was Spike?

"I don't see Spike," he whispered to Tolliver.

"Me neither. Shit, the back window on the pilot cabin's been shot away!" He began to back away.

"Drop that rifle, cigarmouth."

Sullivan's voice. Strickland had never heard it, but somehow, he knew. That was Sullivan. The man they called the Specialist.

The voice had come out of the darkness of the pilot cabin's open doorway. They heard it again—this time making a low, cruel laugh, a laugh that had an edge of insanity to it. Something about that laugh made goosebumps on Strickland's arms. He edged his fingers toward his gun. "Drop it, I said," came the voice again.

This time they saw the snout of an automatic rifle slowly nosing from the darkness of the rear window into the faint light from the château and pointing directly at Laforgue. It was just two yards away, and Laforgue had his gun pointed at the deck. He had no choice but to drop it.

The boat began to move away from the dock.

Shit! Strickland thought. He's taking us out to sea!

But *who* was taking them? Sullivan couldn't drive the boat and keep that gun leveled at them too. Could he? Must be someone else piloting. Spike, maybe? Must be that Sullivan's got one gun pointed at us and the other at Spike. But then he'd have to keep his eyes mostly on us. So maybe he's a little behind Spike, and he's got the gun shoved in his back. Only he's not looking at Spike.

Maybe this Sullivan underestimates Spike.

"Kick that M16 overboard," came the voice from the darkness.

Laforgue hesitated.

"Do it or I blow you all away right now."

Strickland kicked the gun toward the opening—for drainage when they were washed over by waves—under the railing. It slid into the ocean.

Laforgue glared at him.

"We . . . we gotta cooperate," Strickland said, hoping Sullivan heard him. "He said get rid of the gun, so we do it. He's a right guy. He won't shoot us down if we cooperate."

The boat had picked up speed. They were nearly out of sight of the château.

"That's right, punk," Sullivan said. "You'd better co-operate. You, cigarface: Drop your pistol and come in here."

Laforgue reluctantly unbuckled his belt, let it slide to the deck. He went toward the cabin, walking slowly and carefully. The gun snout disappeared from the back window and reappeared in the doorway. They still couldn't see the man behind it.

"Go to the radio, cigarface. Call the château. Tell them you're deserting. Do it now or you're a dead man."

Sullivan waited in the darkness of the pilot's cabin, rifle in hand. Laforgue was a shadow shape in the doorway.

"Careful," Sullivan whispered.

Moving slowly, Laforgue went to the boat's radio. He picked up the hand mike and pressed the send button. "Château Borne, read me," he said.

The radio crackled and a voice inquired, "*Oui?* Laforgue?"

"*Nous partons—*" Laforgue began.

"In English," Sullivan hissed.

"This is Laforgue, we are taking the new job. We are going from Ottoowa."

The crackle cut short as Laforgue switched off the radio.

"Good enough. Now, go back—"

A shadow came alive: Spike was on him, knocking the Beretta to the floor, punching at his gut, trying to twist the rifle away. Sullivan jabbed out with the butt of the rifle, cracking Spike in the sternum. Spike wheezed and staggered back just as Laforgue came in swinging. It was hard to see, but Sullivan managed to duck Laforgue's jab, then moved aside, allowing Laforgue's momentum to carry him off balance. Spike was up, coming at him again—but this time Sullivan had room to fire. He cut loose with the rifle; it chattered, lighting up the cabin for a moment with its blaze, and Spike grunted and fell back, his chest punched through in three places.

Sullivan spun to face Laforgue, who was just getting to his feet. He squeezed the trigger—nothing. The rifle was jammed. Laforgue didn't have to know that. "Get out there," Sullivan growled. He pointed the rifle at Laforgue's head.

Laforgue nodded and slowly sidled past the rifle muzzle, then backed onto the deck.

Sullivan glanced through the window. Two of the mercenaries were crouched, guns in hand, moving toward the cabin.

Sullivan laughed his calculated laugh, and it made them freeze in their tracks.

"Well, gentlemen," he called out, "it seems The Specialist played a little joke on himself. I've bought myself a defective weapon. This rifle isn't working. But . . ." He paused to find the Beretta, then tossed the rifle out the window onto the deck. "I have my Beretta. It's loaded and it's not jammed. It's all I've got. I'm telling you this so you know you'll have the edge when I make my proposal. I propose you either come after me one by one or two at once, and try to hit me in here—but I'm shooting from cover—or you can have a clear shot at me out on the deck. The three of you. If you back up away from the door, I'll come on deck. I'll holster my pistol."

The one with the shaky speed freak's voice babbled, "You kidding? What you trying to put over, huh? You can't put nothing over. We back up and you'll have a clear shot at us through the window!"

"No! Back up just enough to see the door clear. There's a little moonlight just inside the doorway. I'll holster my pistol. You'll see that. If you holster yours too—I see Monsieur Laforgue has picked up his again—I'll come out on the deck. And I'll draw against all three of you. There's enough moonlight to shoot with. What do you say?"

He could almost hear them thinking. They probably thought it would be a sure thing—he couldn't outgun all three of them. And from inside the cabin he might pick them off. Why not?

The one with the British accent called out, "It's all the same to me, mate, if you want to die like a bloody cowboy."

The others said "Yeah" and *"Oui."*

Sullivan holstered his gun, then moved to the door. He showed enough of his right hip in the door so they could see his gun was holstered, but not enough of him so they could get a good shot at him. He heard them holstering their guns, backing toward the stern. Sullivan reached back and cut the engine. The boat drifted in near-silence. There were only a faint whisper of wind and the murmur of waves.

Sullivan thought: Time for the late show. Tonight they're showing *High Noon*.

He stepped through the door and onto the deck. Three men faced him, their hands resting on the gun butts of their automatic pistols.

The American reacted spasmodically, snatching his gun up, shakily trying to level it.

Sullivan had relaxed and turned the action over to his reflexes. He let his reflexes take care of it, and he watched with near-detachment as his hand, moving almost with a will of its own, drew and squeezed off three shots.

Something punched Strickland hard in the chest, and it didn't feel the way he'd imagined the bullet should feel—he felt as if that blow had opened up his chest like a keg, letting his soul pour out into the open, so for the first time he could see it, and in impossibly fast instant replay he could see everything he'd ever done in his life.

It wasn't pleasant viewing.

The next thing he saw was the sky—the moon was falling! No, it wasn't falling, he realized, it just *looked* that way because *he* was falling, falling over backward, pitching over the rail into the darkness, into the cool embrace of the sea, while the pain surged up in his chest at the same moment that the roar of Sullivan's gun—delayed beyond the flash and the bullet—echoed over the water.

He thought: He hit me in the right lung. But not through the heart. I might live through it. I might live. . . .

And then, when he tried to take a breath, and foul brine burned into his throat, he remembered that he'd fallen into the sea.

And he remembered that he couldn't swim.

Sullivan checked the two bodies remaining on the deck: Laforgue and Tolliver. Laforgue had slumped in one corner, Tolliver in the other. He'd shot Tolliver through the forehead, just above the left eye. Laforgue he'd caught squarely between the eyes. But Strickland had moved quickly, spasmodically—like a man on amphetamines—so Sullivan hadn't hit him as precisely as he'd wanted to. He might still be alive.

He found Strickland a few minutes later, bobbing face-up under a foot of water, fish already nibbling on him.

He was dead, probably drowned before he could bleed to

death. Sullivan hauled the body aboard and started the engine, to take the boat to the lagoon where he'd hidden the other bodies. He'd have to dig this grave himself.

He turned on the running lights and began to pilot carefully through the maze of outcroppings.

He had reached the lagoon and anchored, was just fetching the small shovel, when he heard a voice from the heap of corpses behind him. A chill ran through him. He spun, clutching the shovel like an ax, its blade over his shoulder.

He'd laid Spike's body across the other three, and it was Spike who was talking.

"You . . . thought I was . . . dead," Spike rasped.

"Yes," Sullivan said, laying the shovel aside. He drew his gun.

"Wanted to tell you, me'n the Blue Man, we blew up your precious Lily, and if you want to know why—then fuck off, mate. Fuck off. Fu . . . Fu . . ." He made a choking sound. And then he was gone, really gone. Sullivan tried to revive him, to demand: Who's the Blue Man? *Why?* Why did you plant the bomb on the boat?

But he was screaming these questions into the face of a dead man. A face that wore a triumphant smirk.

Sullivan dragged the body into a shallow grave and dumped a shovel load of dirt on that smirk.

And he thought: He told me that to tantalize me, to get his revenge against me. But maybe, deliriously, he gave me a lead. Someday I'll find the Blue Man. . . .

But just now he had Ottoowa to deal with. And Hayden.

Hayden scowled as they came to dock under the château, seeing the cabin cruiser was gone. Why the hell had they taken the cabin cruiser out? That would leave the château underguarded.

Had Sullivan come after all?

He went to the radio and called the château's radio watch. "Hayden here. Status?"

"We're okay here. But Laforgue and a couple of other fellows took off about forty-five minutes ago in a boat. Said they had a new job—called me on the radio. Spike too. And . . . there's only six guys here now."

"What?" Seven more deserters? "Any sign of Sullivan? Any attack?"

"No . . . not attack. There was a strange boat here earlier today. Spike and some guys went out to check it out. I told 'em you wouldn't like that, but Laforgue gave 'em permission . . . and they didn't come back. Except Spike came back to pick up—"

"Okay, never mind. Christ. We're docking. Over and out."

This gave him an excuse to disturb Ottoowa. Maybe the girl was still alive.

As the two-man crew tied up the boat, Hayden went below.

"I got to talk to Ottoowa," he told the bodyguard. "You understand? We're here, back at home base. And something's come up. We . . . Thanks." The bodyguard had shrugged and moved aside.

He forced himself to open the door.

Inside, it looked as if someone had picked the room up and shaken it in a cocktail shaker. Everything was mixed up. The bunk was overturned, the clothing in torn heaps on the floor, a chair overturned, bottles and glasses smashed.

Ottoowa lay on his stomach, breathing deeply. He snored.

The girl was curled up fetuslike in the corner, just beyond Ottoowa's outstretched arms.

Her lips were swollen where he'd hit her. There was a cut over one eye, and bruises on her shoulders. Her dress had been torn away. "How bad are you hurt?" Hayden asked her.

"A little bruised. He hit me—maybe wanted to rape me. Then he fell asleep. Drunk." Slowly she sat up, looking Hayden in the face. She looked like she wanted to cry but had decided that would be giving in to the enemy. She stared defiance at him.

The bodyguard came in, muttering, and bent over Ottoowa. Ottoowa snored.

The bodyguard shook him. Ottoowa groaned and opened one eye a crack. The guard spoke in his native language; Ottoowa growled back in the same, and then shut the eye, resumed snoring.

The bodyguard looked at Hayden and shrugged.

Hayden sighed. "Well, let's carry him to his cabin. Put him in bed. But when he wakes, I've got to talk to him. I'll be in the château. We've got to hire new men—fast."

Hayden took Ottoowa's ankles, the bodyguard took him

under the shoulders, and, grunting, they carried M'lord Edge, "Emperor" of Maggia, to his bed, just as if they were carrying a gutter drunk.

When Hayden returned, Edie was doing a makeshift repair job on her dress by knotting the torn pieces together. Her movements were abrupt, her mouth set rigidly. She was angry. That could be dangerous. It would be a mistake to underestimate her. She might grab a gun somewhere. And after all, she'd put a bullet in ol' Strickland. He grinned, remembering, and said, mostly to discourage her from doing anything rash, "I'll tell you a secret."

He closed the door behind him, listened for a moment. He heard no one move in the hall outside. He went on, "You don't breathe a word about this. But your friend Sullivan hasn't forgotten you. He's been up to some fun and games while we were gone. He took seven men out."

The anger stayed in her face, but it was mixed with a look of cynical pleasure. "*Oui?* Good! But . . . how do you know?"

He snorted. "I just heard that they 'deserted.' " He shook his head. "For your sake, baby, I'm gonna try to see if I can get Ottoowa to believe that—though that ain't doing the job the best way. If I was smart, I'd tell him what happened. He might get shook up enough to get the hell out of this country. That's the best way to protect him from Sullivan—hide 'im."

"You are this much worried about Mr. Sullivan?"

He shrugged. "The guy's a fanatic."

"You won't tell M'lord Edge about the . . . 'desertions'?"

"I'll act like they were real desertions. But ten-to-one those poor sons of bitches are food for the fishes by now." He chuckled. " 'Poor' sons of bitches? Sure, they deserved it. As much as anyone deserves the so-called 'justice' self-righteous bastards like Sullivan want to deal out. . . . But, no, I won't tell M'lord Edge what musta really happened. I'll fake him out that I heard those guys talkin' about deserting. Partly to keep him from offing you in retaliation—I said I'd try to prevent that, and my word's good—and partly because . . ." He hesitated.

"Yes?" She went to the mirror and tried to straighten her hair. She had to squat down to do it, since the mirror was on the floor, part of the wreckage.

"And partly because I guess I'd like to come up against Sullivan. That self-righteous bastard."

"Monsieur Hayden . . ." She stood and faced him. Her face was battered, and for some reason it gave him a gut-wrenching feeling to look at it. That look of smugness she had now, too. He could do without that.

"Yeah? What? What you looking so smug about?"

"I think I understand something about you now. I think you are going to fight very hard against Mr. Sullivan. But I think you are secretly hoping that he is the one who wins."

"*Bullshit!*" Hayden roared, without thinking.

She stepped back, alarmed by the violence of his reaction.

He shook himself and growled, "Forget it. Come on. Let's go ashore."

It was dark when Sullivan brought the boat into the harbor at Bandol. He was tired. But he was ready. Ready to move against Ottoowa.

He'd rest—and go after him about three A.M. if Malta could arrange the police observation to turn their backs tonight.

There was a good chance, Sullivan knew, that as soon as Ottoowa realized he was being attacked, he'd take Edie out onto the balcony where Sullivan would see her and cut her throat. Or do something worse to her.

But suppose he put a knife to her throat and demanded that Sullivan surrender or withdraw?

What would he do then?

Thinking about it, Sullivan tightened his fingers on the wheel.

If he retreated, Ottoowa would kill her anyway—eventually. He'd have to go on. But there was a chance, if he judged Hayden right, that the guy just wouldn't stomach seeing the girl executed. Probably he'd try to find some way to prevent it and keep his job too.

Ottoowa might be too busy with the assault, with giving orders and maybe taking up a weapon himself, to bring the girl into it. If Sullivan could keep Ottoowa distracted enough, he might be able to break into the château and do the job before they hurt her.

And then, there was another possibility. She might already be dead.

Sullivan put it out of his mind. With a discipline learned in firefights, in jungle stalking, and in years of developing a survivor's reflexes, he focused his mind on the objective.

He had twice done reconnaissance of the terrain around Château Borne. He'd charged Malta with obtaining aerial photos.

Tonight he'd double-check the photos against his tactical plans.

He brought the cabin cruiser slowly around, into the lane of seawater between the fingers of docks extending from the main jetty. To either side small yachts and sailboats bulked in the darkness, rocking gently in his wash, like sleeping sea beasts. The lights of Bandol, to his right, twinkled between the naked masts and threw bright smears on the inky water between the boats.

He found the docking space he'd rented, backed into it, cut the engine to let momentum carry the boat the rest of the way. The boat bumped gently against the dock.

He stowed his weapons, except for the Beretta, and secured the boat to the piles. As he was cinching the rope, he noticed four men walking toward him on the wooden dock between the boats. He couldn't see them clearly. The only light came from the cafés across the highway, half-muted by the palm trees, and a single dock lamp at the end of the pier. But all four of the men were big, and they wore suits. They were looking at him, and if he hadn't been so tired, he'd have known instantly what they were.

But just then, all he knew was that something about these men told him: Get the hell out of here.

But to where? There was only one way off the dock, if you didn't swim, and that was by walking past those four men. Unless he could get the boat started.

"Excuse me, monsieur," the man in the lead said, walking up to him.

Sullivan's hand leaped inside his jacket to the butt of his Beretta, under his left arm.

Then he realized that the other three men already had him covered. And the one who had spoken was holding a wallet-badge under his nose. Ministry of the Interior. Federal police.

The men closed in around him.

"You'd better come with us, monsieur," said the man with the badge.

10

The Long Harm of the Law

It was the damned cabin cruiser he'd taken from Ottoowa's boys, he decided, that had got him busted. Someone at sea had seen the gunfight, or part of it, and had noted down the numbers and descriptions of the two boats. Malta had taken the other boat to the more secluded boat garage, and no one had seen him come in there—probably. But Sullivan had brought the enemy boat into Bandol, where the police were already looking for it. He'd underestimated the French cops. They'd seen him coming in, and alerted the feds who were in the area.

Should have ditched the boat up the coast. Should have, should have. Should have isn't good enough. Too many mistakes—too long out of action before taking this one on. And unused to fighting in so civilized a place as France.

Sullivan was riding in a small patrol car, a man—gun in hand—on either side of him. Two men in the front seat. One of them had his .45 automatic drawn, was half-turned to point it at Sullivan, his pale long-nosed face blank but his eyes sharp. They were taking no chances with Sullivan. He wondered if they knew who he was. Maybe. Maybe not—not yet. When they'd demanded his passport, he'd said, ''Haven't got it here, man. It's . . . in my boat. A friend of mine has the boat out. Don't know when he's coming back. My name's Tanner. James Tanner.'' He had a passport in that name, in the other boat, a beautiful falsification job. You never knew when you might need one.

"You gentlemen like to let me in on what this is all about?" Sullivan asked.

"Perhaps," said the man in the front seat, "you'd like to tell *us* why you were carrying a pistol. One that's been fired recently."

"The world's a dangerous place."

"I see." He had only a little accent. Probably had studied at some American university. "I have an intuition that your gun is unregistered, monsieur. This alone is very much illegal."

Sullivan sighed. "Got a smoke?"

The man to his right gave him a cigarette and lit it for him with a disposable lighter. He opened the window to let the smoke out. Just as if they were sharing a cab.

Sullivan was thinking hard.

They hadn't come equipped with handcuffs, which was surprising. That showed they were probably here as an observation team. It was Sullivan's only edge, that lack of handcuffs. That, and the fact that he was probably better at hand-to-hand fighting than these men. But there were guns on all sides. No chance now. Getting out of the car, though, he might be able to break away. It depended on the terrain. These men were no amateurs, however. They'd probably keep him carefully covered when they got out of the car. . . . And suppose he grabbed a gun, took one of them as hostage? He could end up having to kill one of them. Or more. (He didn't bother thinking about the possibility he might get killed himself. That was always with him, a permanent part of his life. Sullivan lived perpetually in the shadow of death.) It would be bad in more ways than one if he had to kill a cop. It would mark him for good. They'd hunt him endlessly. As long as he killed vermin like Morlaine, the cops probably tried only halfheartedly to catch him. But a cop—they'd come down hard. On top of that, he sympathized with the police. They were only doing their job by taking him in. No, he couldn't bring himself to off them.

But he had to get away. The French cops were different from American. In France you were assumed guilty until proved innocent. You could stay in jail for up to a year before being prosecuted. And he'd be a sitting duck in jail. It would be easy for Ottoowa to bribe some corrupt guard to arrange his death "while trying to escape." Ottoowa would escape. Edie would die horribly at Ottoowa's hands.

No, there was no use waiting to see if he could slip through the legal noose and talk his way out. They'd eventually get around to searching the coastline near the shooting. Or someone might stumble on those bodies.

Sullivan wondered if the death penalty was still operative in France.

"I was going to tell the police about that boat anyway," Sullivan said blandly. "How I found it drifting, all those bullet holes in it, decided to take it in. My friend took off in my boat."

"What is your friend's name?" asked the man in the front seat.

But the driver broke in—to Sullivan's relief—telling the other, in French (Sullivan had picked up just enough to make out the gist of it): "Stop asking him questions here. Wait till we get him to the station, and we can get it on tape."

They were in the country now, driving through a high-cliffed canyon of bone-white stone. It was the road to Toulon—probably they were taking him to the Toulon police department for temporary safekeeping. The bone-white bosses of rock rose sheer to either side of the winding road, flecked with bushes; the cliff faces looked like photo negatives, their shadows deeply etched in the bright moonlight. Full moon tonight.

To the left, beyond the oncoming-traffic lane of the two-lane highway, a low stone wall snaked along the road's edge, marking a drop-off into a boulder-strewn dry wash. At certain times of the year, that wash roared with rushing water. Now it was empty but for a few brackish, mosquito-hazed puddles. On the far side of the wash the bank rose steeply to become a pine- and scrub-covered slope which broke abruptly into upthrusting cliffs. Here and there, the crevices between bosses of rock widened into cave mouths.

To the right, the cliff rose just a yard off the roadside. Signs warned of falling rocks.

The driver had to take the curves slowly in places where the road doubled back like the ripples of a sidewinder. The headlights swept over the gray-green bracken as they swung around a corner, lighting fires in the eyes of what appeared to be—from the brief glimpse he had—a pack of wild dogs crouched at the mouth of a cave on the far bank of the dry wash.

The road began to climb, and they slowed, delayed by a chuffing semitruck muscling up the curving grade. The police driver swore. Trying to find a long, straight stretch where he could pass the truck, he swerved out into the other lane, ducking back in again behind the truck as oncoming cars rushed at them. They were so close behind the truck that its exhaust fumes came thickly through the open window, making them cough. The cop on Sullivan's right began to roll the window up. Sullivan flicked his cigarette butt past his nose, out the narrowing open space in the window, just before it closed; the motion was so quick it startled the cops, and Sullivan found himself looking at three gun muzzles held in his face by three tensed French policemen.

Sullivan smiled and said casually, "Really, gentlemen. You should learn not to be so nervous. Bad for the blood pressure."

The man in the front seat snorted, and lowered his gun—a little. The other two, looking a bit sheepish, dropped their guns back in their laps but kept their hands firmly on the grips.

That tells me something about their reflexes, anyway, Sullivan thought. I've got to be damn fast.

Sullivan had forgotten his weariness. It was as if some inner driver had stepped on his accelerator pedal, priming his engine with adrenaline. He was revved and ready to jump. He only needed the opportunity.

That opportunity was tailing them in a long, dark Bentley.

Sullivan watched the headlights in the rearview mirror, thinking: Am I clutching at straws—or is that him?

As he watched, the Bentley cut into the oncoming-traffic lane and with a burst of speed shot up parallel to the police car. Sullivan risked a look. Malta looked casually back at him from behind the wheel of the Bentley. He gave no signal—the cops were looking at him, too—but showing himself was signal enough.

He urged the Bentley ahead, passing the truck just in time to avoid collision with an oncoming Citroën. The Citroën passed, and the police car took the opportunity to whip by the semi.

Sullivan peered along the road ahead, but now there was no sign of Malta. What was he up to?

There was another hairpin curve just ahead.

Suddenly, as they came to the curve, Sullivan understood. Without seeming to, he braced himself. Abruptly the police car swerved, cutting hard to the right, tires screaming, to avoid the Bentley, now stopped in the middle of the road. Malta had the hood up, was frowning down at the motor—faking a stalled car. Sullivan caught only a fleeting glimpse of this before the world began to smear around him, as it does around a fast carnival ride—the police car was skating sideways, then spinning, the driver shouting as he tried to regain control. They'd gone off the road onto a wide, gravelly shoulder—Malta had picked the spot well—where the cliff momentarily bowed inward. The car lurched to a halt, pointing backward from the way it had been going, and the inertia jerked the four men in the car forward and then back.

But Sullivan, prepared, had snatched up the gun from the man on the right, and as the car lurched, he shattered the window with four quick gunshots. Before the cops recovered, he jammed his arm through the broken glass, reached out to open the door from the outside, though he had to lean across the right-hand cop to do it. (There was no other way—the back doors lacked inside handles, to discourage attempted escapes.) At the same moment, he slammed a boot against the gun arm of the cop on his left, a paunchy man with side whiskers, catching him in the wrist. He heard a crack, and the man howled. The whiskered cop's gun fell to the floor. The cop in the front seat had been thrown against the windshield. He was dazed, was trying to right himself, blinking. The other cop was fumbling for his gun as Sullivan shoved the door open and rolled across the shouting man on that side, shoulder-rolling down, out the door, turning a somersault, coming up on his feet and dodging behind the car.

The cop he'd just flung himself over recovered first, snatching up his partner's gun and jumping free of the police car, whirling, plunking three shots at Sullivan. It was dark here, the moonlight broken up by long rough-edged patches of shadow. The shots whined off the rock of the wall.

Sullivan was sprinting across the road toward that wall, past the Bentley—where Malta put on a great show of being confused and horrified, a frightened "innocent bystander."

In a moment Sullivan had vaulted the wall and was skidding down a steep hillside into the dry wash. He still carried the .45, which he jammed into his waistband. His right arm felt slightly numb, and there was a familiar wetness on his wrist. He'd lacerated his forearm forcing it through the broken window. He paused, held the arm up so the moonlight caught it. Not a deep slash. He tore a piece of a shirt sleeve off and made it into a rude bandage, at the same time bounding from rock to rounded rock, working his way down the ravine. He found a branching in the wash and scuttled off to the left, leaping from rock to rock like a goat, trying to put as much distance as possible between himself and the road. He heard the unmistakable sound of the Bentley starting, the cops shouting after it. But Malta, pretending terror, drove quickly away. His part was done; the rest was up to Sullivan.

He was climbing now up a deposit of mailbox-size boulders in the crotch between two rocky hillsides.

Men being pursued go instinctively to high places, which is not always the best escape route. Sullivan had no other place to go. So he let his instincts carry him along.

He reached another shelf of rock and climbed out of the dry wash, heading generally back toward Bandol, north.

He was uncomfortably aware that his dark clothing would show up well against the white cliff face. He tried to keep to the shadow and make as little noise as possible. They'd be coming after him.

He paused, his slashed arm throbbing, and crouched behind a gnarled pine tree. From here he could see the cop car on the road's shoulder, below, on the other side of the ravine. One cop stood beside the car on the driver's side, holding his broken wrist and arguing with the man behind the wheel. The seated cop gave in, got out of the car, and let the other take his place. Sullivan heard the sputter of the car's radio. Reinforcements would be coming. The man with the fractured wrist started the car with his good hand and swung onto the road, driving mostly one-handedly, holding the steering wheel with his knee when he wanted to change gears. He drove off. The other man checked the chamber of his pistol, nodded to himself, and started across the road to join the other two, who were probably just out of sight, in the dry wash below.

Sullivan pondered his options. He could go over the top of the cliff, make his way to the village he knew to be on the other side, and steal a car. But he'd be an easy target going up the cliff face. He could hole up somewhere and hope they passed him in the darkness—but the probing beam of a flashlight below canceled that idea. They had a flashlight, so there was a good chance they'd find him if he hid.

He could take them on one by one and . . . finish them.

He shook his head. No, that would be the tactic if they weren't cops. But it was bad enough already. He'd broken a cop's arm and resisted arrest. And stolen a firearm from a policeman.

"Murphy's goddamn Law proved right again," he muttered.

He'd just have to try to slip by them, maybe jump aboard a truck when it slowed for a curve. So it was back to the road. If he could get past the three men searching for him, they might assume he'd gone up to hide in the rocks. Searching there, they'd be distracted. He hoped.

He hesitated, listening, hearing the muted crunch and clatter as the three cops searched for him below. His instincts screamed at him to climb, like a cat running up a tree when a dog is after it. He told his instincts to go to hell and moving in a crouch, began to work his way down the hill.

The only sounds were the occasional hum of a passing car and the call of nightbirds. He thought he heard dogs howling once, and then a snarl. After that, all was quiet—even the birds had fallen silent. The air smelled strongly of pine and rock dust.

He came to a rocky promontory that overhung the dry wash. He bellied down, wormed along the ground through a thin cover of brush to the lip of the rock, and looked cautiously over the edge. There was a cop four or five yards below. He was looking to the north, his gun in his hand. Looking south, Sullivan could see the other two, together, moving in the opposite direction, their backs to him, figures in charcoal against the darkness of the ravine. They disappeared around a corner. They were far enough away so that the sound of a scuffle might not reach them. Maybe he could subdue the cop below him without hurting him.

It was Sullivan's way, whenever he was the hunted, to turn hunter. To pursue his pursuer.

He withdrew from the edge of the boulder, lowered himself off it, on the south side. He dropped soundlessly to the dirt, and drew his gun, turning it so he held it by the barrel, to use the butt end as a club. He hefted it, and crept through the shadow, breathing deeply but very slowly, moving on the balls of his feet.

He came around the corner of an out-jut of rock, and saw something that made his blood freeze.

Wild dogs. Two of them were big mongrels, spotted and thick-coated, maybe half bird dog and half husky. Probably from the same litter. The other two were big German shepherds, maybe runaways, their fur matted, patchy, their jaws open, tongues lolling, teeth white, eyes yellow. They had the cop ringed in, had him trapped against the concrete underpinning of the roadbed on the left.

The dogs were half-mad with hunger and—perhaps—hatred from the former owners who'd abused them. Sullivan had heard stories of wild dogs, more vicious than wolves, that had torn isolated men to pieces on the Mediterranean. This pack looked ready to confirm that story.

The cop raised his pistol, but apparently he was not an experienced gunman. He forgot to take the safety off. The dogs rushed him. One bore him down with a lunge at his chest. Another tore at the wrist of the gun hand, and the gun clattered to the rocks. The other two darted in with jaws open, seizing the man's legs. They seemed to work almost as a practiced team.

Sullivan's instinct told him: Use this opportunity to get away! Beat it!

For the second time that night, he told his instincts where to go.

He rushed in, reversing the .45 and firing. One dog yelped and backed away, favoring a wounded front paw, snarling at him. The other three, startled, leaped back from the fallen cop. Sullivan ran at them, returning snarls with snarls, firing twice more. Two dogs went down, a bullet in each skull. But the third, the biggest of the two German shepherds, crouched and sprang. Sullivan had a flash image of its wide-open mouth, its yellow eyes, the wrinkled snout running with rank saliva—and then it hit him in the chest like a freight train. He was surprised at its weight and force. He felt himself flung backward, his gun arm thrown back, the dog coming down atop his chest, cocking its big demonic head—ruff bristling behind its ears like a halo of sheer hatred—to snap at his throat.

There was a gunshot, and another, and the animal, convulsing, rolled off him, blood pumping from its shattered ribs. The one he'd wounded barked twice, and then another gunshot sent it yelping into the brush.

Sullivan, grunting, rolled over and got to his feet.

The French cop, bleeding from gashes on his legs and his right arm, stood staring at him, his face white with shock. He'd picked up his gun and shot the dogs, despite his wounds and his confusion. A brave man, Sullivan thought.

Sullivan heard the other men approaching. But they were still some distance off. There might be time . . .

"You . . . you save me," the Frenchman said brokenly. "You did not run—you could have run."

"I've got nothing against you gents," Sullivan said softly, rubbing his chest. The dog had smashed into his bruise, and it hurt bad as the bullet wound he'd taken in the gut in Nam. "I'm here to stop someone. You know who he is, and you know he should be stopped. Don't stop me—from stopping him."

Sullivan turned to go.

He heard the cop mutter, "True. But . . . I cannot let you go."

Sullivan took a chance. He kept walking. But he kept talking, too. "You'll let me go," he said over his shoulder, "because just now I risked my ass to save you."

He ran up the steep slope, caught a concrete block's corner, pulled himself up to the stone wall edging the road. He felt as if someone had pasted a target to the small of his back. Any second now, the French cop might drill him.

But he climbed over the wall, and was quickly across the road, unmolested. He heard the gabble of excited voices from the ravine behind him. The cop's friends had found him. The explanations would take a moment. He might make it yet.

He sprinted down the road, making for the concealment of the rock face jutting out in the lee of the next curve. He rounded the curve, and found himself on the edge of a dirt road that led off the main highway into a hollow between the cliffs. The road stopped at an abandoned sand-and-gravel mill. It was boarded over, and plants grew up through the lower planks, but someone had swung the wooden gate aside. There were fresh tire tracks on the dusty road, leading behind the gray bulk of the four-story gravel mill's main tower. On a hunch, Sullivan ran for the mill, then peered around the corner of the tower. His hunch had been right.

Malta sat in the Bentley, listening to a Walkman and drinking from a metal flask, his back to Sullivan. He nodded his head to the music.

Sullivan grinned—and nearly burst out laughing.

He got in on the passenger side. Malta glanced up, nodded, and passed the flask. He didn't look at all surprised. He took off the earphones and started the car, backed it quickly down the dirt road, and careened down the highway, hell-bent for Bandol.

"How'd you know what happened?" Sullivan asked. He leaned back against the seat, exhausted, the vodka burning in his stomach.

"I was not far away when they took you. I was watching for you, trying to find some way to warn you, but they got to you first. So I followed. I have an employee who monitors the police bands. He warned me they were onto you."

"You think they know who I am?"

"If not now, they will soon, *mon ami*. They have your gun, with your fingerprints on it. They must be on file somewhere. They can guess your background from your style of fighting, no? So you must—*we* must—move against Ottoowa quickly. I have arranged a 'blindness' in the police surveillance for tomorrow night. The ministry will order the police away from the château for twenty-four hours."

"Yeah? Okay. I just hope they can keep these bluecoats I played hide-and-seek with tonight off my back."

"It will take a little more *lucre*, Sullivan, my friend."

"Money?" Sullivan snorted. "Pour it on them. Just keep them away."

"If you are successful, and if you survive that success, I think we can get you out of the country, despite your little problems today. But I'm afraid, in the final assault, we will have Hayden against us, and . . . ah . . ."

"Yeah?"

"Where, supposing that things turn out badly . . . where . . . ah . . . ?"

"Where *what?*"

"Where would you like your body sent, Jack?"

11

The Killing Terrain

Either Malta had miscounted the number of men working for Ottoowa or he'd managed to hire a few more, Sullivan decided. It was a sunny late afternoon, and Sullivan was squatting in a treehouselike observation post built into one of the higher, more thickly foliaged of the pine trees on the ridge overlooking Château Borne.

Sullivan had watched through two sentry shifts, and he had counted at least eight different sentries. Add to those eight men Ottoowa, Hayden, and Ottoowa's personal bodyguards, and that made an opposition force of twelve.

Sullivan's "nest" was almost thirty yards above the boulder-knotty ridgetop, about a quarter-mile to the east and north of where he'd killed the sentries in his nighttime commando raid. He was outside the zone that—so far as he could tell—Ottoowa had assigned for patrolling. There was only countryside—the ridge, a more gentle hilltop, and then the grounds of the château—between him and Ottoowa's fortress. Behind, farther east about three hundred yards, was a construction site, deserted that Sunday afternoon, for a half-built summerhouse. Across a narrow valley from the summerhouse site were a field of wine grapes and an older house, shutters closed, locked up for the time being. That was lucky; if there were people near enough to hear gunfire, they might call the local gendarmes, who hadn't been "blinded" by Malta's bribes.

The treehouse nest was about a yard and a half square, and camouflaged with netting skillfully interwoven with pine branches. He'd made a sort of igloo of greenery around him, with four observation slits hooded by camouflage at the four points of the compass. The floor was made of wrist-thick branches, which he'd brought from some distance away and lashed together with rope. It wouldn't be smart to let Hayden hear the sounds of someone sawing and hammering nearby, when he probably knew—undoubtedly having done more than one recon—that there was no one around. He'd know the construction site would be deserted today.

Sullivan watched through his field glasses as the two east-side sentries rendezvoused at the patio. He swept the glasses over the terrain, reassessing.

Sullivan was facing the house's east side; the main entrance was actually on the château's south side; the "back" of the house faced the sea. The side and front, the eastern and southern faces, were more modern than the seaward face of the house. Here wooden gables had been installed over broad—but ornately barred—windows. Bright blue shutters and flowerbeds looked deceptively homey, cheerful. At the south side two weathered stone lions flanked the spacious porch of wood and stone. Flowerpots stood on the balustrades around the porch. The flowers in them had withered. Beyond the porch, he could see the deep blue of the Mediterranean, just a triangular section of it between the house and the bent trees lining the cliff. There were whitecaps on the sea, and now and then Sullivan's tree swayed, buffeted in a rising wind. The wind was a phenomenon that came about the same time every summer to the French Mediterranean. It was called the mistral, and despite the summer sun and the blue sky, it blew hard, especially at night. Sullivan was hoping it might provide him with some cover that night. It wailed loudly on the cliff—its wailing might be loud enough to blanket some of the sounds of his attack.

Off the house's east-side patio were weed-grown flowerbeds and a lawn beginning to look shaggy, a grape arbor, the vines gone brown and shriveled for lack of irrigation; a few marble benches, almost randomly placed; a bone-dry fish pond of cracked stone; a half-acre more of overgrown lawn—and the stone wall. The wall was about twelve feet high, two feet thick, and constructed of irregular local stones and mortar. Strands of barbed wire ran along its top, newly emplaced, judging by the silvery gleam of the metal. Still, that stone wall wasn't much of a problem. The real problem was the electric fence recently erected just outside it. A powerful current ran through the ten-foot-high chain-link fence. It was crested with spiraled barbed wire, and there was a dead dog leaned half against the links where the fence turned a corner to encircle the property. The dog was some harmless domestic who'd wandered up and poked his snout against the fence to look through—and been instantly electrocuted.

The stone and electric barriers ran together all the way around the property, stopping only at the cliff edge and breaking for a gate thirty yards from the south entrance. There was a sentry on the gate twenty-four hours, in a stone gatehouse. The gate section of the chain-link fence could be electronically rolled away. Sullivan had seen only one car go in, a bodyguard returning from the village with supplies. There were two rented Citroëns parked in the driveway.

There was a balcony on the house's south side, and another on the east side, facing the lawns. A sentry stood in each, scanning the grounds now and then with binoculars, armed with AK47's.

There was a lot of open ground to move over. There were searchlights mounted on the roof, remote-controlled, and four "anticrime" lights, the daylight-bright blue-white sort, atop high chromium poles at the eastern and southern corners. According to the château's blueprints, it was equipped with emergency power batteries and a generator. So it would give him only a few seconds of darkness if he cut the house's power source. He might be able to shoot out the lamps—though that would tip his hand fairly early. But he recognized the manufacturing style of the searchlights—they were bulletproofed, and at this range the bulletproofing would work.

"All that open ground . . ." he muttered.

Not much cover there. He'd have to hope the decoy plan would continue to work. Knocking out those walls would take time, though. That would give the enemy time to sight in on him. But a wise use of his mortars might give him the time he needed.

Briefly he considered attacking from above. He might find a reliable pilot—Malta had no air-pilot experience—and parachute onto the roof. If they spotted him from those balconies, though, he'd be an easy target as he came down. But the real problem would be finding a pilot in time—he had to move against the château *tonight*. The pressure from the cops had made that necessary. And there was also the mistral to consider. A wind like that would make parachuting unreliable.

Reluctantly he shelved the air-attack contingency.

He'd have to go infantry. He lowered the field glasses and thoughtfully lit a cigarette. All around him the air was rich with the scent of pine sap. The swelling breeze sang through the slits in his camouflaged nest and whipped the cigarette smoke into oblivion. The tree creaked in the wind and rustled where its branches, farther down, touched the branches of other trees.

He got to his knees, cigarette in his lips, and checked the ground-drop wire running from the east side of the nest to the base of a smaller tree far below, slanting down in a straight line, taut, at a forty-five-degree angle. A little steep, maybe. The thumb-thick cable whined in the gusts of the mistral. It seemed secure—he'd worried a little that the wind might be loosening it. That cable was Sullivan's emergency exit. It was securely looped around the tree trunk, just above the thick branch that supported his observation nest. On the rough floor beside the opening over the wire was a palm-size metal wheel with a grooved rim—a groove that fit snugly onto the cable—rather like a pulley wheel. An axle ran through the center of the wheel's flat face, with handles on either side, for a quick ride down.

Malta had sneered at the wheel and cable. "A child's toy," he said. "You'll break your neck, my friend. Or it will stick halfway. And you will be moving too fast when you get to the bottom, no? I mean *if* you get to the bottom."

"It can be braked a little by squeezing the handles inward," Sullivan explained. "Certain commandos have used them successfully—"

"And others," Malta had interrupted, "have probably broken their bones on it."

Sullivan looked dubiously down the length of cable. He had never used one in a fight situation. And it *did* look like an unusually long way down. He discarded the idea of testing it now. Too big a chance Malta was right, and he needed his limbs intact tonight.

While Sullivan was distracted, pondering his escape cable, the mistral had picked up, blowing harder, making the tree sway yet more. And its persistent gusts were working at Sullivan's camouflage, plucking bits of branches away. His carefully constructed hooding over the observation slits had blocked off the sun, preventing reflection off his field glasses—a flash off those glasses could expose his position. But the mistral stripped part of that hooding away.

Sullivan scrupulously ground out his cigarette on his boot heel, making sure it was completely out, then lifted the field glasses to peer through the observation slit.

Hayden, carrying an M16 in his right hand, stalked moodily across the lawn to the two sentries standing under the fig tree near the fence. He came quietly up behind them, and when he was nearly at arm's reach, barked, "You assholes had enough *figs* yet?"

The two men jumped and whirled, reflexively jerking their guns around toward him. They relaxed—but not completely—when they saw it was Hayden. "Geez, boss," said Cornell, "you shouldn't startle me like that. I might've—"

"You wouldn't *be* goddamned startled if you'd been doing your fucking job!"

Hayden broke off his dressing-down, his attention drawn to the trees on the ridgetop overlooking the château. He'd seen a flash of light atop one of those trees—hadn't he? He watched, but it didn't repeat itself. He leaned his gun against the tree, reached for the binoculars hanging around his neck, and then changed his mind. He let his hands drop to his side. If he looked directly at that tree with his binoculars, Sullivan would notice it and would probably retreat. It would be better if he didn't let Sullivan know he'd been spotted. Then he could circle through the woods, come around behind that tree nest—if that's what it was. It might just be a piece of a kid's aluminum kite caught in the tree, or a half-dozen other things. But he had to check it out.

He welcomed the challenge to action. He was getting stir-crazy in the château. "Cornell," he said softly, picking up his rifle, "you come with me. Anderson, you stay here. Keep close watch."

Cornell was a beefcake of a man with a bald head and a thick red beard. He had been fired from the Ethiopian mercenaries for raping the daughter of a village headman during what he'd termed "an interrogation." Before that, he'd served two years in Vietnam, and then had been booted out on a dishonorable. No one was quite sure why. Hayden didn't like having to work with men of Cornell's caliber, but he was resigned to it. It went with the job.

Cornell was an American and a former member of a motorcycle gang. "Boy, I'd like to get me a Harley dirt bike and do a little dirtin' on these here hills," Cornell was saying, smacking the barrel of his AK47 against his palm—it seemed small as a policeman's nightstick in his big hands, and he carried it the same way. "You know what I mean? I—"

"Shut up," said Hayden.

"What?" Cornell was startled. He was bigger than Hayden, and wasn't used to being spoken to that way.

"I said stop rattling off. And listen, when we get into the woods—"

"What we going into—?"

"Shut up. When we get into the woods, try to forget you're a buffalo and try to move like a deer. Quietly."

They had gone into the château by the open patio doors. He led Cornell to the side door that led onto the cliff-side stairway. They passed out through that door and into a small copse of trees. The house, Hayden assumed, was blocking them from Sullivan's view.

There was a padlocked door that opened through the stone wall, and another heavily locked door in the electric fence. They unlocked the door in the wall, passed through, locked it behind them. Then Hayden paused to call the gatehouse with his walkie-talkie. "Turn off the juice," he ordered. There was a click, and then the fence stopped its faint humming. He spat at a link where it touched the ground—there was no answering spark. He unlocked the gate, and they passed through. He double-locked the gate behind them, then called for the electricity to be restored. The fence resumed its ominous humming. Hayden led the way into the woods.

"Listen, Hayden," Cornell whispered, following Hayden along the faint path, "what say you tell me—?"

"We're on a recon sortie, that's all. I've got to check something out. A possible observation nest. It's probably not what I think it is, but we got to be sure. And don't make any noise. Sullivan's got ears like an Indian."

"Hell, you ask me, the guy's overrated."

Hayden stopped and turned on Cornell in a sudden fury.

"Overrated!" he hissed. "That man's worth three of you! I oughta know. I trained him myself."

Cornell stared defiance back at him for a second, then shrugged and dropped his eyes.

Hayden went back to work, thinking: I got to stay cool. I'm getting too tense on this job. Damn Sullivan gets a man shaken up.

They moved through pines, palm trees, a scattering of acacias, the terrain gradually rising. They followed the thin trail through what had once been an olive grove, now abandoned. The trunks of the crooked olive trees were like gray smoke against the yellow grass. The orchard was in terraces, each level of the terrace given its shape by a supporting wall of stones, to prevent erosion. They climbed this stair-cut slope, like an Aztec pyramid, moving up the ridge on which Hayden thought he'd seen the tree with the telltale flash in it.

That tree was the highest, but real bushy—it'd be ideal, he thought. Maybe he's up there—or that black buddy of his.

If Malta was in the post, then Sullivan might be on the ground nearby, scouting on foot. He might be anywhere.

Hayden felt a chill, and peered more sharply at the undergrowth, his finger hovering near the trigger of his M16. He checked to see that the gun was ready. The magazine was full. Thirty rounds. He had another magazine clipped to his belt.

"What we looking for?" Cornell asked. He was breathing hard and sweating, blinking stupidly at the trees around him.

Hayden pointed up the hill. "You see that thicket of trees? The tallest one there. He's got a technique for building a sort of treehouse observation post—works real good, when you put it together right."

"You think he's up there?" Cornell's tone was doubtful.

Hayden shrugged. He raised the binocs and focused on the treetop. He couldn't see anyone, but the foliage, after thinning a bit on the way up the trunk, suddenly got thicker about three-fourths the way to the top. There was a ball of greenery there.

He lowered the binoculars and nodded. "Yeah, it's just possible." The target tree was about a hundred and fifty yards away, and farther up the ridge. There was a great untidy spill of boulders swelling from the brush between them. That and the trees between would make good cover.

"You got your walkie-talkie?" Hayden asked softly.

Cornell patted the instrument on his left hip.

"Good. Then . . . you see that dead tree there? You work your way up to that tree. Take a position just underneath it. Try to move so you won't be seen from that treetop. Keep low, and stay close to the bigger boulders. Move quietly. When you get to your position, take a bead on the target tree, but don't fire till I tell you to—unless you see he's firing at me. I'll call you on the walkie and tell you when to open up on that nest. You got it?"

"Sure. I ain't dumb."

Hayden thought better of the reply that occurred to him. "Get going," was all he said aloud. He watched Cornell lumber off into the brush, and shook his head. He'd always told Sullivan: Pick your patrol partner carefully. He'd gotten careless, and picked badly. But then, the others weren't much better than Cornell.

It was a good thing they had Sullivan outnumbered more than ten to one. Even Sullivan couldn't come out on top against that kind of odds. Even though he was up against dolts like Cornell.

And maybe, just maybe, they had a chance to pick him off now, the easy way.

He started up the ridge, circling around behind the target tree. They'd catch that treetop in a crossfire, and whatever was in it—bird, raccoon, or mercenary—was done for.

Sullivan lowered his field glasses, frowning. Why had Hayden gone into the house that way, so suddenly, after looking in his direction? Coincidence? But he'd taken that sentry with him, and the man hadn't come back to his post. What was up?

He shivered, and reached out a hand to steady himself on the tree trunk beside him—the tree was swaying again in the wind. He blinked, and realized that the wind had torn away a piece of his camouflage "roof"—the sunlight was slanting through, hitting him in the face.

He was struck by a sudden worry. Maybe the rest of the camouflaging had been damaged. Maybe he was exposed.

He moved on hands and knees through the cramped spaces

around the tree trunk, inspecting the netting. Yeah, about a fourth of the branches had been torn away. He decided to abandon the nest rather than trying a repair. He was getting cramps in his legs, anyway.

He slung his Ingram submachine gun over his shoulder and moved toward the hole in the floor—covered with boughs just now—through which he could lower himself onto the branches beneath. He'd chosen the submachine gun because it was easier to carry in the cramped spaces of the nest and the tree boughs and because he'd planned no sniping. He had it along in case he ran into a patrol on the ground. It was good for that kind of skirmish.

But it wasn't much use to him when Cornell opened up on the nest.

The tree trunk close behind him spat splinters, two bullet holes appearing, the yellow wood beneath the bark showing like flesh in the wound of some exotic animal.

"Shit!" Sullivan blurted, flattening. He heard, then, the twin cracks and rolling booms of the gunshots.

The air around him whistled with a hail of slugs. Wood splinters leaped like fireworks sparks. A bullet smashed into his canteen and stopped on a metal plate in his belt. Water spurted from the canteen, like a premonition of his blood.

"Idiot!" Hayden burst out when he heard the shots. He jerked the walkie-talkie from his belt. "Cornell? Cornell! You read me? Dammit, Cornell, you—"

"Yeah, I hear ya."

"What the hell are you doing? I told you not to fire till I—"

"Yeah, but I saw him through the branches, see, boss, the wind blew some of that shit away and I saw him and I saw a rifle barrel, so I figured, that's our chance—"

"You're too far to be sure of hitting him alone! I wanted you to fire only to drive him out to me when I was in position, dammit! If there's only one of us shooting, he can duck behind the trunk, you . . . Oh, forget it. Try to keep him pinned down and I'll try to get in firing position."

Swerving, Hayden clambered onto a boulder, hoping to get a bead on the treetop from there. He had planned to move much closer; now there was too much in the way. Trees, and more trees.

He leaped to another boulder, climbed higher, and found a shooting angle. He raised his rifle to his shoulder and aimed.

The fusillade let up just long enough for Sullivan to scramble to the other side of the trunk. He started breathing again.

He hadn't been hit himself, but he'd heard an ominous snapping sound when a bullet had struck the Ingram on his back. He unslung the SMG and swore. Its breech was cracked. It'd blow up in his face if he tried to fire it now. He tossed it aside. At least he had the Beretta in his belt. He couldn't go down the trunk—they'd have a clear shot at him that way. The ground-drop cable was the only way out. He fitted the wheel onto the cable, then kicked the netting and boughs aside, making a wider opening. He took the handles on either side of the wheel in his hands . . . and hesitated.

This is crazy, he thought. I'm too high up for this.

But just then the boughs and tree trunk began spitting splinters again, bullets whining past his head.

He took a deep breath and lowered himself from the nest so he was hanging beneath the cable. For one instant he was a perfect target. And then he released the brake on the wheel—and the world rushed up at him.

At first he thought he'd fallen from the cable, was free-falling to the ground. But that was an illusion of his speed along the steeply down-slanting line. The wind whistled around him, boughs stung his face, trees seemed to throw their tops at him as if flinging spears. His wrists ached, and then the mistral tugged at him, trying to pull the wheel from the cable. A bullet grazed his chest, but he scarcely noticed it. He was consumed with the whipping speed of that mad plunge downward, hearing only the *zz-zz-zz-zz* of the wheel on the cable. And then a wall of greenery smashed into him, knocking the breath out of him. He fell, cartwheeling through a green whirlpool. And then blackness.

"You see that?" Cornell blurted as Hayden ran up to him. "He flew outta the tree! The motherfucker can fly!"

Hayden groaned. "That was a ground-drop cable, idiot! Come on, I think maybe I winged him when he came down. I saw him fall off the cable about two-thirds of the way down—or maybe the wind knocked him off." They ran like two hunters eager to see their downed buck, weaving in and out of the boulders and trees. "I think he's down in that thicket somewhere."

The cable had passed over the lip of a short drop-off and was fixed to the base of a tree on a shelf of rock below. They found the wheel lying on the edge of the drop-off. No sign of Sullivan. Hayden had assumed Sullivan was badly hurt, at least. Now he began to wonder. Maybe he'd come down on his feet and had already retreated. Or maybe he was sighting in on them from cover at that very moment. . . .

There was a thicket of bamboo and stunted fig trees just below the tree the cable was cinched to. Probably he was down there.

Palms sweating, the gun sticky in his hands, Hayden led Cornell to a trail that cut across the hillside and doubled back, down, below the bottom end of the cable. When they'd crept down the trail, jumping at small animal noises in the brush every few seconds, and come to the dense thicket, Hayden whispered, "You circle around, we'll get him between us. Watch out you don't let fly at me by mistake."

Cornell nodded and disappeared behind a brake of bamboo.

When Sullivan woke, some instinct told him: Don't move. Lie quiet and listen first.

He opened his eyes, and he listened.

He heard a bird squawking somewhere above him. He heard the wind sighing. He heard . . .

Twigs crackling under a man's boots.

He blinked, and his eyes came into focus. He was lying between two rocks on a bed of fallen twigs and pine needles. The rocks nearly came together just in front of him, leaving an opening between them just big enough for a man to slip through sideways. Through that opening he could see yellow and green stalks of bamboo, and a fig tree heavy with overripe fruit. He was lying in shadow under a tree he couldn't see without moving. His head throbbed. He wondered if he'd broken any bones.

He heard the twigs crackling again. Slowly he inched his arm around behind him, feeling for the Beretta.

It was gone.

It must have fallen off when he hit the trees. The wind had jerked him off the cable, and he'd fallen into trees before reaching the cable's end. He moved his hand like a spider searching for prey, making no quick motions, to his belt. The knife was still there, at least. He drew the long double-bladed weapon from its sheath.

The light came mostly through the opening between the rocks. Something blotted that light for a moment—a man standing in the bamboo thicket on the other side of the rock gate. A big man wearing a khaki T-shirt and fatigues. On a biceps comparable to a side of ham was a tattoo of a flaming skull; beneath the skull was the legend "DEATH ON WHEELS." The man stood with his back half-turned to Sullivan.

Sullivan gripped the knife, tried to gather his energy together in case he had to spring. The man was carrying an assault rifle—maybe an AK47. He'd probably plug Sullivan before the knife could be brought into useful action.

So Sullivan pretended he was a sleeping snake. A sleeping snake is as still as a rock. But if you wake it . . .

The big man moved on, without looking in Sullivan's direction. He wasn't doing a very good job of searching. A dim bulb. But probably Hayden would be nearby. And if Hayden came past, he'd find Sullivan for sure.

Moving as noiselessly as possible, Sullivan got to his hands and knees. He had to stifle a groan. Maybe nothing was broken, but he was bruised and lacerated in half a dozen places, and there were scratches from branch ends beginning to welt on the left side of his face and neck. His head throbbed; there was a knot over his left temple.

Still, he was intact. He could fight.

He took deep breaths and stretched a little, trying to get oxygen into his bruised limbs.

He moved in a crouch out through the rock opening, and paused, looking around. He saw nothing but bamboo and a group of fig trees, a clump of bracken to the left. He moved toward the bracken, since it was the better cover.

He wriggled with a faint crackling into the bracken, keeping his head below its upper stems. Then he went stone-still. He'd heard Hayden speaking. From maybe thirty feet away. He could make out only part of what he was saying. ". . . Cornell, you . . . impression of his body here . . . twigs warm, dammit . . . dumb fuck. . . . Okay, he's in there, so . . . and bring back at least four. . . . I'll watch it. . . . Here, I can . . . Just shut up and . . ."

Despite his aches, Sullivan grinned. He sidled out of the

bracken, moved to put a boulder between himself and the position downslope from which Hayden's voice had come. Hayden assumed he was still in the bamboo thicket. But he was on the outer edge of it, and moving into the trees.

He hunched down behind a tangle of fallen trees when he heard heavy foot steps and a man's muttered curses. "Bastard shouldn't talk to me that way," Cornell said, walking past.

Sullivan didn't dare jump the man now. The ex-biker might let out a yell and alert Hayden. So Sullivan followed him down the hill toward the château. Apparently he was going for reinforcements. He'd tell the others they'd seen Sullivan, and that would endanger Edie. No, that wouldn't do at all.

Cornell stopped just outside the chain-link electric fence, now within walkie-talkie range. He unhooked the walkie-talkie from his belt . . .

Sullivan lunged at him from behind, jabbing downward with the knife.

But Cornell's reflexes were quicker than his mind. He'd heard the sound as Sullivan burst from the brush, and he turned to meet him. He dropped the walkie-talkie and brought the rifle up like a quarterstaff to block Sullivan's knife, catching Sullivan's forearm on the barrel.

Sullivan grabbed the rifle stock with his left hand and twisted it at an angle he'd learned in disarming training in Special Forces. He was using the force of his arm to turn Cornell's fingers backward. Cornell had to let go or they'd break. Cornell let go with his right hand, but with his left jerked the rifle free and leaped back. He swung the rifle like a club at Sullivan's head. Sullivan ducked—the metal swished so close some of his hair caught on the breech and was yanked out by the roots. Cornell was thrown off balance for an instant by the momentum of his swing.

Sullivan saw his chance.

He ran hard at Cornell and slammed the big man in his heavy gut with his right shoulder, like a football player in a hard block.

Cornell said "Uff" and staggered backward, flailing for balance. He fell against the chain-link fence, dropping the rifle.

The powerful current running through the fence seized the ex-biker and snapped him to rigid attention. He stood at a cruel parody of military attention, arms straight down at his sides, chest outthrust, chin lifted, as he was electrocuted. His eyes, as he smoked, his flesh sizzling, his fingers vibrating like tuning forks, seemed to be focusing on the ultimate superior officer. Death.

Sullivan picked up the walkie-talkie and experimentally thumbed its transmitter; in his best imitation of Hayden's voice he said, "Hayden here. Shut off the power in the fence, I'm coming through."

The humming went out of the fence. Cornell's body slumped, and he tumbled to the earth. His face was drawn back in a grinning rictus. There was a cross-hatch pattern where the chain links had burned into his back.

Sullivan looked toward the château. He was on a side that had two windows and a door but no balcony. He could see two sentries with their backs to him on the far side of the acreage. No one had seen him.

He moved forward, took Cornell by the ankles, and dragged him into the brush. He concealed the AK47 under some leaves. The walkie-talkie he clipped to his belt.

He dragged Cornell's body a short distance to the edge of the cliff. Sea churned into breakers far below. He stuffed a number of fist-sized stones in Cornell's shirt and down his trousers, then kicked him over the edge. The body flapped its arms in the wind as it fell. It struck headfirst on a large fang-shaped outcropping, making a vivid splash of blood on the black stone. Then the waves rushed in again and washed the blood away, tumbling the body into the sea's secret depths.

Sullivan retrieved the AK47, checked it out, then slipped into the woods. He circled widely, moving back up the hill, hoping to ambush Hayden from above.

But Hayden had already realized that Sullivan was no longer in the thicket. He suspected Sullivan had followed Cornell. He guessed the outcome. If he went that way too, Sullivan would probably ambush him. He grunted and began to jog to the southeast, circling to come out on the private road that led to the château's front entrance.

He hurried up the road to the front gate. The man in the gatehouse looked out at him in surprise. He was a stubby man with big eyes and, it was said, some technical expertise with electronic gear. Flanders. "What the hell you doing here, Hayden?" Flanders asked, his mouth drooping, as he came out of the gatehouse.

"Never fucking mind. Just turn off the power on the fence and lemme through."

"I already turned it off. You didn't tell me to turn it back on."

Hayden stared at him. "When?"

"Oh . . . ten, twenty minutes ago. Maybe a little more."

"That was Cornell."

"No. Wasn't Cornell. Said it was you, and sounded like you."

"Ah . . . shit. Yeah . . . oh, yeah, I forgot . . . Uh . . . you seen Cornell?"

"Nope."

"Well, open the goddamn gate, I'm tired of standing here."

"Sure, sure . . ." The gate whirred aside. He passed through the stone wall's gate and circled the house to the far side, to the gate through which Cornell was supposed to have come. No sign of him. He ordered Flanders to let him through, then went to search the ground outside the fence. There—signs of a scuffle. A spot of blood. So that was it for Cornell. They probably wouldn't even find his body.

He went back into the château's grounds, and thought: Better order Flanders to ignore all walkie-talkie messages from here on out. He's got to see me in front of him before he shuts off that fence.

Ottoowa was waiting on the back patio.

"You shouldn't be out in the open, M'lord," Hayden said. Having to call the guy M'lord was beginning to annoy him deeply. He debated telling Ottoowa about Sullivan. If he did, Ottoowa might off the girl. "M'lord, a sniper might . . ."

Grudgingly Ottoowa stepped back into the shelter of the house. Hayden followed him inside.

"Well? Report!" Ottoowa barked.

"Thought I saw an observation nest. We checked it out, fired a few shots at it. Just a kid's treehouse. No one there."

"Where is Cornell?"

Hayden hesitated. "Uh . . . didn't he come back here? I guess he did what he was talking about—said he wanted to go into town for a little R and R. I told him to forget it, but when my back was turned, he slipped out. Probably be gone for hours, or all night, if I know that guy."

"He will have a good time, I hope," Ottoowa said, turning away. "Because he will pay for that good time when he returns."

"M'lord . . ." Hayden winced. "Did you think about . . . those extra men?"

"Yes. I have made arrangements. We may have two more tomorrow. But when so many know I'm here, it's a great danger. I have decided to leave the château. We will leave France tomorrow night. As soon as the new men arrive."

Hayden knew he ought to urge Ottoowa to leave today.

But that would mean no confrontation with Sullivan. No finishing the fight.

Hayden said nothing, but thought: Tomorrow will be too late. . . .

12

Assault on a Fortress

"We've got to time it as perfectly as humanly possible," Sullivan said, tightening a nut on the stand that held the machine gun to the prow of the cabin cruiser. He and Malta were working over the boat in its "garage" on a private jetty south of Bandol. "We should hit them both at the same time—only the decoy ought to start firing about thirty seconds earlier. Make it a minute. That'll give them time to move their firepower from the front of the house to the seaward side."

"I understand, Jack," said Malta solemnly.

Sullivan tossed the wrench aside. "What do you look so damn sad about, Malta?"

"Sad?" Malta grinned. "Not at all!" But his eyes belied his grin.

"You figure I'm gonna get blown away on this mission. Look, even if I had fifty men on my side, fifty *good* men, it could still happen. One bad-luck ricochet, and . . . well, if the bullet's got your name on it . . ." He shrugged. "Hell, I could get it almost as easily crossing the street, the way the damn taxis drive over here."

"But the *odds*, Jack!"

"There are ways a good tactician can tilt the odds a little. Anyhow, it was *you* who suckered me into this game!"

"Yes. *Mea culpa*. But I thought you would be able to do the job from a distance. With a well-placed mortar shell or a sniper's bullet. I didn't know the man would hide himself in this château and . . ." He shook his head. "Well, *c'est la vie.*"

"Yeah. Great."

Sullivan finished attaching the machine gun and stepped back to admire his work. The gun was raked up at the steepest possible angle, as it would have to hit the château's upper windows from far below. "You sure the remote-control mechanism for this thing is going to work?" Sullivan asked dubiously. Malta had jury-rigged it.

"I think so. I've rigged it so that when I shift the remote-control box into high gear, the signal will not only cause the boat's gears to shift, it will also signal the compression spring—"

"I know, but . . ." He shrugged. "The way I understand it, you've attached a battery-operated spring compressor that—after it releases—forces this little metal flange to press the trigger. Right?"

"Yes, essentially."

"It seems to me that the spray from the prow would interfere with the electrical connections—I mean, the compression box is right here on the damn hood of the boat—"

"Yes, yes," Malta replied somewhat abstractedly, "I've insulated it against that. I've tested it—without rounds in the weapon. It compresses the trigger. It may not work for long, *mon ami*. All that shaking . . . But it will work long enough to focus attention on the boat."

"What is it, Malta? You look like you're not all here."

"I am thinking that perhaps the better way would be for me to assault the château directly. Personally. I could hit them from another side, draw their fire . . ."

Sullivan laughed. "Sorry for laughing, but you don't *really* want to do that. I gotta respect you for offering, though. Few men would. But, look, firefight and assault just aren't your specialty. You're an intelligence specialist, that's where your skills are. I don't want to lose you to some stray bullet. Anyway, there'll be plenty to do. You'll be close enough to keep in radio contact with me till I go over the fence. After that I'll leave the radio behind."

"You will try to use their walkie-talkie to deceive them?"

"No. I know Hayden, he'll have figured against that. No, I gotta take that fence out the hard way." Sullivan glanced at his watch. "Gonna be sunset soon, buddy. Time to get to it. . . . You get that backup boat in place?"

"It is there, as of about an hour ago, Jack. It's just an outboard skiff, I'm afraid."

"That'll do. . . . The police trace that boat I stole from Ottoowa to the château?"

"No. It's not registered to that address. . . . I think we can count on the gendarmes taking a little holiday today, my friend. But there's nothing else we can count on."

"Oh, there *is* something else." Sullivan chuckled. "We can count on hell. Tonight the devil's having a bash at the Château Borne."

Some called him Anderson and some called him the Swede. He didn't much care what they called him. He was a man who kept to himself, who'd always felt apart. Maybe he felt different because he was a near-albino. Maybe because he didn't seem to feel a lot of emotions most people felt. He'd never felt love for someone—not since he was a little boy and his dad locked him in that snow-covered shed all night. That night something had frozen in his soul.

There was just one thing that could melt Anderson the Swede a little inside. Sex. Not romance—but sex. He could go at it for hours. And he could think about it for hours when there wasn't someone to go at it with.

So it was ironic that Magg Ottoowa had chosen the Swede to guard Edie. Ottoowa had the impression that the Swede was a sort of eunuch. Maybe because Anderson seemed, most of the time, to be chipped out of ice. Never showed expression. But everyone's got some kind of feeling. Anderson's was lust, and he was having a tough time controlling it.

Anderson stood outside the door to Edie's room, face blank as an erased blackboard; the direction of his thinking was hinted at only by the tightness of his fingers on the breech of his M16.

She'd tell Ottoowa, he was thinking. Ottoowa would kill me ugly.

He was thinking about the kind of death Ottoowa would arrange for him if he had his way with Edie, when the banging came on the door behind him.

"Shit!" he burst out, startled. He turned halfway around. "Yeah, lady, what you want?"

"I want to talk with you, please!" Edie shouted through the door.

Anderson hesitated.

"About what? What you need? You got a bathroom in there, you had your dinner—"

"Please, I've got to have a word with you. I've been wondering what you look like—I want to see."

That was too much for Anderson. "Okay, but keep your mouth shut about this. . . ." He looked up and down the hall, then leaned his rifle against the doorjamb. He fumbled in his pocket with clammy, nervous fingers, found the old-fashioned key, and unlocked the door. He pocketed the key, opened the door, picked up the rifle, and stepped through with it. Staring at Edie, he closed the door behind him.

He licked his lips.

She was wearing a man's bathrobe Hayden had given her, tied at the waist. It showed her long golden legs below the thighs, and the tanned swell of her cleavage at the lapels. She'd brushed her hair, and washed. Even the bruises on her cheek looked good. It might be nice to give her a few more while he—

"Hey!" Anderson snapped as she tried to press past him to the unlocked door.

"I want to talk to Ottoowa," she said, smiling at him, running her fingers softly along his jawline. She tried again to sidle past, and he felt the warmth of her breasts against his right shoulder. He dropped the rifle to the rug and clapped his fingers to her upper arms.

"What you mean, Ottoowa? I thought you said you wanted to talk to *me?* It's me or nothing. 'Cause I ain't gonna let you talk to Ottoowa till he asks to see you. He wouldn't like that."

She squirmed away from him, and he let her, because he liked watching her move. He stared at her heavy, dessert-sweet lips, and wanted to taste them. He wanted to taste every part of her, bad. So bad it hurt.

"You're hurting me," Anderson said breathlessly. "You hurt me just with the way you look. So it's my turn to hurt you now. But I think you're gonna like it."

She was backing away from him, but he didn't mind that either. He liked watching her legs move, the jounce of her breasts as she half-turned to reach behind her.

"You know what I'd like, *mon amour?*" she said huskily.

"No—you tell me what it is you'd like, babe. I just might give it to you."

"I'd like you to press your face into my breasts. I'd like you to . . . to kiss them."

She opened the bathrobe. She had a slip on under the bathrobe, and that was all. Her big round breasts were bare and begging him for attention. They semed to grow, to fill up the whole room for him, just then. He moved toward her, bent over her, reaching for them . . .

And then he thought: What was she reaching behind her for?

Too late. Fireworks burst in his head, and an explosive pain. He had time to think: The bitch hit me with the goddamn lamp. Then he blacked out.

After Sullivan had installed and primed the plastic explosives in the prow of the boat, Malta went to swing the doors of the boat garage wide, opening the way to the pewter-colored waters of the little estuary.

Sullivan went forward to the machine gun, still brooding about the explosives. He wondered if he should install additional armor atop them—but that might interfere with the collision-triggered detonation. Still, it could throw things off if gunfire from the château triggered the explosive prematurely. Probably he'd arranged the armoring to protect it from that, though. Yeah, they'd be shooting downward.

Sullivan covered the machine gun with a tarp and lashed the tarp down tightly so the wind wouldn't pry it up and "drop their pants" in front of all the weekend boaters. It was a crude Soviet-made weapon, a piece of "surplus" confiscated from terrorists two years before: a 7.62mm caliber USSR RPD, gas-operated, with a hundred-round metallic link belt in a metal drum. They'd removed the stock and bolted the ammo drum to the deck, plus added an unusually high muzzle stand for the raked shooting angle. It was a nearly obsolete weapon, mostly useful as a decoy-prop. And maybe it would confuse Ottoowa about who was attacking him. It would be a good thing if he thought, looking at the Soviet weapon, that the KGB was the attacker.

Malta returned to the boat, stepping over the water from the wooden walkway around the edges of the garage, and a minute later they were cutting across the waves to follow the coastline north.

Sullivan's head ached; his scratches stung, and the bullet graze across his left pectoral, where Hayden's bullet had licked him on the way down the cable drop, burned like a branding iron.

But there was a grim smile on Sullivan's lips. He'd let them put him off long enough. Now rage gave him a singing inner strength that made all his aches into a ghostly, dimly felt echo. He shifted into battle consciousness. He was no longer a personality, no longer an ordinary human being with the usual misgivings and uncontrolled mental associations. Now he was a killing machine. He was a tactical computer. He was an automatic weapon. And the only human feeling in him—aside from loyalty to those who stood with him—was the rage of the vengeance-taker. That rage was the fuel for the killing machine's engine.

His armored cabin cruiser shot toward the château like a hard-on.

The sun was shimmering at the horizon. Sullivan hurried to help Malta unload the boat so they could get it out to sea, to use that sunset's glare to their advantage. They'd treated the windows so they were opaque—no one would be able to see that the boat had no pilot. But it would be better if the glare hid the boat's details and made it just that much harder to hit.

Sullivan had moved his attack time up—from three A.M. to eight P.M.—partly to take advantage of that glare and partly to take advantage of the momentum of his inner rage. The attack at the observation nest had infuriated him. Years before, he'd learned that rage can be two things to a warrior. It can be the raw energy that pulls him through, or it can be his death if he allows it to overwhelm his tactical judgment. Rage was something a good warrior learned how to use. Like a weapon.

He moved the battlefield shortwave, the eagle-eye missiles, and a couple of backup rifles to Malta's remote-control post ashore, atop the ridge overlooking the château. "You don't think they will send sentries outside the fence now, Jack?" Malta asked when they'd gotten the gear stored safely behind the blind of camouflaging and twigs.

"No, I cut their forces back too much. They'll need the

survivors to stay in close to the château. . . . Okay, I'm headin' out."

Solemnly they shook hands.

"Bonne chance, mon ami," Malta murmured as Sullivan moved off down the hill.

Sullivan would need that luck.

Hayden had thought better of his decision to keep quiet about the coming battle. To do the job right, he'd decided, he had to give his commander the facts. It tasted bad in his mouth, but he said it. "M'lord, I think we ought to move out tonight. As soon as possible." He couldn't tell Ottoowa, at this point, about the treehouse encounter with Sullivan. But he could tell him what it foreshadowed: "I think someone's going to hit us tonight."

"What makes you certain of that, Mr. Hayden?" Ottoowa asked.

Ottoowa was sitting at dinner on the balcony overlooking the sea. He had at last discarded the formal red military attire—for white formal military attire. With even bigger gold braids. He chewed lustily at a steak so rare it nearly screamed, blood running from the corners of his mouth, all the time watching Hayden.

That made Hayden nervous.

"Uh . . . hard to explain. Just call it the trained instinct of long experience, M'lord. I *know*."

"Indeed?" Ottoowa spat a bone over the railing. It tumbled, trailing blood droplets, to the sea far, far below. "I wonder if you are keeping something from me, Mr. Hayden."

Hayden stiffened. He knew what that meant. When Ottoowa started to wonder about you, you were probably as good as dead. With Ottoowa, even a suspicion of treachery was enough to condemn you.

"I think that tonight," Hayden went on doggedly, "it's going to come down on us. I can't explain."

Ottoowa barked for wine, then turned back to Hayden. "Very well. We will leave in one hour, if we can get the yacht loaded quickly."

"I'd advise *now*, M'lord—and I advise once again against appearing on this balcony. You are a target here."

"A target? No one could get close enough to—"

The wine bottle the steward had just set on the table

exploded. The steward exploded too. Bullet holes ripped him open at the middle, splashing his white jacket with red.

Hayden stared down at the man's twitching body in momentary shock. Shock—but not regret. The man had been Ottoowa's servant for years, the only one Ottoowa hadn't killed, and it was said he himself had been a skilled torturer, had killed dozens while his master looked greedily on.

Hayden's shock melted away a second later and he dived to the flagstone floor of the balcony as another spray from below raked across the balcony.

Ottoowa was down on his hands and knees. He was completely unhurt—physically. But his pride had been dealt a nasty blow. Hayden noted that with some satisfaction. It was good to see Ottoowa on his hands and knees, waddling through the open doors into the cover of the living room.

Ottoowa stood, dusting his knees.

Hayden joined him. "It seems you were right, Mr. Hayden," Ottoowa said. His voice was like a wire pulled taut till it was about to snap. His hands trembled with a fury barely in check. "It's Sullivan, isn't it?"

Hayden moved to a window and peered out from a lower corner. He saw the cabin cruiser below, coming back around to strafe the balcony again. There was a machine gun mounted on the hood—but no one operating it. Must have it rigged so he can press the trigger from the pilot's cabin. Some kind of remote. Funny, Sullivan attacking that way—from the sea. So vulnerable down there. And that had been a lucky hit, that strafe. He couldn't hope to shoot at all accurately—not on those waves, and with no way to aim the muzzle of the machine gun precisely. Funny. Must have seen Ottoowa out there, and it was too much of a temptation. Nearly got him, too. But why was Sullivan sticking around? What could he hope to accomplish from down there now, except knock out a few windows? Sooner or later some boat would pass and see the action and radio the cops. Crazy way to work. But maybe that was it—the unexpected. But how could Sullivan hope to—

Ottoowa's shuddering roar interrupted his pondering. "I *asked* you, *is* that Sullivan?"

Hayden nodded. "I think so. That's the boat that—"

"Then get the girl! Quickly! Bring her here!"

Gunmen were running into the room, babbling questions, unslinging rifles.

Hayden watched them dubiously. But then again, maybe it wasn't Sullivan down there. Maybe—

"Hayden!" Ottoowa bellowed. "Get the girl! I'll oversee our defense!"

"If you say so, M'lord. But I don't think . . ."

His words were drowned out by gunfire. Three sentries and the two bodyguards had taken up firing positions in the window and were laying down a heavy fire pattern on the little boat below. They'd cut it to pieces in minutes, Hayden figured.

Ottoowa gestured spasmodically, a pistol in each hand. "*Go!*"

Hayden shrugged. "Yes, sir."

He moved down the hall, took the stairs three at a time, zigzagging three flights below to the second floor.

Strange—the guard was gone from her door. And it was open.

He found the guard out cold on the floor of her room. Hayden slapped the man's cheeks, waking him.

"Whuh?" The guard was Anderson, a man with nearly albino-white hair, crewcut, and white-blond eyebrows, a classically Swedish face. "Where the hell . . . ?" He sat up and looked at Hayden. He blinked, and then his eyes focused. "Hayden?"

"Yeah, brilliant observation, asshole, it's Hayden!" He grabbed the man by the shirt collar and dragged him to his feet. Then he saw the gash on the side of Anderson's head, matting his hair with blood. "What happened?"

"The bitch. The *bitch!* Started to come outside, said she had to talk to Ottoowa. I told her to forget it. She came at me with . . ." He pointed.

Hayden looked. There was a broken table lamp behind the door. He looked back at Anderson, and despite the gunshots racketing from above, grinned. "She busted your head open? Hell, man, she musta stood on her tiptoes! And it wasn't even from behind!" He nodded to himself. The woman had courage. Admirable.

"Yeah, but shit, she . . ." He winced. "She pulled open her robe. Them big boobies—"

Hayden laughed. "She fucking hypnotized you, Anderson! You dumb ass."

"Look, don't tell Ottoowa what happened, okay? I'll find her—"

"No, uh . . . forget it. I'll find her. You go outside and report to Bates. Gotta beef up that back sentry watch."

"That gunfire I hear?"

"No, that's the little drummer boy playing a march. Get going, and watch your dumb ass—we're under attack. Keep your eyes open. I got a feeling he'll hit us from the back, no matter what it looks like now."

Anderson got to his feet. "Where's my gun?"

"Naturally, dumb ass, she took it. Get another from the basement, and *move*!"

Anderson moved, groaning, holding his lumped head.

Hayden went up the hall to the stairway and paused beside the door of one of the unused bedrooms. He heard a noise from in there. Sure, Edie was probably holed up in there—she'd been in the hall, heard him coming, was waiting for him to go.

He hesitated, then shrugged. It wouldn't help their defense to bring her out. Sullivan wouldn't let a hostage stop him now.

The hell with her. Let her go.

Smiling just a little, he went upstairs. "She's not there," he began, stepping into the living room. "Anderson . . ." He broke off, looking around. "What's going on? Bates! What're you doing here?"

Bates and the other sentries, all but Flanders, were at the windows, firing at the boat outside. Ottoowa was at the telephone. He threw the phone onto the floor and kicked it against a wall. "Someone cut the lines!" he bellowed.

"Naturally," Hayden said dryly. "M'lord . . ." That time he really had to force it out. "Why are the sentries up here? We need to guard our rear—"

"What? They came because they heard the shooting, you fool!"

"But that's . . ." A light dawned on him. "That's what Sullivan wants!"

"What?" Ottoowa stalked toward him, waving the pistols. "What are you talking about?"

"Hold your fire!" Hayden shouted at the sentries. He had

to repeat it three times. The men stepped away from the windows, blinking at him through a haze of blue gunsmoke.

Hayden pushed Bates aside with a curse, snatched a pair of binoculars off a table, and looked through the window.

Incredibly, the boat was still there. It looked half shot to pieces, but it was still running. The machine gun had been knocked off, but the boat kept zipping back and forth across the little inlet, working its way in toward the dock . . .

"Armored!" Hayden burst out. "I can see camouflaged armoring! And look—where that right windshield's shot out—there's no one driving that thing! It's remote-controlled, a fucking decoy! You idiots! What's it doing now? . . . It's heading toward the yacht!"

The cabin cruiser hit the yacht broadside, and the big load of plastic explosives in its prow exploded thunderously, consuming the smaller boat in a ball of black-shot red flame; they could see the shock wave make a sort of inverted bubble in the water around the exploding boat. And then the smoke hid the wreckage and part of the sinking yacht. "He's blown up the yacht!" Bates shouted. "He—"

A voice crackled from Bates' walkie-talkie. "Anyone there? This is Anderson—somebody just blew up the gatehouse! Looked like a mortar shell! Shit, Flanders is dead. He . . . The electric fence is knocked down, somebody's coming through. . . . *Shit!*"

And then silence.

Malta lowered the binoculars, grinning. That was one yacht Ottoowa would not be using for an escape. Already its deck was completely awash, and it was heeling over to port. By now Sullivan should have penetrated the fence. Time to back him up.

He quickly checked the eagle-eye missile launcher one last time. He activated the TV cameras. The little TV screen on the control unit showed only dark sky, a black-and-white image—mostly black. Luckily there were powerful outside lights at the château. Lights designed for the château's defense—which would help him destroy it.

He stood well back from the launching tubes and activated number one with the thumb switch. The missile's tail shooshed out white smoke and flame, and then it was gone, rocketing almost straight up. Malta bent over the screen, twiddling knobs to signal the missile's computerized navigator—the image on the screen changed. There was a confused blur of coastline, the lights of the château, the horizon, then a dark gray face of rock rushing at him. He jerked the joystick back—too late. The missile plowed into the cliff below the château, exploding brilliantly but uselessly.

Malta cursed himself in French, Algerian, and English, wishing he'd done more research on operating these missiles. He fired number two—and lost that one as well, ran it into a treetop.

But now he was beginning to get the feel of it. His third missile shot straight for the château. The image whirled, and the little screen showed the roof of the château, the spotlights slicing across the back lawns. He veered downward, then forced the missile into a wide circle over the treetops till he could get his bearings. It was not unlike a video game. Once you got the feel for it . . .

But the image on the screen moved so quickly! What if he brought the missile down too close to Sullivan? He'd never have time to be sure who was in the target area. . . .

He took a deep breath, twiddled the knobs, and pressed the joystick forward. The rear lights of the château leaped toward the camera in the snout of the missile. The target grew.

Sullivan heard the explosions of the first two missiles and grimaced. The eagle-eyes, it seemed, were harder to operate than they'd supposed. He was crouched in the rubble of the stone wall, inside the electric-fence perimeter. He'd blown the wall—but then the sentry with the white hair had pinned him down here before he could get through the still-smoking gap.

There was about twenty yards of lawn between Sullivan and the corner of the house where Anderson crouched, sheltered by a stone buttress, firing M16 bursts at Sullivan's position. The rear and side grounds were lighted in swaths of light from the swiveling searchlights on the roof, and from the one remaining anticrime lamp. Sullivan had shot three lamps out, to give partial cover to his assault area. He'd left the remaining lamps intact to guide Malta—but now it seemed that Malta wasn't going to be much help.

Sullivan carried a semiautomatic assault rifle, the Beretta, a knife, and six grenades. He yanked two grenades free, holding their pressure clamps tightly, one in each hand. He waited till Anderson's latest gun burst ended, then jumped up and lobbed both grenades over the wall, one shortly after the other. He was too far and tossing at a difficult angle—he probably couldn't blow the sentry away with those grenades. But the son of a bitch would keep his head down, maybe just long enough . . .

The grenades exploded close together near the corner of the house; the buttress protected Anderson from the flak, but Sullivan was up and running, clearing the crust of wall, zigzagging across the lawn under cover of the smoke from the grenade blasts. Pieces of sod were still pattering to the ground around him as he ran. He peered through the blue-gray smoke, glimpsed the sentry getting up, raising his M16 muzzle . . .

Sullivan threw himself down and to the right, rolling. Bullets screamed into the turf where he'd been a second before, ripping it brutally. He kept rolling, coming into a wide patch of shadow. Then he sprang to his feet, and keeping low, rifle spitting flame in his hands, sprinted for the shelter of the stone porch railings. Anderson ducked back to avoid Sullivan's burst. Sullivan made the porch, then jumped over the railing into the flowerbed, working smoothly with the motion to shoulder-roll, somersault, and snap up into firing position—as the door to the porch was flung open from inside and three men rushed out. At the same moment, Anderson rushed Sullivan from the side of the house, shouting, "He's there, to your left, the bastard's on the other side of the porch!"

The three men—Bates, one of the black bodyguards, and a French mercenary—turned as one to begin firing at him. He was already opening up on them, but he knew it was too late.

The dirt kicked up powder around him as they fired at him, at first inaccurately in the darkness.

Sullivan knew he had only two or three seconds to live.

The air split with a violent shriek—and the porch erupted in flame and smoke, pieces of hot debris flying outward to trail vapor. Malta had scored a bull's-eye.

The shock wave from the eagle-eye missile's blast kicked Sullivan in the gut and tumbled him backward. He found himself lying on his back, staring up at the stars, his head ringing, gasping for air. He forced himself to take a breath, and swearing, got to his knees, fumbling for his rifle. He scooped it up from the dirt in front of him, checked to see that the barrel was clear, put in a fresh clip, and got shakily to his feet. He started forward, moving through a spreading cloud of smoke and dust. Small tongues of flame—finding no foothold on the stone walls—licked futilely at the ragged gap four yards high and three wide where the front door and the porch had been. He counted three dead—or pieces of men that amounted to three dead—in the rubble. He'd killed two others that day, so that left six or seven fighting men against him. Unless the white-haired sentry . . .

A goulish figure, a thing out of nightmares, loomed up in the smoke cloud to Sullivan's left—the white-haired guard, the right half of his face torn away by flying debris, his teeth and the bone of his jaw showing within the wound, muscles exposed and hanging, one eye socket a puddle of red. Yammering maniacally, he charged Sullivan with an M16. Sullivan dodged, and fired from the hip, zippering the disfigured sentry with six slugs at close range. The man was lifted off his feet by the impact of the bullets and thrown back over the snaggletooth remains of the railing. Sullivan turned away, flattened himself against the wall beside the missile-impact hole, and lobbed a grenade into the house. The wall at his back shivered with the explosion, and fragments of stone fell from the edge of the break overhead.

Sullivan ducked down and spun on his heel to spray the anteroom—just a scorched and rubbled cave now—with a double burst from his semiautomatic.

There was no return fire.

He unsnapped a flashlight from his belt and shone it into the smoke-filled room. Not even a corpse. But there would be at least half a dozen more men to deal with somewhere in the house.

The air shuddered, a long *boooom* shivering through the walls of the château. Malta had used the fourth missile, mostly as a diversion—probably on the balcony.

Sullivan stepped through the broken-down door into the ground-floor living room. To the right, a cracked picture window showed only darkness—the view off the cliff's edge. A few stars. Ahead, a wide staircase, twisting upward. Sullivan ran across the open space to the stairs, ducked back against the wall of the stairwell, half a flight up, looking for the enemy. No one yet. The overhead lights glowed as if nothing had happened, though they were slightly muted by smoke from the detonations; smoke that stung his eyes, made him cough.

He began to move up the stairs, and with his left hand started to return the flashlight to his belt—when the lights went out. Probably a complication of that last missile strike—it must have caused a fire or broken a water pipe, shorted out the system. If it was a short, even the backup would be useless.

Sullivan smiled coldly. He was used to working in darkness.

He kept the flashlight in his left hand, but turned off. In his right he carried the Beretta. The rifle was slung over his shoulder. The pistol would serve him better at this close range. Too bad he hadn't had time to get another submachine gun.

Knees bent, almost squatting, Sullivan moved up the stairs. He was above the thickest smoke now, and could breathe almost freely.

The darkness was deep on the stairwell, but broken by patches of gray above at the landing where light—moonlight, starlight, and a flicker that suggested fire, possibly from flames on the tar roof—came in through windows at the end of the corridor.

Sullivan kept to the pits of darkness, moving cat-soft, breathing deeply but so slowly it would be hard to hear.

But the men coming down the hall toward the stairway weren't so careful to move quietly. In fact, they were arguing.

The tall, angular one was saying, "I think we oughta stick with Hayden. He knows what he's doing, man, and—"

"No, no," said the shorter, stockier man in a heavy French accent. "That Hayden is crazy to go the back stairs."

Sullivan, when he'd first heard their voices, had swung over the stair railing. He was perched atop the switchback of the railing below the landing, balancing on the balls of his feet, hidden behind the balustrade, holding on to it with his left hand, the automatic pistol at the ready in his right. He was counting on the two men looking first down the stairway itself, and not beyond the railing.

He had guessed right. The men paused at the landing, just at the top of the stairs, the short one, nearer the outside rail, flashing his light down the stairs. He carried an AK47; the other carried a shotgun.

Sullivan was poised on the railing of the flight beneath them. If they'd looked down at their boots, they'd probably have noticed him looking through the rail posts. He could almost have bitten their ankles.

He shot the first one through the crotch, because he couldn't hit the heart or head—the railing was in the way. The man shrieked and dropped his rifle. It banged down the stairs. He clutched at the close-range wound where his groin had been, and doubled over—that made it easy to finish him. Sullivan put a bullet through the side of the man's head; it split open like the proverbial ripe melon, jerking on his neck as he fell away.

The taller man, confused—the floor seemed to be shooting at them—swung around and let loose with the shotgun. The double-barreled combat shotgun roared, but it was too high, taking a chunk out of the railing well over Sullivan's head. Sullivan fired twice between the railing posts. This man was farther from him and he could sight in on him clearly. Two bullets crunched through the tall man's skull and he fell over backward with a single short yelp. The flashlight looped from his nerveless fingers, and flaring light wildly, bumped down the stairs to the next landing. It came to a stop leaning against the bottom step, pointed upward, shining its light over the stairs and up onto the sprawled head-downward corpse of the Frenchman.

Sullivan swung himself over the railing, alighting neatly on the steps. He picked up the shotgun and with his own flashlight briefly looked it over. Double-barreled twelve-gauge with a bandolier containing four more shells fixed to the stock with duck tape. Looked to be in good shape. He holstered his Beretta, reloaded the shotgun, and cocked it.

Carrying the shotgun, he crept up to the landing. A large grandfather clock faced him across the corridor, ticking sullenly. He heard footsteps approaching from his right. Someone coming down the stairs.

He crossed the corridor with a single long stride and turned to flatten against the wall beside the clock. The big clock stood between him and whoever was coming down the stairs. Sullivan held the shotgun upright, feeling its cold metal barrel against his cheek. He held his breath.

A middle-sized man with long stringy black hair and a Slavic face walked past without seeing him. The man's attention was fixed on the stairs—the flashlight propped up at the bottom shone up toward him, and he assumed, probably, that someone was lying there holding it. The glare from the big flashlight made it hard to be sure no one was behind it. He shouted, "Who's there?" as he pointed his M16 at the light. Sullivan, behind him, dropped the shotgun down into firing position. The motion made a slight noise and the man whirled to face him, M16 spurting flame and slugs.

He'd fired spasmodically, without aiming, and the bullets crashed into the glass face of the clock, sending shards flying, bits of springs and wood jumping out.

But with the shotgun at a range of two yards, Sullivan couldn't miss. The shotgun bucked violently in his hands, disgorging hellfire—he fired from the hip, the stock against the meat of his thigh. The big gun's kick jabbed him painfully. But that was nothing to what the shotgun did to his enemy; even Sullivan was a little sickened.

The double barrels tore the man in half, so that blood splashed on the ceiling and the walls. The man's insides, shredded, sprang out from a hole big as a basketball as his body was rag-dolled backward over the stair railing, heels-over-head, tumbling to hit the stairs a flight below with a sickening *snap-squish* sound.

Sullivan nodded to himself with a professional's satisfaction. Good close spread on that shot. Effective weapon—but only at very close range. He reloaded it—just two rounds left—and moved off down the hall to the stairs at the end.

But he hesitated at the bottom of the stairs. What had that French guy said? Something about Hayden on the back stairs. Where *were* these back stairs? And what was Hayden doing there?

Probably he'd gone downstairs, and would be working back up, behind Sullivan. Hit him from behind while he was distracted by this cannon fodder.

Sullivan went to the vertical gray rectangle behind the stairs—the window of the corridor. He looked out, but he could see no one moving on the lawns.

He decided against going farther upstairs this way. He moved off down the hall to the other end, opening doors, firing a burst through, fishing for a reaction. Nothing. He had laid his hand on a doorknob—when the door behind him opened. He spun. One of the black bodyguards, armed with an SMG, stood silhouetted against the gray light filtering up from a narrow stairway. The back stairway?

Both Sullivan and the African were startled—neither had expected the other. But, unlike the bodyguard, Sullivan didn't allow his surprise to slow his reactions. He snapped the shotgun up and fired a split second before the other man would have squeezed his own trigger.

The range was even closer here. The double blast caught the man full force in the teeth. His head split into two halves, separated at the two jaws, the upper half exploding backward, the lower clacking a few times before, almost headless, the corpse sagged and tumbled down the stairs.

Sullivan tossed the exhausted shotgun aside and caught up the bodyguard's SMG. There was a fresh clip in the submachine gun. He looked down the stairs.

Where was that dim light coming from?

He moved down the stairs, submachine gun hard and cold in his hands. They were stone stairs, and very old. This was the oldest part of the château, judging by the cracked stone walls and the narrowness of the stairwell. He stepped over the shattered body of the dead bodyguard and continued down, taking the steps slowly and carefully, flattened against the back wall of the dank, twisting stairwell.

He came around another bend—and saw a man standing against the light of a doorway five steps below. The doorway looked out onto an anteroom, this one bare of furniture, with only a single electric light bulb overhead. Sullivan felt a breeze on his cheek, faintly damp and salty. So the anteroom opened onto the outdoors, probably at the stairway that led down the cliffside.

The man in the doorway had his back turned to Sullivan. He was a tall, wiry black man in fatigues and a headband. The second bodyguard. The man was looking out past the anteroom.

Voices floated up the stairs. Someone talking outside. Sullivan guessed whoever it was had to be at least eight yards distant. Maybe more. So if he shot the bodyguard now, they'd hear him, and they'd pin him down here—he'd have to retreat up the stairs.

He heard Hayden's voice then. ". . . says he heard

gunshots up the stairs. . . . Your other man hasn't come back . . ."

"Then we move quickly . . ." Ottoowa's voice.

"You get in that boat and get the hell away from here, and I'll take care of—"

"No! He is a worm and I will step on him."

"If you inflate the boat, you can—"

"I will not scuttle away in this filthy rubber raft—I have run enough! I am the Emperor!"

"M'lord, he's . . ."

Sullivan moved quietly down the stairs. He slung the SMG over one shoulder, took a garrote out of one of the pouches on his belt, and wound its ends around his two hands, then stretched it taut between them. He moved up behind the bodyguard and with a swift, fluid, circular motion looped the wire around the man's neck and jerked it tight, at the same time dragging him backward into the shadows, so his struggles wouldn't attract the attention of the men outside. Pulling the man off balance served to tighten the garrote, the victim's body weight itself strangling him. The guard had time only for a startled squeak before the wire shut off his windpipe just above the larynx. He struggled like a trapped black panther in Sullivan's grasp—twice Sullivan nearly lost control of the man, the thrashings almost throwing him off balance. But he stood braced against the wall, pectorals, biceps, and forearms working together like the three parts of a gallows.

Four muscle-aching minutes later, the man stopped thrashing. He went limp in Sullivan's arms, eyes bulging, staring at the ceiling, tongue half-sawed-through between clenched teeth.

Sullivan lowered him noiselessly to the floor, abandoned the garrote, and unslung his appropriated submachine gun.

He moved forward toward the doorway to the anteroom—and froze.

It was too quiet outside now.

Hayden was there. Sullivan was sure of it. He could feel it. The son of a bitch had probably convinced Ottoowa that it was time to retreat. The mass murderer would be down those steps carved into the cliffside, inflating a raft for an escape down the coast.

And Hayden would be under cover outside the door, waiting. Hayden had realized that both bodyguards had disappeared—

and that meant Sullivan had found the back stairs. Hayden knew where Sullivan was.

Sullivan thought: If I retreat up the stairs and try to circle around behind Hayden, Ottoowa will get away. I've got to get past Hayden now, or the job's blown.

He squatted down, moved through the shadows to the open doorway, peered around the doorframe.

The anteroom was dark. No one around. Hayden would be just outside that half-open door. Sullivan could see a watered-down milky light throwing a pale shaft through the other doorway onto the stone floor. He slipped through the door from the stairway, moved toward the outside door. He flattened against the wall beside the outside door, jerked a grenade from his belt, and tossed it through.

A flash of light and a *whump*. Shrapnel whining off the stone of the outer wall.

Sullivan launched himself through the door, SMG chattering in his hands, slicing into the woods, shadows, anyplace a man could hide. Then he flung himself down to the right, rolling behind a boulder that marked the stairway leading down the cliffside.

Breathing hard, gun hot in his hands, muzzle smoking, Sullivan scanned the woods. No return fire. Hayden must be there—but playing it cagey. Or . . . Sullivan looked down the stairway. Down there? Covering Ottoowa's retreat? That must be it. He turned to head down the stairs.

A boot crunch behind him. He turned just in time to see Hayden, grinning, stepping from the doorway of the château, an M16 in his hands spitting flame.

Something smashed into Sullivan's left shoulder; its brother dug hungrily into his left thigh, spinning him around. He fell, cursing with the pain in his wounds as he struck the stone stairway. He rolled down five steps, came to rest at a wide place where the stairs switched back—where a zig became a zag.

He would have liked to lie there staring up at the stairs, the blue-white moon, resting, falling into the pit of darkness opening up in his mind . . .

But he cursed himself and forced his right arm to prop him up, his right leg to work. Summoning the rage that would ride roughshod over the pain, he got to his feet. His left thigh was bullet-slashed and bloody—but the slug had missed the bone.

He thought: Hayden must've run around to the hole I blasted on the far side, gone into the house and come out of it behind me.

Sullivan fired a burst up the steep cliffside. Bullets spanged off stone—he glimpsed Hayden running to hide behind a boulder.

Sullivan knew he was a sitting duck.

He looked for cover. Hayden fired, strafing the stone at Sullivan's feet; in a moment he would draw a bead on him and cut him down.

But Hayden's firing ceased, cut off by another burst. A burst from the château, behind.

Sullivan forced himself to move up the steps, peering through the darkness. Malta? No. . . . He saw her then at a window on the second floor, a rifle in her hands. Edie. She'd fired through the window glass, forcing Hayden to cover himself.

Which gave Sullivan time to move up two flights, circle the boulder Hayden was behind—Sullivan moving crabwise across an outcropping of rock just below the boulder, the cliff dropping away sheer beneath him—and come out face to face with Hayden, two yards distant.

Hayden grinned and raised the M16. But Sullivan had his weapon already leveled. He squeezed the trigger, and his old friend jerked with the impact of the bullets, bouncing four times against the boulder, then flopping sideways. The M16 lay at his feet.

Hayden was on his left side, shuddering, breathing raggedly.

Sullivan bent over him, his mouth dry with regret.

"Sam—" Sullivan began.

"Don't say it, Jack—don't say . . . that you're . . . sorry. You done a good . . . job . . . but you wouldn't . . . wouldn't need that girl to . . . to bail you out if you'd . . . paid attention when I . . . was . . ."

He coughed and closed his eyes.

"Sam, you bastard, I didn't want to—"

"I know." Hayden opened his eyes. "But you . . . did me . . . favor . . ."

One more shudder. That was all. The life went out of him.

* * *

Rage. It was Ottoowa's fault. Hayden's death. Ottoowa had corrupted him. Ottoowa and his kind.

The rage guided Sullivan's hands as he staunched his wounds, applied a tourniquet, put a fresh clip in the SMG. And the rage gave him the strength, despite his blood loss, to move down that cliffside, searching for Ottoowa.

Sullivan reached the jetty, teeth grating with fury. The bastard had escaped. He'd gotten clean away.

And then he saw the raft. It was just a hat-shaped silhouette against the moon-silvered sea—the rubber raft was the rim of the hat, and the man sitting in it was the crown. Ottoowa, rowing away to the north, thinking to follow the coastline to the next town and hire a boat there.

Sullivan smiled, and figured the range. The raft was big enough . . . Yeah. It was just possible.

He tossed the SMG aside and drew his Beretta. He extended his arm straight from the shoulder, took a full ten seconds to aim, and fired. Three times.

The raft shrieked like a wounded cow, and began to shrivel, to shrink. A minute later Ottoowa, bellowing in fury, was thrashing through the water away from the deflated raft toward the shore. Sullivan withdrew to the cover of shadows and began to pick his way across the tumble of boulders at the base of the cliff.

There was a small, pebbly scallop of beach, just a few yards across, between two of the boulders. Periodically the waves rushed up over it, raked pebbles clattering back down when the water retreated.

As Sullivan expected, Ottoowa made for that tiny beach.

Sullivan was there waiting behind a rock, breathing shallowly, nursing the rage that was his strength.

In five minutes Ottoowa had reached the beach and lay sputtering on the shingles. He wore only fatigues and a T-shirt now. He was barefoot, and drenched.

Sullivan stepped into the open and stood over the madman. "Get on your knees," Sullivan said.

Ottoowa snorted, then got to his knees—and slashed at Sullivan with a knife.

Sullivan had been expecting that. He leaped back, then snapped his left leg up, a karate kick, striking Ottoowa's knife hand at the wrist. Bone crunched. Ottoowa groaned, and the knife arced away to splash into the surf.

Then Sullivan braced himself and took Ottoowa by the throat with his right hand. He held him out at arm's length and began to squeeze. Ottoowa on his knees; Sullivan standing over him.

"I execute you," Sullivan said between clenched teeth as the waves surged in to drench his ankles. "I execute you in the name of all the people you tortured, and killed, and exploited, and robbed, and tyrannized."

Ottoowa choked, slapping at Sullivan's ramrod arm, clawing at that implacable vise grip, his face swelling, eyes protruding, gagging.

"I execute you," Sullivan continued, "in the name of every black man I ever served with . . . I execute you for Julia Penn and Sam Hayden . . ."

"Jack!"

Sullivan looked up, a mist clearing from his eyes. "Who . . . ?"

It was Malta, pulling the outboard skiff up to the beach through the water, the surf lashing about his ankles.

"Jack, he's dead. Let the body go. You've been strangling him for five minutes after he died. You're wounded, my friend, don't waste your strength on a corpse!"

"He's dead . . . five minutes ago?" When the rage took control of him, he lost all track of time. "Funny how time flies when you're having fun," he said, letting the body fall to the shingles.

Neither of them laughed at that.

They dragged the body into the boat and pushed off. Sullivan climbed in, and sagged on a bench, the body curled at his feet, as Malta started the outboard. "Got to . . ." Sullivan began, then licked his lips. He felt dizzy. "Got to pick up Edie . . ."

"She's waiting on the dock, Jack. We'll pick her up and go. The police are coming—someone heard the explosions. We have to hurry."

He said something more, but Sullivan didn't hear it. He was swallowed up by that pit opening once more in his mind. He thought: Poor Edie. She got involved in this mess, had to see all this ugliness. And all she wanted in life was to be a singer . . . just to sing to people. Poor . . .

And then the darkness swallowed him whole.

* * *

Three days later, Sullivan was strong enough to move about.

"You lost a lot of blood, my friend," Malta said that sunny afternoon as they rode along the shore in the Bentley. "I'm not so sure you should be out of bed."

"I'm okay," Sullivan said.

Malta glanced at him and shrugged.

Sullivan hadn't said much for the last three days.

They drove south along the Mediterranean, in no great hurry. Sullivan glanced at his watch. Two o'clock. They were due to meet Julia Penn at her yacht on the docks in Toulon at three-thirty.

They drove through some striking countryside, past two-hundred-year-old villas covered with baroque gimcrackery, and past rustic graystone roadside inns. Another time, Sullivan might have enjoyed the scenery. Now he was looking inward. He was thinking about Edie.

She was waiting for him in Paris, where she'd gone to avoid answering the questions asked by the Toulon police. He had her address on a piece of paper folded and tucked in his shirt pocket. She expected him to meet her at that address in two days. She talked about going away with him to America. She wanted to get a job singing in an American nightclub. They'd live together there, and—

But he knew it just wasn't in the cards.

He had a job to do. Not just a mercenary's job. A vigilante's job. The world needed cleansing, so innocents like Edie could have the chance to sing.

Malta carried the Styrofoam cooler onto the deck of the elegant yacht. Julia Penn, wearing a clinging blue dress, came out of the cabin when she heard them arriving. Her eyes widened, seeing the ice-packed cooler. Sullivan shivered.

"Bring . . . bring it below," she said breathlessly.

Malta carried the cooler down the narrow steps, along a hallway, and into a stateroom. It was a plush room with satin draperies around the portholes, silk covers on the queen-size bed, a rack of cut-crystal decanters and a well-stocked liquor cabinet.

"Put it there." Her voice was hardly more than a whisper. She'd gone paler than ever.

Malta put the cooler on a small table and stepped back.

She stood staring at it. "Take it out where I can see it," she said.

Sullivan shrugged. He removed the top of the cooler, set it to one side, then reached in and pulled out a black plastic garbage sack, twisted shut with a wire. He shook the ice water off the sack—which was weighted down at the bottom by something inside—and set it on the tabletop beside the cooler.

He could just make out the outline of Ottoowa's features pressing against the plastic from within.

Moving in slow motion, her eyes wide, her lips parted, Julia Penn went to the table and untwisted the wire that held the sack shut. She opened it and looked in—she saw, Sullivan guessed, just the top of Ottoowa's head and maybe one of his eyes. Enough to know. She closed the sack by twisting it, but didn't replace the wire.

"It's him," she whispered to herself. "It's *him*. I know it is."

She went to a cabinet and took out three snifters.

"Not for me," Sullivan said. "No drinking for a while. Slows recovery."

For the first time, she seemed to notice the sling on his left arm. "You were wounded . . ." Her eyes drifted to his cane.

Malta nodded. "His leg too. He should be in bed now. But he's stubborn."

"Job's not done till the kill is confirmed," Sullivan said.

"It's confirmed," she said huskily, pouring brandy for herself and Malta. She glanced toward Sullivan. "What about the police?"

"They're looking for Jack," Malta said. "But not very hard. He killed a lot of men they wanted to kill themselves. And I've arranged for him to get through customs when he goes. He has a false passport . . ." He sipped his brandy, then added, "All he needs is his money."

She nodded, and, her hands shaking a little, opened a cabinet and took out a slip of paper. She gave it to Sullivan.

It was a check for an immense amount of money. He scarcely looked at it. He tucked it in his shirt pocket absentmindedly.

"You'll have no trouble cashing that?" she asked.

"I don't think so. Not in the States. No one will be looking for me there."

There was no question of her canceling the check after he was gone. They both knew that. Even if she'd been inclined to do so, she'd have been afraid to.

She drained her brandy, set the glass down decisively, then went to her bed. She reached beneath it and took out a shiny new hatchet.

She hefted the hatchet and looked at the sack containing the head of the man who'd decapitated her twin sister.

Sullivan and Malta looked at each other. Malta put his glass down and said, "*Au revoir*, Madam Penn."

She'd lost interest in them. She was opening the sack, taking the grisly prize from within by its hair.

Malta and Sullivan left the room.

But they came running back when they heard a shriek.

Julia Penn was standing over the severed head, her hands over her eyes, screaming. The head was rocking slightly on the floor, the hatchet buried in its skull, between the eyes. "Look at it!" she shrieked, wailing, sobbing. "Look at him! He's laughing! He's laughing at me! *Make him stop laughing!*"

Sullivan looked down at the severed, half-rotted head of Magg Ottoowa. Its mouth was drawn back in a hideous grin, a rictus that made it look as if it were laughing.

Epilogue

Sullivan sat in the backseat of a taxi, on his way to Charles de Gaulle Airport in the suburbs of Paris. He was humming. The sun was shining through the window, and it felt good on his face.

He felt better today, almost a month after they'd delivered the kill confirmation to Julia Penn. His wounded leg and arm were still stiff, but he could move them about. The bullets had made flesh wounds, nasty-looking but not as bad as they might have been.

And he felt better, too, about Edie. Sure, she'd felt bad. But she had eyes for that young record engineer she'd cut her demo single with. She'd forget Jack Sullivan. Especially after that record producer he'd paid off got her career started. That is, *if* the guy came through. Maybe he'd skip out with the twenty-five thousand dollars Sullivan had given him and do nothing for her.

He wondered, too, if Julia Penn were still in the sanatorium. He doubted it. She was tough, inside. And the doctor had said she'd had a nervous breakdown of the sort that could be good for a person in the long run. It let you work some things out of yourself. She'd probably come out of it stronger.

He looked at his airline ticket for New York. He'd heard that Rusty Spike had done "some kinda work" in Manhattan just before signing on with Ottoowa. Maybe he could pick up the trail of Lily's killers there. And there was another job in New York. He didn't know what it would be yet. But he knew there was work for him there.

The cabdriver turned on the radio. Sullivan heard a familiar voice. Edie's voice, singing from the radio.

Sullivan smiled. So the producer had come through. He'd gotten that demo single on the radio. That would generate interest, and some record company would snap her up.

The cabdriver was humming along with the song. It was clear he liked it.

Sullivan leaned back and, against doctor's orders, lit a cigarette. He put Edie out of his mind and started thinking again about New York.

Yeah. There was work to do there.

Special work—for The Specialist.

DON'T MISS . . .

The following is an exciting excerpt from the next novel in the new *Specialist* series from Signet:

THE SPECIALIST #2:
MANHATTAN REVENGE

The night was cool; a few stars, directly overhead, managed to brave the glare of the city lights, marking with celestial clockwork the inevitable course of Sullivan's mission of vengeance. . . .

He pulled the knit cap over his head, down crookedly over his eyes, to make a partial mask, then showed himself in the front door of the building just as the group of Meat Hooks was passing.

Sullivan had his jacket sleeve unbuttoned and pulled back; he was rolling it back down now, as if he'd just shot up. Junkies sometimes carried their own small bottles of mixing water and used the empty buildings in the neighborhood for a quick sheltered fix after a score. Sullivan had seen them at it more than once; he knew how to play the part by now.

He stood swaying, as if he'd taken a heavy hit and was uncertain on his feet. "Good shit," he called to them. "They're open on Second Street, fourth onna right. You guys oughta try it. Fuck it, I'm gonna do up some more."

Such shallow street camaraderie was common because users liked to establish themselves with others on the street, in case they needed a score one day and were unable to find it. If they were known, they could be more or less trusted.

Sullivan reeled back into the building, but not before he'd seen the Meat Hooks grin at one another and start after him. All four were Caucasian, sunken-eyed, pock-faced, sallow.

Borderline junkies themselves, hoping to roll him for dope and money.

He waited just long enough so the first one could see him stagger up the stairs.

The one in the lead, the slender one with his knife already in his hand, ran up the flight ahead of the others, maybe hoping to grab the dope and hide it so he could keep it for himself.

When he reached the second floor, the only way to go was left, around the corner jutting out behind the stair banister. He came in a hurry, and ran into Sullivan's eight-inch Solingen-steel razor-honed blade, his hurry impaling him on it, the cold metal sliding as if through butter into his belly, and up into his heart.

The knife was in Sullivan's left hand—he'd simply held his left arm out, braced, the knife waiting like a booby trap. He clamped his right hand over the punk's mouth to stifle his scream, and dragged him into the room behind, elbowing the door shut a moment before the other three came onto the landing.

The Meat Hook in his arms spasmed a moment, then sagged, his eyes glazing. Sullivan eased him to the floor, using the Meat Hook colors to wipe the blood from his arm and knife blade.

"Where'd he go?" someone said in the hall on the other side of the door.

" 'Nother floor up."

More footsteps pounding up the stairs. But only two of them went—the third was suspicious. He stood muttering to himself just outside the door.

Sullivan said, just loud enough for the one in the hall to hear, "Yeah, that's some good shit. Yeah."

Sudden silence outside the door.

Then it swung inward.

Sullivan was flattened against the wall behind the door. The Meat Hook stepped into the room, a .32 in his left hand, and stood staring in shock at the remains of his friend. Sullivan silently shut the door and moved in close behind him.

Sullivan had sheathed the knife. Now he had the garrote wire wrapped many times around his hands, the strangling length taut between them. With one fluid motion he encircled the target's throat with his garrote and jerked the loop tight before his victim could do more than squeak. He squeaked again, and again, for perhaps three minutes, as the noose dug into his throat, cutting off his trachea. His face swelled, purpling, mottling scarlet, his eyes bulged, his fingers clawed in pathetic futility at the wire—then his brain shut down for lack of oxygen, and in a minute more he was dead.

Sullivan untwisted the wire and let the body sag to the floor. The noise of its falling covered the faint sound of the door opening behind him.

The Best in Fiction from SIGNET

(0451)

- ☐ **THE DARK FOUNTAIN by Jay Robert Nash.** (126122—$2.95)*
- ☐ **SOMEONE ELSE'S MONEY by Michael M.Thomas.** (126009—$3.95)*
- ☐ **LOVE AND TREASON by David Osborn.** (125002—$3.50)*
- ☐ **TOUCH THE DEVIL by Jack Higgins.** (124685—$3.95)†
- ☐ **FAMILY TRADE by James Carroll.** (123255—$3.95)*
- ☐ **THE FALL OF THE RUSSIAN EMPIRE by Donald James.** (123271—$3.50)*
- ☐ **FORGOTTEN IMPULSES by Todd Walton.** (098021—$2.75)*
- ☐ **INSIDE MOVES by Todd Walton.** (096614—$2.50)*
- ☐ **FOOLS DIE by Mario Puzo.** (088816—$3.50)
- ☐ **THE GODFATHER by Mario Puzo.** (125800—$3.50)*
- ☐ **THE GIRL IN A SWING by Richard Adams.** (124324—$3.75)
- ☐ **SOME KIND OF HERO by James Kirkwood.** (115767—$2.95)*

*Price slightly higher in Canada.

†Not available in Canada

Buy them at your local bookstore or use this convenient coupon for ordering.

THE NEW AMERICAN LIBRARY, INC.,
P.O. Box 999, Bergenfield, New Jersey 07621

Please send me the books I have checked above. I am enclosing $________ (please add $1.00 to this order to cover postage and handling). Send check or money order—no cash or C.O.D.'s. Prices and numbers are subject to change without notice.

Name____________________

Address____________________

City ________ State ________ Zip Code ________

Allow 4-6 weeks for delivery.

This offer is subject to withdrawal without notice.

The Specialist Questionnaire

Win A Free Gift! Fill out this questionnaire and mail it today. All entries must be received by June 30, 1984. A drawing will be held in the New American Library offices in New York City on July 30, 1984. 100 winners will be randomly selected and sent a gift.

1. Book title:__________________________________

   Book #:____________

2. Using the scale below, how would you rate this book on the following features? Please write in one rating from 0-10 for each feature in the spaces provided.

POOR		NOT SO GOOD		AVERAGE			GOOD		EXCEL-LENT	
0	1	2	3	4	5	6	7	8	9	10

	RATING
Overall opinion of book.	______
Plot/Story	______
Setting/Location.	______
Writing style	______
Dialogue	______
Suspense.	______
Conclusion/ending.	______
Character development	______
Hero	______
Scene on front cover.	______
Colors of front cover.	______
Back cover story outline.	______
First page excerpts.	______

3. How likely are you to buy another title in The Specialist series? (Circle one number on the scale below.)

DEFI-NITELY NOT BUY		PROB-ABLY NOT BUY		NOT SURE			PROB-ABLY BUY		DEFI-NITELY BUY	
0	1	2	3	4	5	6	7	8	9	10

4. Listed below are various Action Adventure lines. Rate only those you have read using the 0-10 scale below.

POOR		NOT SO GOOD		AVERAGE			GOOD		EXCEL-LENT	
0	1	2	3	4	5	6	7	8	9	10

	RATING
Able Team..........................	______
Death Merchant	______
Destroyer............................	______
Dirty Harry..........................	______
Mack Bolan (Executioner).............	______
Penetrator	______
Phoenix Force........................	______
Specialist	______
Survivalist	______
______________	______
______________	______

5. Where do you usually buy your books (check one or more):
   ( ) Bookstore
   ( ) Supermarket
   ( ) Variety Store
   ( ) Dug Store
   ( ) Discount Store
   ( ) Department Store
   ( ) Other:______________

6. What are the names of two of your favorite magazines?
   1) ______________
   2) ______________

7. What is your age? ______ Sex: ( ) Male
   ( ) Female

8. Marital Status:
   ( ) Single
   ( ) Married
   ( ) Divorced
   ( ) Separated
   ( ) Widowed

Education:
   ( ) Grammar school or less
   ( ) Some high school
   ( ) H. S. graduate
   ( ) 2 yrs. college
   ( ) 4 yrs. college

If you would like to participate in future research projects, please complete the following:

PRINT NAME:______________

ADDRESS:______________

CITY:__________ STATE__________ ZIP__________

PHONE: ( ) ______________

Thank you. Please send to: New American Library, Action Adventure Research Dept., 1633 Broadway, New York, New York 10019.